HOT *Italian* NIGHTS

BOOKS 4 to 6

ANNIE
WEST

HOT ITALIAN NIGHTS ANTHOLOGY 2, BOOKS 4-6
ISBN: 978-0-6484551-3-4
Copyright © 2018 by Annie West

THE ITALIAN'S BOLD RECKONING
Copyright © 2017 by Annie West
First published electronically 2017
First paperback edition 2018 ISBN: 978-0-6484551-3-4

AT THE ITALIAN'S BIDDING
Copyright © 2017 by Annie West
First published electronically 2017
First paperback edition 2018 ISBN: 978-0-6484551-3-4

FALLING FOR THE BROODING ITALIAN
Copyright © 2017 by Annie West
First published electronically 2017
First paperback edition 2018 ISBN: 978-0-6484551-3-4

Cover Design and Interior Format

THE ITALIAN'S
Bold Reckoning

Book 4, Hot Italian Nights

Chapter One

THE FIRST TIME ANGELA SAW Matteo De Laurentis after a year's separation he was kissing another woman.

Well, not kissing, precisely, but it was clear that was what he intended. The beautiful redhead was backed against a crumbling wall in the Venetian alley, with one of those picturesque arched bridges just beyond her.

But Angela barely took in their surroundings. Her staring gaze locked on Matteo's wide shoulders and the lean strength of that tall body as it hemmed the woman in. He even had one hand braced beside her head, reinforcing his passionate, almost predatory stance. And the redhead, far from seeming threatened, wore an expression that signalled she was ready for his kiss. Ready for anything he demanded of her.

Angela's heart stalled high in her throat. Shock ripped the air from her lungs.

Shock, it was definitely shock.

It could *not* be jealousy.

Angela was over him. Had been over him for ages.

So why did her blood rush so fast in her arteries? She tensed, heart pounding, ready to flee. Or perhaps to stalk over, grab Matteo's shoulder and drag him away from that…female. And then she'd—

What?

Slap him?

Yell at him?

Wrap her arms around his neck and kiss him till he didn't know what day it was? Till he gathered her close and whispered she was the only woman he wanted, the only woman he'd ever want?

As if.

Angela swallowed convulsively but couldn't dislodge the bitter tang of hurt, and of shattered, foolish dreams.

The strength of her emotions stunned her. She'd convinced herself she'd washed her hands of him.

She had to put out a hand to the stone wall for support, her palm registering chill dampness and crumbling grit. A little like her relationship with Matteo, she thought with a grimace — cold and disintegrating. For surely this punch of emotion to the belly was an aberration. He felt nothing for her and soon she'd be calm and in control of herself.

She'd better be, or her time in Venice would be torture.

'Cut!' The deep voice resonated in the narrow alley.

Instantly there was movement, a murmur of voices, people going about their jobs. The lights were dimmed, the camera stopped and someone moved forward with a warm cloak to wrap around the redhead's creamy, bare shoulders. Because it wouldn't do to have one of the film's stars come down with a chill.

Angela barely noticed. Her attention was on Matteo. He'd dropped the arm that imprisoned his co-star against the wall, but he hadn't moved away. They were engrossed in a murmured discussion Angela couldn't hear.

But the fact they stood so close, their heads inclined together, their body language intimate, made raw hurt gouge through her insides.

Angela shut her eyes, willing the pain away. This could not be happening. She was a professional. Here only to work.

Her relationship with Matteo had been over for twelve months, since the day she'd learned he'd been unfaithful.

She'd known this job was going to be tough. Had fought against coming here till every avenue had been cut off and she had no choice but to obey the summons. Now, with no options left, she had to be strong. Immune. Professional.

Her eyes snapped open just as Matteo turned his head and caught sight of her.

Electricity jolted through her, making her muscles tighten, her soles tingle and her nipples peak. Even from this distance his dark blue eyes had a magnetic quality, making it impossible to turn away.

Was it imagination or did he tense too, his conversation momentarily faltering? Certainly he stilled long enough that his companion turned her head to look. Angela had known Gina Moretti was beautiful. She'd seen the photos. But in the flesh she was exquisite.

Angela's pulse thrummed fiercely, as if daring her to stride over there and plant herself between the pair.

But you gave up any right to him a year ago, didn't you? And good riddance. He's not the man for you.

'Angela? Is that you?'

She turned to see one of the cameramen beside her. A tall, skinny guy with a sweet smile.

'Davide! I didn't know you were working on this film. It's lovely to see you again.' Genuine pleasure helped her fix a smile on her face. She and Davide had met years before on what had been the first film for the pair of them. Both introverts with a shared sense of the ridiculous, they'd soon bonded.

'And you.' His smile slipped. 'I was sorry to hear about your mother. It sounds like it's been a tough time.' His gaze darted towards the bridge where the actors stood, then quickly back.

'Thank you, Davide.' Angela put her hand on his arm. It felt good to know there was at least one person on set she could relax with. 'It has been tough.' With a conscious effort she stopped herself from glancing towards Matteo. 'She died too young, but she didn't suffer. And now I'm back, ready to work.'

If only she could hang onto that, she'd get through even this trial. Right now her work was all she had, and after months when she'd been unable to concentrate on stringing words together, much less writing a viable screenplay, her recent return to writing was a blessing.

All she had to do was get this job out of the way and then she could get back to the new project she'd started, the one she hoped would help her recover from her emotional and writing slump.

'So what have you been up to? Did I hear you worked on that job in Palermo?'

Davide's smile turned to a grin. 'I did. And everything went wrong from the first day. It's a wonder we ever finished. I'll tell you over a drink if you like.'

'Sounds great. I'll have to check my schedule of script meetings but then I'm yours.'

Matteo's scalp prickled. And his nape and shoulders. Ants crawled across his back. Even his legs tingled. He fought the urge to whip his head around and instead focused on his stance, on Gina, on the story they were telling together.

But his concentration was shot. Something had changed, the atmosphere grew charged and it had nothing to do with the faux passion between him and Gina.

This was visceral. Matteo felt the drag of tension deep in his gut and knew she'd come. At last!

He'd waited for this day so long. He needed…

Belatedly he became aware that Gina's expression had changed as she'd picked up his tension.

Hell! The scene had been going so well. Now he'd killed it.

'Cut!' One thing about being director as well as actor, he had a level of control that had been missing before.

If he wanted he could stride over to Angela — he knew she was here, watching him, he sensed it in every taut nerve — and drag her away for the private discussion they had to have. But that would show his hand, and his desperation. He had no intention of revealing that and losing his slight advantage now he finally had her almost where he wanted her.

He'd worked too long and too hard to get her

here.

'Everything okay, Matteo?' Gina frowned up at him, concern clear in her gorgeous face.

It struck him anew that despite her beauty, he felt nothing for her but friendship and respect. Absolutely nothing.

'Fine. Just got distracted. I'm sorry.'

She shrugged. 'These things happen. But I think it's going well so far, don't you? The story is excellent and it feels…right.'

Matteo nodded. The story was excellent. Angela should be proud of it. Instead she'd been hiding on the other side of the world, refusing to participate in the pre-shoot collaboration till absolutely forced by the contract lawyers.

'It's early days, but yes, I'm hopeful.' Just as well. He'd sunk most of his savings and a lot of investors' money into this, his first foray into directing. True, some of the investors, like his eldest brother, Luca, and Matteo's best friend, Niccolo Marchesi, were extremely wealthy, but Matteo was determined to produce a film that would reward their faith in him.

There was one person whose faith in him seemed to have died completely. But that was another matter and he had a plan to deal with it.

Unable to resist any longer, he turned.

There she was, watching him. Reaction smacked him square in the gut. It was like taking a step onto a bridge and finding it wasn't there, that instead he was in freefall.

She was gorgeous. More gorgeous than he remembered.

He'd fallen for a woman who hid her natural

beauty, who dressed in neutral colours as if trying to blend into the background. But Matteo had seen beneath the camouflage.

There was no camouflage now. She wore a jacket the colour of amber that glowed like a beacon in the shadows of the alley. Long boots and closely-fitted jeans hugged her slim legs, making her a magnet for any red-blooded male.

Her face was flawless, her eyes wide and those lips... Matteo shivered, recalling the taste of her pouting mouth, and the wicked, wicked things she'd done with it. She might be reserved with strangers, but Angela was a passionate woman.

His heart clenched.

How he'd missed her!

He couldn't believe they'd come to this, after all they'd meant to each other. He'd been reduced to using her contractual obligations to get her in the same city as him!

'Matteo? Are you okay?'

'Of course.' He turned to Gina, now shrugging into warmer clothes. 'We're finished here. Why don't you head back?'

Her gaze strayed over his shoulder and he read her curiosity, but Gina merely nodded and turned away.

Hauling much-needed air into his lungs, Matteo turned and instantly froze. Angela had her arm on the cameraman's arm. She was leaning in, smiling at him.

Matteo wanted to break the guy's legs and throw him in the canal!

Another breath, deeper this time, as he pulled on an expression of calm. But his stride was quick as he crossed to the pair.

Each step revealed something new. Her hair, once light brown with warm honey tints, was now sleeker, a pale blonde. She'd grown it too. It fell in tempting waves past her shoulders, down towards her pert breasts. At her throat, on a narrow black ribbon, glinted a golden heart locket.

Matteo's gaze narrowed on it. Who'd given it to her? Whose photo rested inside?

The instant fizz of fury propelled him forward, just in time to hear her say to the scrawny cameraman, 'But then I'm yours.'.

Like hell she was!

Matteo had prepared for this meeting carefully. He'd planned to be calm and relaxed, putting her at ease, charming her into trusting him. But all that flew out the window when she looked up into Davide's dazzled eyes with the sort of smile she'd once reserved for Matteo.

Before the cameraman could speak Matteo stepped between them, his hand shooting out to encircle her wrist, warm and fragile, tugging it away from the other man.

Instantly she drew a sharp, hissing breath. Her head swung round, eyes widening and pupils dilating as she saw him. Those soft brown eyes had once, too long ago, looked adoringly at him. And he, like a fool, had thought they always would.

Matteo had learned his lesson. He took nothing for granted anymore.

'Hello, Angela.' His face felt tight as he smiled. Was he smiling or grimacing? He didn't give a damn.

He turned to the lanky crew member who, up

till this point, he'd been so pleased to have work on this project. Now Matteo wished him to the devil, despite his cinematic skill.

All trace of a smile disintegrated as he stared at the other man. 'I see you already know my wife.'

Chapter Two

*H*IS WIFE!

Angela flung open the lid of her suitcase and grabbed a pile of neatly folded clothes. She stalked across the vast, opulent room and pulled open an antique door, looking for the wardrobe. Instead she found a palatial dressing room, with sleek modern shelves and endless hanging spaces.

She shoved her clothes onto a random shelf and pivoted on her heel.

Matteo had referred to her as his wife, just as if he hadn't received her request for a divorce. The paparazzi who'd snooped around for a story behind their separation would have a field day if they heard that. But more, Matteo had her checked into this extraordinary private hotel that was more like a palace than a place for a cash-strapped screenwriter.

The walls were hung in exquisite *eau de nil* silk. The wide tester bed was topped with a gilt crown from which hung matching silk. Antiques, elegant and perfectly positioned, turned the room into a suite fit for royalty. Even the fresh flowers in their crystal vases were so gorgeous it was a shame she'd be the only one to see them.

When she was met at the vaporetto stop on the Grand Canal, fresh off the plane, she'd been only too grateful to relinquish her luggage, not knowing it would be taken somewhere like this. Having it taken on ahead had been a luxury, for dragging a heavy case over the quaint cobbled streets wasn't fun. Besides, despite herself, she'd been eager to detour and catch a glimpse of the filming.

Angela's step faltered in the doorway of the dressing room and she sagged against the door frame.

Face the truth.

You wanted to see Matteo.

Even now, even after his betrayal. Even knowing the pair of you were never meant to be together.

Her heart crashed against her ribs and her knees turned to jelly as the full impact of this afternoon took its toll.

She'd taken one look at Matteo and all her fine self-talk about independence and strength had vanished.

The old, terrible yearning was back full force.

Angela squeezed her eyes shut. She *couldn't* want a man who'd betrayed her.

But at the same time she remembered how she'd withdrawn from him before that. She hadn't been much of a wife for him, had she? The further he'd invited her into his glamorous world, the more uncomfortable she'd become. Wooden, stilted, nervous — she'd hated the way she froze in front of the paparazzi cameras and couldn't find a thing to say to interviewers or to Matteo's socialite friends.

She'd even retreated from *him*, sure he'd soon realise he'd made a mistake insisting on their whirlwind marriage. For if she withdrew first, then surely their inevitable separation wouldn't hurt as much. It was a lesson she'd learned from her distant, domineering father.

But it hadn't worked out like that, had it?

Bitterness tasted sharp on her tongue as she recalled Matteo's then co-star on the final day of shooting just over a year ago. Her platinum blonde hair was rumpled, her lips swollen and lipstick smeared. And she'd worn nothing, absolutely nothing, beneath her silk robe as she stepped out of Matteo's trailer. She'd stumbled on the bottom step and the robe had parted, leaving Angela in no doubt of that. Besides, the cat-that-got-the-cream smile on Vittoria's face as she met Angela's frozen stare had said it all.

Angela pressed a palm to her writhing stomach. Just as well she'd missed lunch, or she'd probably bring it up.

She'd found Matteo De Laurentis heart-stoppingly attractive and hadn't been able to resist him. But that was only one side of Matteo. Behind the gloss and glamour he was intense, hard-working and surprisingly down-to-earth.

She hadn't been the right wife for a movie star who attracted the press wherever he went and whose smile made women the world over swoon.

But nor had she deserved infidelity.

She straightened her shoulders and stood tall, forcing herself to cross the room and unpack.

There'd been faults on both sides. The marriage was a mistake. A complete mismatch. The only sensible thing was to end it.

Stoically, Angela ignored the hollow feeling inside, as if her body caved in on itself. She'd get through this, do the work necessary on the screenplay and leave.

She caught sight of herself in a huge mirror edged with silver gilt. Beneath her brave, bright jacket and the new look, Angela was still the shy, geekish introvert she'd always been. Holding her own against Matteo's forceful personality and his raw charisma would be hard. But she'd toughened up this last year. She could do it.

She *had* to do it.

He had to knock a second time before she answered the door.

'You!' Her lush mouth tightened and her eyes narrowed as she took him in.

Had he really hoped this would be easy? That she'd fall at his feet, or better yet, into his arms?

Dream on, De Laurentis.

She'd already engineered an excuse to leave the set before he could get away, as if determined to avoid him.

'Me.' He moved to enter the room but halted when she blocked his way.

Matteo could force his way in. He might even be able to persuade her to let him in. But, though her action was like a smack in the face, he decided not to push. Why make an issue out of this when more important things were at stake?

Like finding out the real reason his wife had deserted him.

'Ready for the script meeting? I came to show you the way.' He kept his expression bland and his tone easy.

She was so skittish he knew any suggestion they meet to discuss their relationship would fail. But she couldn't refuse to work with him.

Matteo hated that he'd had to use that as an excuse to lure his wife to Venice.

Slowly she nodded. 'Just a second.' She turned and hurried to the elegant antique desk over by the window, snatching up a laptop bag. She almost ran back.

Because she was worried he'd cross the threshold into the sanctuary of her room?

Matteo glanced at the wide, silk-covered bed against the far wall, his jaw clenching. When he entered his wife's room it wouldn't be because he forced his way in. It would be because she *begged* him to. And begged for a whole lot more besides.

'This way.' He spun on his heel and marched down the hall. Behind him he heard the snap of her heels on the marble floor. Since when had Angela worn high heels during the day?

Face it. You have no idea what she's been doing these last twelve months. How she's lived and who she's been with.

His stride faltered at the idea of another man in her life. But he couldn't believe it. Not Angela. She might infuriate him with her obstinate refusal to return to him, but she wasn't a cheat. Her honesty, the knowledge she was utterly genuine, without the guile he'd found in so many women, was one of the things that had first attracted him.

'This is a very quiet hotel,' she said as he strode down the grand staircase. Her tone of voice made him wonder if she was nervous.

'That's because it's not officially open. My brother, Luca, bought the palazzo recently and is still refurbishing. There's more work to do before it's officially open. But he knew I wanted somewhere private, away from the crowds.'

Matteo pushed open a door and gestured for her to enter the conference room with its vast oval table. One wall displayed a series of old maps and sketches of the city. On the far side, windows gave a tantalising view of the Grand Canal, but Matteo had more important things on his mind than the beauties of Venice.

One beauty at a time.

He breathed deep as Angela passed him, catching the faintest, shockingly familiar scent of her favourite fig and cinnamon soap. His hand tightened on the door. He hadn't smelled that in so long.

It hurled him instantly back to those heady, ecstatic days when Angela was rarely out of his arms. When she'd been as eager for him as he was for her. She hadn't been able to sleep unless she was curled against him. Even in sleep she'd kept a proprietorial hand on him and he, who'd spent years revelling in the fun of casual affairs with an endless supply of eager women, had surrendered himself willingly. He'd wanted no-one but her.

That hadn't changed.

No wonder he was strung so tight he felt he might snap.

'Yet he could fit in all the crew?' She put her case on the end of the long table and drew out a gilded chair, her movements stiff. She'd never been good at hiding her feelings. He was grateful for that now. It gave him at least one advantage.

'Sadly, no.' Matteo shut the door then took the chair beside hers.

Instantly she stiffened. But instead of shuffling the chair further along the table, she merely concentrated on getting out her laptop and a paper copy of the script.

'Filming seems to be going well. That scene I saw today…you and Gina work well together.' Angela kept her eyes down, as if the most compelling thing in the room was the text before her, not the fact she was alone with her husband for the first time in ages.

Matteo slapped his own copy down on the table, thrusting aside impatience. He couldn't tell if she was just nervous or trying to reinforce the point that they were no longer intimate.

But surely her nerves meant her emotions were engaged. She still *felt* something for him.

That, combined with the flash of response he'd seen in her eyes at the shoot, told him she wasn't immune to him, as she pretended. In fact, the way she'd stared at him back in the alley told him she still desired him.

The question was, did she love him?

'It's going well enough,' he said finally, when he could unlock his clenched teeth. It grated that she wanted to talk about the film, not *them*.

'So some of the crew are staying elsewhere?' Angela seemed desperate to keep the conversation rolling. Was she afraid what would happen if she didn't fill the silence? Surely she knew she couldn't avoid the moment of truth between them.

Yet she continued to busy herself, starting up her laptop. She was trying too hard to be impervious. That was a good sign.

Matteo leaned back in his chair, repressing a smile as he read her body language. 'Actually, all the crew are in another hotel.'

'What?' That made her look around. Her eyes, a delicious mix of toffee brown with amber, were wide with shock.

'There was a problem with the other hotel fitting us all in.' The problem being that he, Matteo, wanted privacy for his reunion with his wife. This place gave him all the privacy he wanted. His plan was to cut her off from other distractions and resolve the problems keeping them apart.

'You mean we're *alone* here?' Her horrified expression tore at his ego.

It was on the tip of his tongue to retort that he was her husband, not a serial killer. *And* that he'd done what most husbands wouldn't and allowed her a separate room. *For now.*

He wanted her to come to him of her own volition, not because he forced her. Though at the moment, compulsion was tempting. Restraining himself, chatting like polite strangers, took its toll.

'Of course not. The manager is here and several staff. And there are decorators coming and going, finalising the other rooms.'

Matteo saw she was about to protest, perhaps demand new accommodation, and pre-empted her with raised hand.

He'd used the script as an excuse to get her alone. Now, pride wounded that she continued to make small talk, he changed tactics. He refused to let her see his desperation. Let her wait as he'd had to wait. Let her stew, wondering when he'd broach the real reason he'd brought her here. It was time Angela tasted a dose of her own medicine.

'Let's not waste time discussing domestic arrangements. There's a problem with the script we need to sort out. It all seemed fine on paper, but filming in Venice presents some unique issues.'

If Angela had feared her husband would sweep her into his arms and seduce her, or even interrogate her on why she'd deserted him, she was doomed to… Was that *disappointment?*

What had she expected? That he'd welcome her with open arms? He was a proud man, a man who could and did have his pick of glamorous women. Clearly he'd moved on.

Angela blinked and tried to focus on the dialogue on the page before her. After an hour working next to Matteo, of him treating her as nothing more than a work colleague, her nerves were at breaking point. It became impossible to maintain her pretence of concentration on the text. The words swam before her eyes. Her mind kept straying to the man at her side and the pain engulfing her.

She was tired and heart sore.

She'd prayed she could remain professional in front of Matteo but it became harder with every second. She bit her lip and tried to find her place.

'Let's break for a bit.' His voice, soft, yet with a distinctive husky edge that was far too seductive, was like a caress.

'Good idea.' Angela nodded, closing the script and raising an unsteady hand to push her hair back from her face. It had been a long day. The stress of sitting close to Matteo, and the perverse disappointment that he didn't care that this was the first time they'd seen each other in ages, was too much to bear.

His chair scraped back from the table and she sucked in a breath of relief. Soon she'd be back in her room, able to regroup.

But instead of standing he turned the chair round to face her, his knees brushing her thigh.

Startled, Angela swung her head round and was instantly captured by his brilliant indigo stare. She couldn't look away, no matter how hard she tried. Her heart tripped to a frantic beat and her breath seized somewhere north of her lungs.

There was a tension in him that hadn't been there before. His sculpted cheekbones looked higher than ever, tight flesh emphasising his charismatic looks. A familiar, tiny line appeared at the centre of his forehead — a sign he was perplexed or thinking hard. His supple mouth thinned and beneath the close-cropped beard he wore for his current part, Angela saw his jaw clench.

Matteo braced his hands on his splayed legs and leaned close, invading her space, filling her senses with the addictive scent of pine and exotic spice and hot male flesh that she'd missed so long.

Yearning flickered through her. A desire to channel her hands through that glossy black hair and haul him in for a hungry, open-mouthed kiss so she could lose herself in the riot of pleasure he always delivered.

'Now, *wife*, you can tell me why you left me. And why you refused to come back.'

Chapter Three

IT HIT ANGELA THEN THAT Matteo's enviable calm had been a front.

This close, she read the turbulent emotion in his eyes, in the pinch of his haughty nostrils and the angle of his head. Suppressed energy hummed through him, congesting the air between them, making adrenaline course through her body in instant response.

The question was, did she want to run, or stay and see this out?

A lifetime's habit in avoiding confrontation made her imagine shoving back her chair and making for the door.

But she couldn't keep running. She'd realised that when she was in Australia, trying to mend herself and find the strength to imagine the future without Matteo.

It was time to face this. Wasn't that why she'd returned? The lawyers' messages about breach of contract had given her impetus but she'd already known she had to…finish this with Matteo.

Finish. It was such a cold, depressing word.

She swallowed hard, throat muscles chafing as if they closed over shards of glass.

'Well?' One black eyebrow slashed upwards.

Angela pushed her chair back from the table,

moving enough that his knees no longer touched her thigh. Pretending she didn't still feel his nearness like a physical weight, branding her skin.

She leaned back as far as she could in her straight-backed chair and clasped her hands together.

'I told you before, Matteo, we're mismatched. It was never going to work.'

'That's no answer and you know it.' His voice was calm but Angela sensed something dark and barely leashed beneath the even tones.

'You want me to be specific?' She dragged in a breath and shifted her gaze so she stared at a point just past his ear. It was too hard, meeting those searing eyes. 'You need a woman who can accept your…sophisticated lifestyle.' She tasted bitterness on her tongue and grimaced, swallowing hard. 'Who can thrive in it.' She paused, choosing her words. 'I'm not that woman. I let…passion blind me.'

It had been love, not merely passion that had made her hope, if not quite believe, they could made a go of it. But she'd been sorely mistaken.

'You're still talking in generalities that make no sense.' His voice was terse but Angela refused to look directly at him. This was hard enough already.

She spread her hands. 'I'm not comfortable on a red carpet. I can't handle the press—'

Angela couldn't miss his wide, slicing gesture. 'That means nothing! You think I married you for *that*? Besides, coping with public attention is something you learn over time. And I was there to help you, if you'd only let me.'

It was true. Matteo had been patient and understanding, not pushing her beyond her limits.

Cossetting her, in fact, when some would have expected her to sink or swim. The clamour of press speculation about their unlikely union was part of the PR wheel that kept his career progressing. Naturally he'd expect her to make the most of it.

'That doesn't explain why you deserted me.'

Unthinking, Angela swivelled to look at him, tugged by the hint of vulnerability she heard in his roughened voice. Almost as if he *hurt*.

Angela had assumed his pride had been dented by her leaving. But since he'd turned to another woman so soon after their whirlwind wedding, she'd never considered he'd feel real pain when she walked out on him. A man truly in love wouldn't have betrayed his wife.

Was he acting? His phenomenal success wasn't merely due to his sexy good looks. Matteo was one of the most talented actors she'd seen.

She was the one torn apart by grief at his betrayal. And at her own naivety in believing he could ever have loved her. She'd been a challenge, a twenty-five year old virgin who'd thought the sun and the moon shone out of his eyes. She'd inadvertently piqued his hunter's instinct when she'd shyly withdrawn from his advances instead of opening her arms.

That had come later. Matteo's passion had been an education. Angela had, to her amazement, discovered that beneath her natural shyness and the reserve she'd acquired in order to keep the peace with her father, lurked a lusty woman whose appetite for sexual pleasure, and specifically for Matteo, knew few boundaries.

'Talk to me, Angela! I understand you flying to

Australia when your mother needed you. But you could at least have come to me on set to tell me the news, instead of leaving a note for me to find when I got home. I had no idea how sick she was. I would have gone with you.' He paused, his chest rising as he pulled air deep into his lungs.

'Then when I flew out later for the funeral you were changed. So…cold and withdrawn.' His expression was so bleak Angela almost believed he was hurting as much as her.

'I didn't believe it at first when you said our marriage wasn't working for you. It came completely out of the blue.'

Angela bit the inside of her cheek. She remembered that day with absolute clarity, right down to the pinch of the new black shoes she'd worn to her mother's funeral and the disbelief in Matteo's face at her declaration. And the fact that, despite everything, she'd wanted to throw herself into his arms and pretend everything could be all right again. That *they'd* be all right.

That she hadn't seen what she'd seen.

It had taken every ounce of courage she had, to face Matteo and tell him the marriage wasn't working and she needed space. Even then she knew he wouldn't have accepted that if it weren't for Sonia intervening. Sonia, her protective older sister, who'd come to her aid and convinced Matteo that Angela wasn't up to any more stress.

Angela should have told him then that she wanted a divorce, but she knew how determined he was, how persistent. She hadn't had the strength to finish it then, going through all the distressing details. Besides, despite her misery, despite knowing her dream of love had been an illusion, she hadn't been ready to talk of divorce.

'I know you were mourning and you needed time to get over your mother's death. I understood you weren't yourself, and Sonia confirmed you had had a lot of family stuff weighing on you that you needed to work through.'

He leaned closer, his gaze pinioning her. 'So even though it went against every instinct, I took her advice and gave you space. But I never meant for it to last this long. You don't answer calls or emails. Whenever I've planned to fly out you've flat out rejected me, finding some excuse not to be available. You don't even want to talk about us, must less fight for us!'

His voice rose on a note of impatience and indignation, but Angela heard more too. That echo of hurt in his husky, deep voice. As if *she* were at fault. As if *she'd* broken their marriage. When all she was trying to do was put an end to the disaster that enmeshed them both.

It was too much.

'You want to know why I don't want to be with you?' Her spine stiffened and her jaw jutted.

For so long she'd tried to put this behind her, knowing the recollection could only hurt, but there was no stuffing this back into the dark recesses of her soul where she'd tried to hide it. That hadn't worked. The poison had seeped right through her, making her feel *tainted*.

It was he who should feel tainted, not her.

'I've tried to be…civilised about this,' she said, catching his frown of confusion. 'It's clear we just don't work as a couple so it seemed simpler to go with that.'

Because after living much of her life in the shadow of her bullying father, she naturally took the line of least resistance and emotional upheaval. After her parents divorced, Angela, still a young schoolgirl, had moved to Italy with her father, while Sonia stayed in Australia with their mother. Which meant Angela bore the full brunt of her father's oppressive, controlling ways.

But now, suddenly Angela could no longer tamp down the raw, biting agony over the way Matteo had betrayed her.

'I *did* come to see you. As soon as I got the call from Australia.'

Matteo's eyes rounded. 'I never saw you. I was on set the whole day.'

Angela's lips widened in a tight tug of facial muscles that was probably more grimace than smile. 'I came to your trailer. But when I got there your co-star, Vittoria, was leaving it.'

Instantly Matteo stilled, his expression freezing.

Angela supposed she should feel triumph, seeing he knew the game was up. He couldn't play the innocent, deserted husband any longer. But instead it was a terrible sense of despair she experienced, turning her insides into a vast, empty space.

Had she hoped, even now, that he'd deny it? That she hadn't seen what she had?

'Go on.' He bit the words out so sharply Angela flinched.

He was angry.

But Angela had come a long way. It had taken twenty-six years to find the nerve, but she refused to back down now just because she confronted an angry male. She lifted her chin and stared straight back at the man she'd once loved. The man who even now—

'Her hair was mussed and her mouth was swollen. Her lipstick was smeared as if she'd been kissed to within an inch of her life—'

'No!' The word stopped her mid flow. When he spoke again disdain dripped from each word. 'As if she'd kissed someone.'

Angela shrugged. She didn't care about semantics.

'She wore a flimsy silk robe and absolutely nothing under it, as I'm sure you know.' Her tone was every bit as contemptuous as his. 'And before you ask, I know that for a fact. She made sure of it.'

Angela shuddered, remembering the sharp flare in the other woman's eyes and the curl of her lips as she'd accidentally on purpose let her robe gape.

'And?' His eyebrows rose, for all the world as if none of that made a difference.

How dare he?

'And she looked me square in the eye and told me to give you at least another half hour, because even a man of your vigour and strong libido needed time to regroup after your private…celebration.'

Angela's face pinched as a sour taste filled her mouth. Blood rushed in her ears, blocking out all sound but the heavy thud of her pulse. Her clenched hands shook and her eyesight tunnel-visioned. All she saw was Matteo, staring back at her, his expression arrested.

'And?' he said again.

'What?' Angela blinked back hot tears of fury.

'You believed her?' His gaze was as keen as a

knife. Angela felt it like a blade scraping her flesh.

She refused to flinch away. *She'd* done nothing wrong.

'It was pretty hard not to. I saw her with my own eyes.' And heard that syrupy satisfaction, that purr of pleasure with its dark undercurrent of malice. The woman had been brazen about being caught with Angela's husband, flaunting her bountiful beauty. She was a screen siren, famous for her lovers as much as her incredible curves and intensity on the screen.

Angela had looked at her and seen everything she, Angela wasn't. Vittoria *fitted* Matteo's world in ways Angela never could.

'It never crossed your mind to ask *me* what had happened?'

Angela blinked. There was something in his voice she couldn't identify. Something she'd never heard from Matteo.

She sat back, arching her eyebrows. 'So you could lie to me?'

'So I could tell you the truth!' His features drew hard and taut, each line and curve honed blade-sharp.

He shot to his feet, the movement so abrupt his chair toppled back and Angela flinched, half-primed for violence, one arm shooting up instinctively to protect her face.

Matteo had never hurt her but her father had back-handed her if she didn't instantly obey. It was why she'd run away from home so early, refusing to let herself be a victim any longer. Old instinct was slow to die.

Matteo registered her involuntary cringe and

froze.

Then he let loose a stream of words under his breath. Hard, angry words that weren't Italian. She guessed they might be Ladin, the native tongue from his home region in the north of Italy. It was rare, a sign of intense emotion.

Matteo spun away, across the room, as if he couldn't bear to be near her. He slammed to a stop when he reached the window and propped a hand on the sill, leaning against it. His other hand raked his glossy, immaculate hair.

When he turned his dark eyes looked febrile. With anger? Regret?

'You should have come to me. I was never unfaithful to you, Angela.'

Chapter Four

MATTEO COULDN'T GET A GRIP on his emotions. They seesawed between disbelief, compassion and blinding white-hot fury.

'How could you believe that of me?'

He was far from perfect but he'd believed Angela brought out the best in him. He *loved* her! How could she doubt him?

Still she sat, staring up at him with wide eyes, frozen in the spot. Not only had she believed he'd been unfaithful, but the way she'd cringed from him said she feared he might lash out her physically!

He shook his head, vision blurring, not wanting to believe it. Yet there'd been no mistake about her instantaneous reaction. Nausea cramped his stomach and bile rose, at the realisation she actually feared him.

He'd thought a year apart from Angela the worst torture he could endure. Now he found it was nothing to discovering what she believed him capable of.

'You thought I was going to hit you.' The words ground from him.

Immediately she shook her head. 'No! Not that. I…' She got to her feet, her movements stiff, and grabbed the back of the chair as if for balance.

'It was an instinctive reaction. My father…' She spread out one hand in an imploring gesture. 'He used to hit me. If I didn't do what he wanted or if I disagreed with him.'

Shock slammed into Matteo. Shock and anger, and a rush of protectiveness. The need to gather Angela close and reassure her, and himself, was so strong he actually trembled with the effort it took not to reach for her. But probably that would be the worst thing to do.

Suddenly, with appalling clarity, so many things about Angela and her past made sense.

Matteo gritted his teeth. He hadn't liked what he'd heard of the late unlamented Signor Rossi before this, but now…

On his divorce he'd split the family, bringing Angela back to Italy and breaking off all contact with his wife and other daughter in Australia. Angela hadn't spoken about him much but Matteo had gleaned enough to suspect her father had tried to trample any show of spirit and destroy her self-confidence. It was a testament to her strength of character that Angela had succeeded so well in her chosen career.

Now Matteo had some inkling of how difficult that must have been and the emotional scars she hid.

Her core of inner strength, that unyielding honesty, had drawn him to her in the first place.

At the back of his mind a voice whispered that her lack of confidence might be part of the reason she'd believed he'd slept with Vittoria.

He understood that. Intellectually it made sense, but still Matteo couldn't be calm. He was too furious. With Angela for believing him a man who'd lie and betray her. More, who'd beat her!

Furious with her father for what he'd done to her, and for the fact he was dead and beyond Matteo's reach.

Furious with himself too, for not following his instinct and forcing Angela to talk to him properly when he'd been in Australia for the funeral.

His feelings for her had always been bigger, stronger, *more* than anything he'd experienced before. Those feelings were so new and foreign he'd wondered sometimes if his very intensity might make her nervous. So when her sister had pleaded for his patience, he'd let himself be persuaded to back off.

He should have followed his instinct.

But as well as the anger, there was hurt. The anguish tearing at him made it impossible to stand still.

He pivoted on his heel and stormed to the far end of the room, then back again, as if physical action might assuage the roaring wave of emotions threatening to engulf him. But the room wasn't big enough to contain his feelings. He needed to throw himself off a cliff on an abseiling rope, or race a car through the mountains, or do something truly punishing. Even then, he doubted his anger would subside. He strode back to the window, but the scene of the busy canal did nothing to calm him. He turned to survey her, crossing his arms over his pumping chest.

'In the name of all that's holy, why didn't you tell me? We could have sorted this out, instead of spending twelve months on opposite sides of the globe.' His voice reverberated around the room.

Angela anchored herself with both hands on the chair back and leaned towards him. 'Because of this.' Her voice was earnest yet oddly triumphant, her chin high in the air. 'Because I didn't want to face your bluster.'

'Bluster?'

He stalked the width of the room to stand before her, hands on hips and chest heaving. Her eyes widened but she stood her ground. Only a frantic pulse at the base of her throat betrayed her.

For a second Matteo felt a pang of pride at the way she held her own against him. Till he remembered. But while his soul wept at the pain she'd endured at her father's hands, her past didn't excuse her readiness to believe such outrageous untruths about her own husband. The man she'd promised to love and cherish. The man who'd put her at the centre of his world.

'This isn't blustering.' His voice dropped to a silky thread of distaste and disgust. 'You impugn my honour. Accuse me of dishonesty and breaking my vows! Don't I have the right to respond?'

She blinked but stood still, her expression as taut as a soldier in an execution squad. She really believed he'd betrayed her. That pierced him to the heart.

Was there no breaking through to her?

Matteo shook his head. 'What about the promises we made? Do you think I made them lightly?'

'I think you meant them at the time. But you'd become disenchanted with me. I couldn't be the sort of wife—'

'Hold it right there! I *never*, by word or deed, implied you were anything other than the woman

I wanted to spend the rest of my life with. I *loved* you, Angela.'

God help him. He still did. Though how they could move past this to any sort of understanding, Matteo had no idea.

For the first time he saw a chink in that austere expression. Her smooth brow wrinkled into a frown. Had he said something she'd misinterpreted? It didn't seem possible, but this whole scenario was unbelievable.

Matteo curved his hands around the back of the chair she held in front of her like a protective barrier. Again that rapid blink of shining eyes and her chin notched up a fraction more. But she didn't retreat, probably because he was careful not to touch her.

'I haven't made love to another woman since I met you.' He said it slowly, letting her absorb every word. 'Vittoria tried, probably because I was one of the few men to say no to her. She came to my trailer and kissed me, plastered herself over me and I kicked her out. Obviously she didn't accept rejection well, since she took out her anger on you.' He grimaced, remembering the sordid scene. He'd never liked that co-star. It had been a trial from the first working with her. But he'd never expected…

'I haven't wanted another woman since I met you. I've been celibate the whole time you've been away.'

At that Angela *did* react. Her mouth rounded in a perfect O of astonishment.

Matteo wished he hadn't noticed. She had the sexiest mouth. Its natural pout was enough to make him hard at the best of times and right now, despite his fury, he couldn't banish the surge of hunger that reminded him his wife had become the only woman who could satisfy him. Standing this close and not having her was one of the most difficult things he'd done. He could all but feel those soft lips trailing across his skin, heading for—

'This separation, the separation *you* caused because you didn't trust me enough to give me the benefit of the doubt, or even to talk with me, has been driving me insane.' He saw the words hit home but he couldn't pull back. The anger inside him incinerated all caution. After a year of pulling back, giving her space and time as her sister kept urging, of playing nice, he'd reached his limit.

'How would you feel, Angela, if the situation were reversed?' Matteo thrust his head forward, right into her space. Once more he inhaled that fruit spice scent of her soap and more, the underlying fragrance of warm woman that was innate to her. He still woke in the night with the smell of her in his nostrils, his hands shaking from trying to hold her to him even as the dreams ended and the illusion faded.

His need for her even now, only stoked his ire.

'If I saw a guy coming on to you, should I just assume you were complicit? That you'd betrayed me? For all I know you've been sleeping with some man in Austral—'

'No!' She shook her head so forcefully a swathe of gilt hair swung forward, the tips brushing his chin.

Matteo reared back, unprepared for the surge of lust that shook him to the core from that gossamer fine caress.

How could he be so irate and still want the woman who believed he'd betrayed her? Who mocked his honour and his love?

'I haven't slept with anyone else.' Toffee brown eyes with those distinctive shards of amber stared up into his.

'I'm supposed to take your word for that, am I? To trust you? As you didn't trust me?'

She swallowed convulsively. 'It's true. I would never…' Another shake of her head. 'Besides, no man would ever—'

'What? No man would ever want you? Is that the lie you're trying to feed me?'

'I don't lie. I—'

'And nor do I, Angela. I've *never* lied to you.' His stare challenged her to argue and this time she remained silent, her fine eyes shadowed. 'As for other men wanting you, your precious Davide does.'

'Davide is just a friend. He has no interest in—'

'Have you *seen* yourself, Angela? I can't believe you look in the mirror and don't realise you're beautiful.' Though it struck him now that his wife never preened in front of mirrors. It was rare for her even to wear lipstick. The makeup she wore now signified a major change.

Why had she done it? The makeup, the new hair colour, the sexy clothes? They couldn't be for him. He'd had to drag her here kicking and screaming under threat of breach of contract.

So who was she dressing up for?

Jealousy was a juddering avalanche, blasting his body with icy needles of pain that burned right through him. Matteo squeezed his eyes shut, feeling the adrenaline rush abruptly subside.

He was tired, more tired than he'd ever felt in his life. It was an effort to hold in the turmoil of feelings churning through his gut and making nausea rise.

He snapped his eyes open.

Angela hadn't moved. But her face had paled from delicate cream to a parchment white that even makeup couldn't hide.

'I loved and trusted you, Angela.' He drew a heavy breath, ignoring the lance of pain jabbing right through his cramped lungs. 'I thought you loved and trusted me too. But now I wonder if I was mistaken.'

How he wanted to reach for her! Kiss her into softening in his arms. Kiss her till her head spun and she offered herself willingly to him. He could do it, he had no doubt. Always, they'd shared a special closeness in bed.

His grand scheme in bringing her to Venice had revolved around him seducing her back into intimacy, because in the past that part of their relationship had been sheer perfection. He'd assumed that once they were together again they'd be able to work through any issues. Because they loved each other.

Now Matteo saw the glaring flaw in his plan.

He loved his wife. Even now, after she'd hurt, offended and outraged.

But he wasn't sure she loved him.

The knowledge threatened to crush him.

Maybe she'd believed the worst about him because secretly she no longer loved him and subconsciously sought a way out of their marriage.

The testosterone pumping through his body urged him to sweep her off her feet. To overwhelm her with passion, to *make* her want him again. His instinct was to fight for her, win her over by whatever means he could.

Except now he knew her early years had been shadowed by coercion and violence.

Matteo wouldn't, couldn't, force her to behave or feel in the way he wanted. He refused to follow in her bullying father's footsteps. Honour and love demanded better of him.

He needed a new strategy. He needed to give her time to absorb the truth about what had happened with Vittoria. In the meantime there was nothing more he could do here.

Heart heavy, he strode from the room.

Chapter Five

'THANKS, ANGELA. THIS DIALOGUE WORKS much better now.'

From beside her at the table Gina smiled and Angela couldn't help but curve her lips in response. Gina was so genuinely lovely, inside and out, that smiling back was automatic. Despite the raw ache of desolation engulfing Angela.

Three days it had been and nothing had been resolved between her and Matteo. Instead of forcing her to renew their conversation, he'd surprised her by giving her space. He sat across from her now, silently frowning as he marked another section of the screenplay with a slashing stroke.

His plain gold wedding band caught the light and Angela's stomach cramped. Did he still wear it because, like her, he couldn't quite bring himself to remove it?

Or because removing it now, mid shoot, would draw attention that would be sure to attract the ravenous press?

He treated her with the distant politeness he would a stranger. Yet there was a tension in him, a sense of tightly curbed energy, that unsettled. There were no more private discussions, in fact he went out of his way to ensure they were never alone. Every script meeting had at least one other person present, most often Gina, his co-star.

Were they lovers?

Angela's chest squeezed at the thought. After what had passed between her and her husband, she assumed the ties that bound them were now completely unravelled, though obtaining a divorce would take some time yet. What could be more natural than that he'd seek solace in the arms of the gorgeous, Titian-haired actress, after his wife had shunned him?

Angela had been such a fool. Worse, she'd been a coward, running away instead of confronting Matteo straight away. It was no good telling herself discretion rather than valour had been a necessary survival skill, growing up under her father's bullying control.

She was an adult now. She should act like one.

The look on Matteo's face… His tone of voice as he'd declared he'd been with no other woman since they met, had *wanted* no other woman…

Matteo was a consummate actor but Angela had read his pain and surprise, and his outrage at what she'd revealed. She had no doubt he'd told the truth about that scene in his caravan. It was just the sort of malicious thing Vittoria would do if rejected, especially as she'd made it clear several times that she considered Angela to be under par when it came to femininity and attractiveness. Learning Angela's husband preferred his dowdy wife to her own abundant charms must have sliced at her pride.

Angela was still shocked by the discovery. The certainty she'd built her life around for twelve months shifted like crumbling foundations in an earthquake, revealing a whole new, unfamiliar landscape.

It was hard to get her bearings, difficult to know what to do. She'd never felt so out of her depth, with Matteo, her Matteo, so close, yet so distant. She longed for him, ached for him. But the thought of going to him and trying to bridge the gap she'd created between them terrified her. For she was afraid of what the final outcome might be.

Matteo's words had rung with all the force of a pledge in the still air between them.

I loved and trusted you, Angela.

Those words haunted her days, and worse, her lonely nights as she woke again and again from fitful sleep, wracked by memories of their exchange.

I loved you, Angela.

Past tense.

Had she destroyed his feelings for her? Had her too-ready acceptance of his guilt killed what they'd once shared?

Of course it had. There was nothing like love in Matteo's attitude now. Instead he acted as if being with her was a necessary chore. Like brushing his teeth or paying his tax.

'Earth to Angela! Are you with us?' The deep rasp of his voice was a rough caress on the sensitive skin of her nape.

Her head jerked up and she saw Matteo's frown had become a scowl. There were shadows under his eyes and his cheeks looked more hollow than usual, but then they'd only just stopped shooting. It must be the screen makeup making him look... haunted.

'Sorry, I was—'

'Angela was concentrating on the same section you were, Matteo. Now you've interrupted her train of thought.' Gina's tone was smooth.

Angela flashed a sideways glance at her. Was the actress covering for her? It was impossible to tell.

Gina continued. 'You're drinking too much coffee, Matteo. It makes you snappy.'

He mumbled something that might have been an apology and pushed aside his espresso. Gina was right, every time Angela saw him these days he seemed to be sipping coffee.

Angela stole another quick glance at him, wondering if it was exhaustion or stress she'd read in his features. After all, the film was a huge gamble. Branching out into directing as well as acting was an enormous risk. Knowing Matteo, he'd be utterly driven to ensure the film's investors as well as the cast and crew, were rewarded with a success.

Having his almost ex-wife on site might be the straw that broke the camel's back.

'This section.' His eyes locked on hers and Angela felt that old, familiar frisson of connection. If she wasn't careful she'd lose herself in that dark blue gaze, like one of his adoring fans.

Or like a wife who'd tried for twelve months to eradicate him from her heart and failed. Failed phenomenally if the misery sucking her down was any measure.

'Which one?' Angela looked down at his script and back to hers. 'Okay. Yes?'

'It needs more.'

She waited but he didn't elaborate. She was forced to look up again and meet that waiting gaze.

What was going through his mind? When he

looked at her so intently it felt as if Gina wasn't at the table, as if it were just Angela and Matteo. As if it wasn't the script they discussed, but something far more profound.

Did she imagine a charge in the air? A fizz and crackle of awareness?

'We need more sexual tension.'

Angela blinked, her mind slow to process his terse words. Finally, like an oxygen-starved diver coming up to the surface, she rallied. 'The script?'

One black eyebrow rose in haughty astonishment. 'What else?'

Of course. The script. The only reason she was here.

Ruthlessly Angela squashed the hurt welling within, that Matteo could look at her so coldly.

It was her own doing. She'd wrecked their marriage with her lack of trust. Because she couldn't believe a man like Matteo could genuinely care for her.

Well, she didn't have to worry about that now. His demeanour made it clear she was here under sufferance. There'd be no more words of love. Ever.

Angela swallowed and tilted her chin higher. 'You want a sex scene?' Stoically she refused to think of Matteo and Gina, naked and entwined.

'No. Not sex. Sexual *tension*. A sex scene would decrease the tension between them.'

Angela bit her lip. Of course. She wasn't thinking. Well, not about the script. Her mind kept straying to the tension between her and Matteo. To the tug of sexual attraction that grew stronger not less, every second they were together. Or was she the only one to feel it now?

'Matteo,' Gina leaned across the table. 'It's been a long day and I think—'

Angela cast her a grateful smile. The actress was trying to run interference. But she'd deal with this herself.

'It's okay, Gina. I see what Matteo means. I'm sure I can produce something more that will fit the bill. Something to make us question the hero's motivations even further.'

'You don't think he's dark enough?' the other woman said.

Angela sat back in her chair and met Matteo's stare head on. 'He's an ambivalent character, but we could make that stronger. There's already a question mark over his morals. If we ramp up suspicion that he, as the detective assigned to protect the heroine, could be the one stalking her, trying to kill her...' She spread her hands and shrugged. 'We want to use the tipping point between trust and fear, to have the audience unsure which way the story will go.'

Something flickered in Matteo's expression, making Angela press on. 'That seed of doubt is what sells the story. Can she believe him, despite the evidence? Or is she being blinded by sexual attraction? Can she really trust her heart to a man she barely knows? And if she does, will she survive unscathed, or will the man she loves destroy her? Will he protect her or betray her?'

It was ironic that her final project with Matteo mirrored so closely the emotional dilemma she'd faced last year.

Even more telling was the fact she'd written it in that heady period when she'd met Matteo and fallen for him like a ton of bricks. Had it been her subconscious warning her she didn't belong in his world? Or was it mere coincidence?

'I'll work on increasing her distrust and the possibility of his betrayal. You'll have it this afternoon.'

'Well, if anyone's up for the challenge of writing that, you are, Angela.' Matteo's tone was terse, bordering on accusation. He shoved his chair back from the table with a shriek of wood on wood. 'Gina, let's have another try at that last scene. I still don't feel we did it justice.'

Angela stared down at the text blurring before her eyes, not even looking up when Gina gave her clenched hands a sympathetic squeeze and hurried off.

Angela had wanted to know how things stood with Matteo and now she knew. He hadn't forgiven her. That jibe about her being the expert to write about distrust and betrayal proved it.

So that was that.

Since learning the truth about what had happened a year ago, she'd harboured stupid, optimistic hopes. Hopes that he might one day forgive her and they could try again to build on the love they'd once shared.

Now she knew better. She'd bruised his pride, questioned his honour and proved herself a coward. There was no going back.

She'd completely destroyed the single most beautiful thing in her life.

Chapter Six

'YOU WANT ME TO WALK you back, Angela?' Davide swayed a little as he shepherded her out the door of the tiny bar.

For four days Angela had avoided him, remembering Matteo's insinuation that Davide might harbour a hope to become more than a friend. But finally, today, she'd run out of excuses. Or maybe she just hadn't been able to face the prospect of another evening alone, shut up in her lonely hotel room with only her thoughts for company.

She was annoyed at herself too for letting Matteo's sneering remark about Davide stop her from catching up with her old acquaintance.

'I'm fine, Davide. We're in opposite directions.' For a second she wondered if she should offer to see *him* to his hotel. He'd drunk more than she remembered from the old days, but then he was nursing a broken heart too, since his long-term girlfriend had dumped him.

'You're a good friend, Angela.' He wrapped a long arm around her shoulders, giving her a quick squeeze. 'But you should have shut me up so I didn't spend the whole time talking about my problems.'

'I didn't mind.' She smiled and gently extricated herself from his hold. Davide hadn't come on to

her, but she didn't want there to be any misunderstanding between them. 'I value your friendship
too.'

She peered at her watch in the gloom of the narrow alley. She wished there was more light.

'Okay, then. I'll see you tomorrow.' With a wave
he turned, lurching slightly and veered down a tiny
side street.

Angela spun on her heel, ready to step out in
the opposite direction, then wished she hadn't
when her foot skidded on the wet cobbles. Damn
her pride. She should have worn her comfortable
flat shoes with their excellent grip. Except the
one defence she'd had against Matteo's narrowed
judgemental gaze these days was to act, and dress,
as if his dark mood didn't get to her. As if her heart
wasn't breaking all over again.

Instead she put on a show of emotionless professionalism.

So each day she'd worn something from the new
wardrobe her sister Sonia had gathered for her in
Australia. Something bright and funky, fun and
fashionable. Even if her new, electric-blue ankle
boots with their high, narrow heels weren't made
for Venetian back alleys.

She might no longer be the woman Matteo
wanted, but she refused to blend into the background as if ashamed of herself. Her soul-searching
had convinced her she'd spent too long trying to
melt into the shadows, as if she wasn't good enough
to warrant notice. It would be convenient to blame
her father's overbearing ways for that, but it was
time to move on. Angela was no longer a timid
teenager. She'd put on a confident face and hope-

fully one day be as brave as she pretended.

Angela stepped forward, consciously reducing her usual stride to a careful gait. She passed a bar, bright and cheerful, then entered a section that seemed gloomier than before.

Her nape prickled as if tickled by an icy draught and she remembered, with a sudden unwelcome flash, that while *Calle dei Assassini* might be a quaint little street now, its name derived from its ancient reputation as a site for murder. She shivered. Clearly she'd spent too much time immersed in the brooding thriller plot of this screenplay. She needed—

Her thoughts stalled as a dark figure peeled away from the inky blackness near an unlit doorway.

Angela's pulse leapt and her heart slammed up as if trying to escape her body. She was just debating whether to turn back to the brightly lit bar when she registered the familiarity of that loose-hipped walk and those straight shoulders.

'Matteo? What are you doing here?' She wished her voice didn't sound so fragile. So hopeful.

Angela cleared her throat and firmed her lips, wishing she'd remained silent. It was none of her business what he was doing here. Or who he was meeting.

He stopped before her, his face in shadow. 'It's late. You shouldn't be wandering about on your own.' There was no mistaking the steel in his tone. It was like the caress of a sword tip across sensitive flesh, brutally sharp yet with a quality that sent a shudder of stark awareness through her.

Angela blinked, horrified by her reaction. 'I don't need your commentary on my life, Matteo. I get enough judgement from you on my work.'

Angela side-stepped and made to walk past. Instantly his hand snapped out, fingers encircling her wrist.

Sparks ignited, heating his palm and sending shockwaves up his arm.

He hadn't meant to touch her. Physical contact was the last thing he'd planned, even if his brain persisted in torturing him with memories of their bodies sliding together, slick with arousal and eager with excitement.

'Don't you know how dangerous it is for a woman to prowl the streets of a city alone so late at night?'

Where was her sense? She was asking for trouble.

'I'm not *prowling*. I'm going to my hotel, to bed.'

The mention of her bed predictably made his body tighten. Days fuming over her distrust, and her insult to his character, hadn't stopped his physical desire for her.

If anything, working with Angela every day, sleeping just down the corridor from her, and not having her, merely intensified his craving.

In the first shocked instant after hearing why she'd deserted him, Matteo had genuinely believed she'd destroyed his feelings for her. But he'd been mistaken. He existed on a knife's edge, torn between pride, lust and something that might have been sympathy. Except he refused to let himself examine that softer feeling lest it undercut his determination to keep his distance.

Who was he kidding? He could no more keep

his distance from Angela than he could fly.

She'd buried herself deep in his heart and he couldn't excise her, even if he tried. He didn't want to excise her, he realised.

Angela yanked her arm back and reluctantly he let her go. His fingers closed on air and he made himself drop his arm to his side.

'Davide should have seen you to the hotel.'

Her chin notched up. 'Davide? You know who I was with?'

Matteo shrugged. Of course he knew who she was with. He'd made it his business. They might be estranged but Angela was still his wife. The thought stirred heat through his cramped belly.

'How long have you been here?'

Matteo ignored the question. 'Come on.' He spun on his heel and began walking. 'I'll see you safely back.'

One step and she didn't move. A second step and nothing. On the third he heard the soft thud of her boot and released the pent-up air caught in his chest.

Once upon a time Angela would have done any-thing he asked, ever eager to please him. Strangely, needing to win her compliance was somehow more satisfying than having her agree to every-thing he suggested.

Their tussles over the script, sometimes with a common purpose and at others arguing from opposing positions, had proven stimulating.

Now, there was a word. Matteo felt so stimulated in Angela's presence, it was dangerous.

They walked silently down the lane, turned and soon found themselves passing through a deserted square. They crossed an arched bridge, another turn and another deserted street. As they walked, close but never touching, Matteo felt his ire dissipate. Competing forces battled within him but anger wasn't one of them.

'Matteo?' Her voice had lost that aggressive edge.

'Yes?' He led the way through another narrow alley.

'What were you doing back there?'

It would be easy to lie and say coincidence had led him to the spot just as she emerged from the bar with Davide. But he'd never lied to Angela.

Curse it! Even now, when it would be a simple matter to salvage his pride, he refused to.

'Waiting for you.'

He swung round when he discovered she'd stopped. A light on the corner of a building illuminated her face. Her eyes were wide and her mouth sagged. Her forehead twitched, puckering into a frown.

'You *are* my wife. I promised to protect you.'

Her hand rose to her throat in a nervous gesture. 'But you don't *like* me. You're furious with me.'

'Am I?' Matteo didn't know for sure what he felt anymore. Being patient, giving Angela space and time to come to terms with the truth, was driving him insane.

'You've been stomping around the set for days like a bear with toothache.'

His lips twitched. 'Just because I've been exacting?'

'Exacting?' Her voice rose half an octave and she shook her head, her blonde hair sliding around her shoulders. 'You've turned into a perfectionist.'

He spread his hands, lifting his shoulders. 'I want this film to be the best we can make. Surely we all want that.'

Her jaw tilted higher. 'Then perhaps you should be a bit more patient. You'll get more out of the crew that way.'

Matteo's amusement faded. 'Any member of the crew in particular? Your friend, Davide, perhaps?'

She stepped closer, her hands clasped before her. 'He's just a *friend*, Matteo. That's all he's ever been.' She paused then went on in a voice so soft he needed to incline his head to hear. 'There's never been anyone but you.'

Matteo stared into her earnest, beautiful eyes and knew an urge to pump his fist in the air. Or to wrap his arms around her and haul her close to kiss that ripe mouth.

His pulse hammered. She'd told him that before, just days ago, but he'd been so shocked by the revelation that she'd believed *him* unfaithful, he hadn't known what to believe. He'd been eaten up with jealousy when he saw her with her precious cameraman.

If your wife didn't trust you, what was to prevent her turning to someone else? Suspicion had been a sharpened splinter, driving deeper and deeper into his gut.

His elation at her words was proof, as if he needed it, that he still cared for her. Not just wanted but cared.

'I'm sorry I distrusted you. I can't tell you how sorry.' Her voice grew stronger and her gaze didn't waver. He felt it as a physical thing, a warm touch on his face. 'I'm sorry I ran away. You didn't deserve that.'

Matteo exhaled slowly, feeling some of the brittle carapace around his heart crack. 'No, I didn't.'

He stood, head canted towards her, fingers flexing at his sides, waiting for more. For her to say she regretted the gulf between them now. That she'd missed him. That she wanted him still.

That she wanted to try again.

Instead her gaze dropped away. He watched her swallow, the action jerky, as if that slim throat was razor-lined like his own.

Disappointment welled.

Was that all? Had she nothing more to say to him? So much for him giving her time to realise they belonged together.

Tendrils of mist snaked towards them from the nearby canal, enveloping their legs in a clammy chill. Still neither moved.

Finally, his mouth twisting with the sour tang of disillusionment, Matteo found his voice. 'It's late. We've got an early start.'

He made himself turn, even though it felt as if he turned his back on a lost opportunity. Silently she walked beside him, though not close enough to brush his arm. That distance, in these narrow streets, seemed significant.

Once more Matteo was tempted to force her hand by seducing her into his bed. Adrenaline coursed through his body as he held himself in check, not reaching for her despite the desire beating through him with each pulse of his blood. It would be so easy to make her see what she was missing, for the sexual awareness was there between them, as strong as ever.

From the first the physical side of their relation-ship had been spectacular. Even that initial time when she'd admitted she was a virgin and Matteo had been so wary of hurting her.

But that hadn't happened. It was as if they were made for each other, their bodies attuned in a way he'd never found with any other woman.

Damn it. It was more than sex, at least for him. He loved his wife. Even furious and hurting from her loss of faith in him, he still loved her.

But how did she feel about him?

He wanted more than her regret. Apologies were a poor substitute for the laughing, loving wife he'd had by his side for so short a time.

They'd been apart longer than they'd been together.

Maybe she preferred it that way.

The notion scoured his soul, making him gri-mace as he opened the door to the palazzo and gestured for Angela to precede him.

He was a man who went after what he wanted. He'd built his career with a drive to succeed that saw him taking risks other actors wouldn't. He'd wooed and won Angela because he'd known within a week of meeting her that she was the one for him.

He craved action. To convince Angela they were meant for each other. His palms tingled with the urge to reach for her.

Except he needed Angela to want him, not because he corralled her into it, but because she wanted to fight for what they'd once had. He had to be strong enough to allow her to do that.

'Matteo? Are you still angry?'

They were on their floor now, walking down the

wide corridor with its enormous gilt-edged mirrors and studies in oils of Venice.

Was it anger he felt? Or frustration at realising the rift between them wasn't as easily fixed as he'd hoped? Because even now, Angela regarded him as warily as if he were a stranger.

He turned to face her when they reached her door. 'What do you want from me, Angela?'

'Want from you?' Her head tilted to the side and that delicious mouth pouted in confusion. Heat roared through his belly and Matteo had to step back so as not to reach for her. He could persuade her, he knew it. She'd always been putty in his hands.

Seducing her would ease his terrible physical craving but it wouldn't repair their relationship.

If their marriage were to work he needed *more*.

Angela needed to be more — a woman confident enough to give her trust and her whole heart into his keeping.

A woman willing to take a risk.

A woman who'd meet him halfway, supporting and loving him as he loved her.

A partner.

'What do *you* want from *me*, Matteo?'

'That's easy. Nothing's changed there. I want you to want me. I want you to *believe* in me. And in us.'

Her eyes widened, the expression in them, more than mere shock, reinforcing his determination to be strong and give her space. For he'd swear that was hope he'd read there.

Instantly his heart soared, till he reminded himself he'd been wrong before.

He drew a slow breath into cramped lungs. He'd

never felt so vulnerable. To relinquish control went against his nature. But last time he'd set the pace in their relationship and Angela hadn't been ready.

Perhaps she never would. The idea carved a chasm through his belly.

'The next step is up to you.'

Chapter Seven

THE NEXT STEP IS UP to you.

But what next step?

All night Angela lay, sleepless, staring at the darkened suite. She was torn between memories of him in their bed in Rome, his dark locks rumpled and his stern, sexy features almost boyish in sleep, and the image emblazoned on her brain since he'd left her in the corridor. His expression then had been harsh, with a frown raking his brow and his lips pulled into a flat line that spoke of pain or perhaps disapproval.

She'd wanted, hoped, that her apology would dissipate the tense atmosphere between them. That perhaps he'd reach for her, curl those long fingers around her nape, dip his head and kiss her, dispelling regrets and guilt.

You hoped he'd make it easy for you.

Did you really expect you could just say sorry and he'd welcome you back with open arms?

Angela rolled over, watching the silvery pink light of dawn colour the window.

Matteo had spoken of wanting, of trust. Her heart still ached over the pain she'd caused him, the terrible waste of a year apart when they could have been together. All because of her distrust. Yet through that time, even when she believed the worst, she'd wanted Matteo.

She wanted him still, with every needy cell in her body.

And she trusted him.

It had taken just one proper conversation with him to clarify what she'd thought she'd seen a year ago. That, more than anything else, highlighted how foolish she'd been.

At the end of it Angela knew he was telling the truth about the scene she'd witnessed at his trailer. Because Matteo had always been honest with her. He'd never hidden behind convenient fibs. His honesty was one of the qualities she'd so admired. How had she forgotten that?

Angela had spent her childhood and teens under the harsh authority of a man who demanded obedience. As a result she'd learned to avoid stating the stark truth if it meant keeping the peace. It had been a precaution to protect her safety. Because confrontation was to be avoided at all costs.

Matteo's willingness to be upfront with her had been something new and wondrous.

So new you couldn't really believe it?

No. She was making excuses. Nothing could pardon what she'd done to them.

Angela had been a coward. She'd believed the worst and instead of confronting the situation, and her husband, as he deserved, she'd forgotten all he'd taught her about trust and honesty. She'd reverted to the timid girl she'd been under her father's roof.

Angela pushed aside the bedcovers and padded to the window, resting her arms on the sill and watching the wide, pearly waters of the canal turn peach and rose pink.

It was a new day.

Matteo had given her a second chance at their marriage, bringing her here. It was up to her to grasp it and prove she was up to the challenge of being, not just a lover, but a wife and partner, confident in his love.

Angela had no idea how long it would take to convince him she'd changed, but she'd do it. Hope filled her. And excitement.

She looked at the Grand Canal and smiled, for the first time since she'd arrived fully registering its majestic beauty.

'Wow! This is some scene.' Gina darted a sharp, assessing sideways look at Angela then turned back to the script. 'It doesn't pull any punches.'

Angela leaned towards the actress. 'You have qualms about it?'

Once she'd had the idea for the new scene, she'd been totally focused on how to make it the best it could be, drafting and polishing for hours to get it just right. Her priority had been to make it fit seamlessly and ensure it provided vital new information yet at the same time increased doubts about the characters' real intentions. She'd aimed for a visceral hit of emotion and if Gina's reaction was any indication, she'd succeeded.

'Qualms?' The redhead shook her head. 'Not at all. It's brilliant. I love the hint that my character isn't all she seems. This darker edge is fantastic.' She looked up, her stunning blue eyes catching Angela's. 'What does Matteo say?'

Angela shrugged, ignoring the spike of tension

that kept her back straight as a gondolier's oar. 'I don't know yet. He's been in meetings all day. He hasn't seen it.'

Which had stymied her plan to show him as soon as possible that she'd moved on from her suspicions. For a woman who didn't trust her husband would *not* create a scene like this for him to play with another woman.

'You must trust him more than most wives trust their husbands.' Gina might have read her mind.

'Because it calls for you both to be almost naked?' Despite her excitement at the quality of the work she'd created, Angela's voice turned husky. She didn't want Matteo seducing another woman, even if it was make-believe for the camera.

Gina tilted her head, surveying her. 'Partly that. But more because it's such an emotionally intimate scene. It's all emotion, stark love, raw yearning and terrible distrust. It will strip away distance.' She paused. 'Some women would feel threatened by their husband performing that with another woman.' She flicked the manuscript with immaculately manicured nails. 'At least when it's as incredibly intense as this.'

Slowly Angela nodded. 'The truth is, once I was writing I didn't think about you and Matteo, just the characters and how this is much more effective than what I'd originally written. As for trusting Matteo…'

She paused, chewing her lip, surprised by the urge to unburden herself. But then Gina had proved to be likeable, generous and warm-hearted and without her sister here, Angela needed a confidante. 'It's taken a while and I've made some mistakes, but I do trust him. Now. I'm hoping this script will convince him how much.'

Instantly Gina wrapped her hand over Angela's. There was understanding in her fine eyes and for the first time Angela saw beyond her luminous beauty to the older, wiser woman she was.

'Don't beat yourself up. Trust takes a long time, believe me.' Her mouth tightened at one corner, making Angela wonder fleetingly about the actress's experience of trust and betrayal.

'And if your husband is a national heartthrob...' Gina lifted her shoulders. 'At least that explains why Matteo's been out of sorts. He was like a cat on hot metal before you arrived, unable to settle to anything. Now you're here, he's focused but so edgy.'

Gina sat back, her smile widening. 'I predict by the end of this film he'll be grinning from ear to ear! You both will.'

It was impossible not to feel buoyed by her assessment. 'It's that good?' Angela had hoped but hadn't been sure.

Gina nodded. 'It is. But more than that, if Matteo is looking for a sign you trust him completely, this is it.' She picked up her glass of iced water. 'Now tell me, what are you wearing to this party tonight? We don't want to clash and I'm sure your husband will expect us to do him proud.'

Matteo reached for the black silk bowtie and looped it under his collar. He tied it then checked the mirror.

Crooked.

He straightened it but it twisted back to sit awry.

Mouth tight, he stripped it undone and tied it again, this time watching in the mirror when usually he could do this on autopilot.

It was another disaster. Now he'd somehow managed an oversized knot that, no matter how he tugged and coaxed, refused to sit right. Worse, his collar tightened around his throat like a garrotte.

He swallowed and yanked at the collar, trying to find extra breathing space. Anyone would think he'd never worn formal dinner clothes! While it was true he'd grown up in rural northern Italy, where his mother's family had lived off the land from time immemorial, he'd been to enough galas and first nights to wear a dinner jacket and bowtie with élan.

Not tonight. Tonight he was as nervous as the skinny, eager kid he'd been in his first walk-on role.

His gut twisted in convoluted knots and his hands — he held them out before himself — sure enough they were unsteady.

Swearing under his breath, Matteo tore the tie off and flung it on the bed. The dress code for tonight's party was formal but they weren't going to ban him entry. After all, it was a PR coup to celebrate the filming in Venice, helped along by some high-profile contacts eager to promote both the venture and the city.

His elder brother Luca was one of those backers, and Matteo's best friend, Niccolo, Italy's favourite race driver. For a moment Matteo wondered how Niccolo would react to seeing Angela tonight, but he was astute enough to tread lightly. Frankly, his friend's reaction didn't bother him as much as his own.

The thought of Angela tied him in knots even more tangled than that wrecked bowtie.

He worked his jaw, trying to ease the tension there. He was wound so tight he felt like he might splinter.

All because of his wife. And that script change.

His heart plunged against his ribs in an out-of-control beat that sent blood pulsing too fast round his body.

Had she meant it for the message he'd been waiting for? A sign that she was ready to embrace change, and their marriage?

Running late after a series of meetings with city officials, then with producers, he'd been surprised to find an amended script waiting for him. Angela had already made the changes he'd requested at the last script meeting. But these were different. He hadn't asked for them, they were initiated solely by Angela, and they took the story, and its gut-clenching tension, to a whole new level.

He knew Angela was talented. There had been no favouritism when he'd got the rights to this script. But the twist she'd added, and the outrageous energy of it, was pure brilliance.

Where before there'd been subtlety and innuendo, now there was power and, yes, subtlety, but a whole new landscape of emotion. This was written from the heart. There was no holding back, no playing safe. Nowhere to hide.

And nowhere to hide for the actors either. It was challenging and glorious and if he and Gina could do it justice, would be one of the finest things either of them had done.

It was…brave.

Matteo shrugged into his dinner jacket, thinking of the risks Angela was asking him to take with this script. Not only did it challenge him as an actor, it challenged *them*, as a couple. For it would force him to strip himself bare, emotionally. And Angela had to trust him to do so, convincing an audience he was in love with Gina Moretti, absolutely besotted with her, and then return to his wife, his feelings for her still unassailable.

Did Angela trust him to do it?

If so it meant she was confident of him in a way she hadn't been before. It was a huge step for a woman who, just a year ago, had preferred to run than stand and face him.

There was only one way to find out. Matteo strode to the door, eager to see his wife.

But there was no response to his knock on her door and his tension ratcheted up another half dozen notches, before he recalled the message that she'd wait for him downstairs. He wasn't thinking straight. He hadn't been from the moment he opened the revised manuscript and hope had thundered through him.

Matteo's stride lengthened as he hurried towards the grand staircase, too impatient to wait for the handsomely appointed lift. He was loping as he cleared the stairs and entered the foyer, only to slam to a stop when he discovered Angela wasn't alone.

Two female heads turned to him. Gina Moretti was there. His co-star, with her red hair dressed high, and wearing sapphire blue, would be a treat for the paparazzi.

But she was just a blur to him. It was Angela who held his attention. Her blonde hair glowed like moonlight against the long, dark coat that muffled her from throat to knees. Yet the sight of her, waiting for him, her eyes aglow, made his heart hammer even faster.

Her lips were slicked with a red so vibrant it screamed come-bed-me. But then he'd thought that about all the bright colours she'd worn lately. That she was tantalising him, inviting him.

Matteo was torn between wanting to parade her for all the world to see — *his* woman. Only his. And to take her somewhere private, somewhere he could strip away every damned barrier between them till she admitted she loved him, would always love him.

He'd thought his patience these last four days had been phenomenal, but it was nothing to the effort it took not to sweep her back to the privacy of his bedroom right now. Excitement rode him, and anticipation. Tonight they would resolve this. He could wait no longer.

He dragged in a laboured breath and eyed her sultry pouting mouth. Fire coiled in his belly as he took in the way her lips edged down so sexily at the corners. He wanted—

'Matteo! At last. We were about to leave without you. I promised we'd arrive early for photos.' Gina stepped forward, but he couldn't drag his gaze from Angela.

She met his eyes directly, her own a blaze of... what? Challenge? Or something else? Whatever it was it made his toes curl.

He needed time alone with his wife to talk. And

more. So much more.

After a year without her, his patience was frayed to a single thread.

It would be a miracle if he got through tonight's party without causing a sensation in front of all the VIPs and paparazzi by carrying his wife off to ravish her.

Chapter Eight

ANGELA'S PULSE GALLOPED AT THE intensity of Matteo's scrutiny as he strode towards her across the foyer. She felt that indigo stare from her scalp to her soles and in every inch between.

His touch as he escorted her and Gina across the Grand Canal by private launch seemed to linger at her waist. Possessively? Was that wishful thinking or did he, too, feel that powerful connection between them? As if they were linked by invisible bonds.

Fear vied with excitement as Angela realised she'd have her answer tonight. There was an air of determination about Matteo that told her he'd come to a decision.

Which meant she'd be on tenterhooks all evening since tonight's party couldn't be avoided. It was specifically to promote the film's connection to Venice and they had to do their bit.

The event was every bit as sophisticated as Angela had feared. The grand old hotel was lavish, with no expense spared on furnishings, catering or the huge, formal arrangements of exotic flowers. Most of the frighteningly chic female guests wore black, making her and Gina stand out in their vibrantly-coloured gowns, and the sheer volume of jewels glinting under the chandeliers dazzled the eyes.

Bling was in and Angela would have felt woefully out of place, even in her stunning dress and silver stilettos, if not for the jewellery her sister, Sonia had given her.

Usually Angela wore only her wedding ring and the beautiful yellow sapphire solitaire Matteo had presented on their engagement. But tonight, to match the wide strip of exquisite silver embroidery at her waist, she wore long, sparkling earrings and a glittering ring on her index finger. She had no diamonds but the faux gems shone brilliantly, giving her much needed confidence.

A year ago an event like this, full of wealthy, opinionated people, eager to assess and find her wanting, would have been hell.

Tonight Angela didn't care. The guests faded into insignificance. She was on the verge of losing her husband and perversely, though that was what she'd told herself she wanted when she came to Venice, the idea put everything else into perspective.

What could these people do to her that could possibly be worse than Matteo dismissing her from his life?

No amount of arch looks or snide remarks could hurt the way she did when she contemplated a life without him.

Besides, far from looking down on her, the glamorous crowd seemed friendly. Was it reflected glory from being Matteo's wife?

Or perhaps they really are interested in talking to the screenwriter about the film that's already getting such buzz.

It was time she focused on the encouraging self-talk she'd learned at her positivity and assertiveness course in Australia, rather than fall into old habits of doubt and retreat. That was the old Angela, the one whose confidence bowed under the weight of pressure. That wasn't the woman she was determined to be.

So, while Gina drifted from group to group and Matteo got tied up in a cluster of serious-looking men, Angela was left to mingle.

Clearly Matteo wondered how she'd cope in this crowd. He'd kept her close as they entered, giving her hope that she might breach the barrier between them. She hadn't been able to read his expression, but she did register his tension.

Then, as more and more people had approached to talk business, that tension had increased, making Angela wonder if everything was okay with the investment for the film. So she'd urged him to go with them, almost had to push him away.

Because he thought she couldn't cope on her own?

That thought had sliced through her pleasure at the fledgling hope he wanted to be with her. She didn't need him hovering, no matter how much she preferred having him near.

Since then she'd intercepted several glances her way, Matteo's brow furrowed in concern. That, more than anything, strengthened her resolve not to play the wallflower.

The dress helped. Strapless, with cunningly draped folds and a full length skirt, it was of such an outrageously eye-catching red that when Sonia had first shown her, Angela had been adamant she could never wear it. That *never* had goaded her determined older sister into action. Despite the years they'd spent apart the bond between them had proved strong. She'd reminded Angela it was past time she stopped hiding in the shadows, blaming their father for flattening her self-esteem. It had been Sonia who'd urged her to try the training that had helped her to get a new perspective on her life.

Wearing this provocative dress tested her nerve, since she'd always tried to blend into the background. But she owed her sister and besides, she discovered she liked looking good.

Several women stopped to ask about the designer and Angela forgot her reserve as she raved about the up-and-coming Australian designer Sonia Rossi. Sonia would be thrilled when she messaged her later.

Angela even found herself laughing with a formidably fashionable woman over exactly what shade of red her dress was. The other woman's knowledge of the infinite varieties of colours astounded her. Angela hadn't realised there were so many distinctive shades.

'Will you share the joke?' A deep voice made her spin round. It wasn't Matteo, yet the man before her made her catch her breath. Niccolo Marchesi, the hottest race driver on the international circuit and certified heartthrob, stared down at her from fathomless dark eyes.

It wasn't his good looks or high public profile that stopped the air in her lungs. It was the fact that she'd last seen him at her wedding, when he'd been Matteo's best man.

'We're just trying to pinpoint the exact colour of Angela's dress,' the older woman said.

Niccolo nodded. 'Passion red. Obviously.' He paused. 'Matteo is a lucky man.'

He didn't say any more, just kept his gaze on Angela, and the other woman drifted away, saying something about finding her husband.

Angela lifted her chin. 'How are you, Niccolo? You're looking...good.' He looked good enough to eat, or he would, if she weren't a one man woman.

'Fine. And you? Again, my condolences on the loss of your mother.'

Angela nodded, recalling the flowers and message of sympathy she'd received from him while in Australia. Now she thought of it, Matteo's siblings had all sent similar greetings. There had been an abundance of support, even from across the globe at that distressing time. But she'd been too caught up in misery over her mother's death and her husband's apparent betrayal to really appreciate that.

'Thank you, Niccolo. I'm feeling...better now.'

One eyebrow lifted. 'And you're back in Italy to stay?'

'I am.' Angela refused to think of the possibility Matteo would reject her. She was determined to fight to get him back, no matter what it took.

Suddenly her inquisitor smiled, a flash of blinding white that transformed his face from broodingly handsome to charming in a second. 'Matteo will be pleased.'

'I hope so—'

'Did I hear my name mentioned?'

Heat feathered Angela's bare neck as Matteo moved in to stand on her other side. Instantly her pulse skittered and wildfire ignited to spread through her veins. Her knees trembled so she had to lock them rather than grab at one of the men beside her.

'Do you always assume you're the centre of conversation?' Niccolo's grin widened. 'It must be the actor in you, Matteo. They say performers are narcissistic.'

'At least we have real talent,' her husband said, a laugh in that husky voice that made the bare skin across her shoulders tingle and grow taut. 'As opposed to those who simply drive a machine around a circuit.'

He clasped a hand on his friend's shoulder as his smile broke free.

The sight of that smile up close, after a year without it, made Angela stifle a gasp. Her heart did a silly little jig and sparks of heat ignited all across her body.

It had been so long since he smiled at her. Seeing that grin up close reminded Angela sharply of all she'd thrown away.

How she missed the joy they'd once shared! The enormity of her loss ripped a jagged, gaping hollow in her belly.

Matteo swung his head around, his smile fading to something else as he looked at her. Something she couldn't place.

'Maybe the conversation should be about someone who has the talent and imagination to create a whole world in their head then bring it to life with their writing.' His words stroked her and his eyes were warm.

It was too much.

Angela's throat constricted as she stared up at him.

Since arriving in Venice, perfunctory smiles of thanks had been the most she'd received from

Matteo when she submitted revised lines. Most of the time he seemed so…contained around her, on guard. If you didn't count that day when he'd been absolutely furious with her.

'That's the nicest thing you've said to me in…' Her sandpaper-lined throat finally stopped her words and she had to look away. She felt the prickle of heat at the back of her eyes and refused to let him see.

A silent moment passed. And another. A hot shiver raced down her backbone as she blinked, looking down at the fall of vivid red fabric, trying to compose herself.

Of all the times to fall apart! At a simple compliment! She'd been doing so well too, mixing with so many elegant strangers.

'That's shameful. Your husband should compliment you regularly.' To her surprise Niccolo's firm hand slid around her waist, making her head snap up so she met his gleaming dark eyes. 'Come with me, *cara*,' he murmured. 'I'll ply you with champagne and tell you your eyes are as bright as the stars. Then we can—'

'Enough, Marchesi.' Matteo's voice, though soft, held a rare note that sliced through Niccolo's banter like honed steel through butter. 'If anyone is going to drink champagne with my wife and compliment her, it will be me.'

Angela turned to her husband. There was a fierceness about his features as he watched her that might have frightened her once. But she welcomed it. For she read in it a naked need that matched her own. A physical hunger, and more, at least she hoped it was more. At the moment she'd take whatever she could get from him.

Her pulse raced as hope rose.

'Surely that's for the lady to decide.'

What was Niccolo doing? Being deliberately provoking?

'The lady has decided,' she said as she turned to Niccolo, drawing his arm from her waist. 'Thank you for the offer, Niccolo, but it's my husband I want.'

That was when she understood. When she saw the flicker of triumph in his eyes. First he'd probed her intention to stay in the country, after she'd been separated from Matteo for a year. Now Matteo's best friend had made her admit she wanted her husband.

Instead of being annoyed, she found herself smiling at the handsome man before her. 'I hope one day some woman leads you a merry dance, Niccolo.' Something she'd noticed last year gave her an inkling his days as a fancy free bachelor were numbered.

'So do I,' Matteo said as he hauled her close to his side, up against a wall of bone and lean, hot muscle. 'Now make yourself scarce. There are lots of single women here who for some strange reason are dying to meet you. Leave the married ones alone.'

A frisson of delight rippled through Angela at Matteo's possessive hold, and his words.

Married. Matteo still regarded himself as married. Despite her earlier mention of a divorce and the revelation of her distrust. Despite his fury.

Surely that, and his firm hold, meant he was willing to try again?

Angela was so wrapped up in her thoughts she barely heard Niccolo's farewell before he peeled away to join the party throng.

'Did you mean that, Matteo?'

'Mean what?' His eyes, a rich, velvety dark blue like the last colour in the evening sky before darkness descended, meshed with hers. Angela's breathing turned shallow and swift.

'About my writing.' Not that it was her writing she really wanted to discuss. But his compliment had sideswiped her, taking her by surprise and revealing the true depth of her longing.

For answer Matteo secured one of her hands and lifted it to his lips. 'You're the most talented writer I know.' His kiss shot darts of fire up her arm then down, arrowing sharp and hard straight to her womb, making her tremble.

His thumb toyed with the solitaire he'd given her, his lips curling in a tight smile that looked proprietorial.

'That scene you've just written...' He shook his head. 'It's amazing stuff.' Suddenly his eyes lifted, his gaze meshing with hers and pinioning her to the spot. She couldn't have moved even if the grand old palazzo began to slide into the sea. 'It's *courageous.*'

'You and Gina are up to it.'

He tilted his head as if to view her better. 'Courageous for you too, Angela. There's a lot of you in that script. Others might not recognise that, but I do. You've laid yourself bare in your writing.'

Angela shrugged, the movement tight. Because he was right. She'd delved to the core of her doubts and fears to create this. Trust Matteo to recognise that.

'I want the film to be as good as it could be.' Her voice was a raspy whisper.

'You were only thinking of the film?' Matteo's expression was impenetrable, as if he wore a mask. Only those vibrant eyes hinted at something else going on within.

Angela shook her head, her hair sliding around her bare shoulders. 'No. I was thinking of us.'

Slowly he nodded, the gleam in his eyes pinioning her to the spot. 'It will take real trust for you to watch me film this with another woman and not feel threatened.'

He was right. Angela hadn't added sex scenes, though the characters did become lovers. But the screenplay would require a level of emotional intimacy between the actors that had to be real on some level.

'I can cope.' She lifted her chin to meet his gaze. 'I want to do this.'

Chapter Nine

MATTEO STARED DOWN INTO SOFT, toffee-brown eyes, and felt his heart turn over in his chest.

Here was the woman he'd fallen for, the passionate, strong woman who loved her work...and him.

Others had been fooled by the drab clothes Angela often wore, and her habit of melding into the background when part of a large, noisy group. But Matteo had always been drawn to the fire within her, all the more tantalising as he seemed the only one who knew it was there.

He wanted to believe Angela was that woman again. The one who trusted him enough to marry after a short, whirlwind romance. Who *believed* in him. Or did that other Angela still lurk there, the one who'd believed the worst of him, turned her back and deserted him?

Around them the chatter and laughter of the party filled the air. Someone walked by, jostling Matteo, pushing him closer to her. But he and Angela seemed caught in a web that bound them close, separate from the rest even while in their midst.

'I believe in you, Matteo.' Her words were soft but he felt them pierce his stubborn soul. 'I believe in *us*.'

She swallowed hard. Mesmerised, he watched the convulsive movement of her slim throat, pale gold like her bare shoulders and the upper slopes of her breasts. That expanse of delicious skin had driven him crazy all evening, even while trying to concentrate on business.

No, it was more. *Angela* had driven him crazy and not just because she looked stunning. The woman who'd written that amazing text had made him begin to hope again.

'I'd like to try again. If you can forgive me.'

'It's not about forgiveness,' he growled, simply because his throat had turned rusty. It was true. His pride had taken a beating and he'd been furious. But he'd had time to realise what really mattered. 'It's about trust, about sharing and belief.'

If the moment weren't so serious Matteo would have grimaced at himself. He sounded like some soppy agony aunt giving advice to the lovelorn. But as an actor he spent a lot of time delving into emotion and motivation. He might be as macho as the next Italian male, but he knew what he felt.

Angela pressed closer, so close he felt her slim form against him from the lush cushion of her breasts to the cradle of her hips and down to her thighs.

'I know, but I'm sorry. I really am.'

Matteo caught one slim hand as it rose to her throat. His thumb stroked the once familiar profile of the snug-fitting wedding band and the unique solitaire he'd found for her.

He lifted her hand and pressed his lips to it. 'Apology accepted.'

The sharp hitch in her breathing spoke of relief.

He felt her fingers tremble.

'And us?'

Matteo let his lips curve against her skin. 'I never want to be separated from you again.'

The terrible burden that had weighed on his shoulders so long slid away as Angela's smile broke free, dazzling him. She'd never looked as lovely as in this moment.

Lovely and sexy and *his*.

Urgency filled him and Matteo released her hand, instead sliding his arm round her narrow waist and propelling her across the room. It was tough going with the crowd so thick. He worked on autopilot, smiling, apologising, promising to catch up later. But with every step he headed straight for the enormous, gilded entry doors.

'Matteo, stop.' Her sibilant whisper, her hand on his chest, made him pause.

He looked down and saw Angela frown. Cold lead dropped through his gut. Had she changed her mind?

'Why?'

'Why? We can't just up and leave. The reception is for you, us, for the film. You're the guest of honour.'

Matteo snatched a fortifying breath. 'That's all?'

'All?' Quickly she looked around then leaned closer. 'Isn't that enough? I saw how serious you looked before, when you were talking business. There's a problem with the backing for the film, isn't there?' Her voice was so low she had to lean right up against him to be heard.

Matteo took advantage by wrapping his arm harder around her. Sensation shivered through him and his body grew so taut he had to focus on remembering where they were before he embarrassed himself.

'There's no problem with the backing.' Even talking took too much effort, given the urgent need pulsing through him. 'Everything is fine. More than fine.'

The only way it could get better was if Angela was naked and they could find somewhere private.

Suddenly a year of abstinence became an impossible burden. Especially as each breath drew in Angela's unique aroma, warm female, cinnamon and rich fruit notes.

'But earlier, with those men, you looked…worried.'

Matteo would have laughed if he'd been able. He hadn't realised he was so good an actor. He thought Angela must look at him and see he was torn between worry over how she'd cope at such a high-profile event, and his own desperate yearning to have her.

'Worried for you. And wondering if I could get through the evening without ravishing you.'

Once his pride might have revolted at admitting that, but Matteo had passed the point of no return.

'As for being guest of honour, I've done the necessary, spoken to all the people I need to. Besides, Gina and the others are still here.' He made himself wait, felt his blood pulse once, then again.

'So it's okay to leave?'

This time Matteo leaned in, whispering against her ear, feeling her quiver and arch into him as his lips caressed her. 'More than okay.'

Despite his ambitions as a director, if he had

to think about anything other than himself and Angela right now, he'd go crazy.

To his dismay Angela pulled back, but her ruby lips curved in a wide smile that hit his groin full force. Then she was urging him forward, through the crowd, like a slim, red torpedo racing to its target.

Matteo bit back a laugh of pure delight, ignoring the blur of staring faces. He'd wanted the old Angela, the woman with fire in her veins and passion in her soul. It seemed, against all the odds, he'd found her.

They made it out of the grand reception salon, down the vast, sweeping staircase with its elegant marble steps, through the main door onto the hotel's private jetty where a speedboat waited. Minutes later they reached the tall crimson and gold striped poles that marked the jetty at Luca's hotel. They stepped up, swept through the door and across the lobby. And all the time Matteo kept her at his side, his hand clamped on her hip.

A current of energy ran through them, circling from one to the other and back again, urging them on.

Finally, *finally*, they were in the hotel room.

Matteo didn't know if it was his or hers. There'd been a key card in his hand and moments later they'd tumbled through the tall doors into the dimly lit space beyond.

The door closed softly, reinforcing the fact that, at last, they were alone. That was all that mattered.

Matteo heard rapid breathing and the pounding of his blood and made himself stop, feet braced wide, his arm still wrapped around her.

He was afraid that once he moved he'd shed his civilised self and swoop down on Angela like some barbarian.

The sharp ache of hunger in his belly, the raw need, made him *feel* barbaric. Everything in him was drawn too tight and hard. His hands seemed too big to hold her lithe form.

Yet their year apart, a year of celibacy, of grieving the loss of his wife and wondering if they'd ever again resolve their differences, kept Matteo still. Logic told him to go slowly, carefully, even if the rush of testosterone nearly obliterated the capacity for thought.

Did she feel the same? Angela stared up at him with an expression that was close to adoration. When they'd first married he'd seen that look on her face and it had made him feel like the king of the world. As if he were invincible.

Now Matteo knew he was anything but. If he lost this woman again…

'Matteo?' He watched her lush mouth shape his name. A dart of fire tongued his belly then drove lower.

He'd never needed a woman the way he needed Angela.

His arms lashed around her, drawing her up on her toes, and higher. Fitting that supple body against him. Wide eyes met his. Her breath feathered his mouth, and then her arms were round his neck, pulling his head down to hers.

Angela saw the fire in Matteo's eyes, felt the strung-too-tight rigidity of his tall frame, and expected to be devoured.

She ached for him, was ready to lose himself in a rush of passion.

But her husband had other ideas.

It was as if, after twelve months apart, he was intent on learning her all over again.

His face blotted out the light and his mouth touched hers, gently brushing her lips.

A quiver ran through her from the barely there point of connection where her lips trembled, to the back of her scalp where tiny pinpricks of sensation exploded. It sped right down through her melting vital organs to the soles of her feet in four inch stilettos that waved helplessly somewhere above the polished floor.

Angela had no point of reference but him. His tall frame against her, his arms, rigid as steel girders, lashing her to him, his straight shoulders supporting her arms. His breath warmed her face and the rich scent of mountain pine and spicy male skin teased her nostrils.

Matteo's mouth slid along hers, sealing her lips, but not yet entering. She'd forgotten how soft his mouth was, for in repose his face was all hard masculinity. She felt the brush of his short beard, rasping against her chin, awakening long-dormant nerves.

Eagerly Angela angled her head, pushing closer. Matteo slicked his tongue along the seam of her lips.

Instantly, hungrily, she opened for him, needing the give and take of his open-mouthed kiss. But he'd already moved, his mouth at the corner of hers, then nipping at her bottom lip, making tingles of delight wash through her.

'Matteo.' It was barely a sound, more a vibration on the heavy air between them as he bit gently at her earlobe, then lower, nibbling down the side of her neck. She arched in his hold, her head flung back in abandon.

Angela's heart beat double-quick time. Surely it throbbed too high in her chest, as if seeking to escape.

'You drive me crazy.' The words rasped against her throat, a graze of lips and whiskers and warm lips. She clutched the back of his skull, fingers buried in the thick comfort of his glossy hair. 'I want every part of you, Angela. I want to start at the top and work my way down and then start over again.'

Her breath hitched and for a moment she couldn't make her voice work. She felt too full of emotion. Too full of a happiness she'd thought she'd never experience again.

'That sounds wonderful,' she gasped. 'But please, kiss me now. I can't…' Her feelings overwhelmed her. She'd walked away from this man, believed their love broken into a million discarded fragments. The enormity of what she'd almost lost, of what she'd barely saved, rocked her.

'Angela?'

Through her blurring vision she saw eyes of darkest indigo mesh with hers. 'Kiss me, Matteo. *Please.*'

Her lips were still forming that *Please* when his mouth settled on hers, warm and demanding. His tongue probed and she opened wide for him, losing herself in almost-forgotten pleasure.

The taste of him, utterly unique, burst upon her

like a flash of sheet lightning. How had she existed for twelve months without it?

Their tongues slid and duelled as he angled his head for even better access and Angela revelled in each caress.

This felt so right. As if they'd never been apart.

No, not that. For every cell of her body was more hyperaware of him than she'd ever been. Even in those innocent, heady days when she'd first realised the sexiest, most charming, kindest man on the planet was interested in *her*.

Then she'd been awed and delighted. Now she treasured every familiar touch and taste. The deep hum of satisfaction in the back of his throat, the grab of his fingers, digging through the silky fabric of her dress. The line of hardness along her belly where his erection stood proud and ready.

Angela was torn between relief they had this second chance, the desire to cherish every single moment, and the need to lose herself totally in the pleasure she'd only ever known with Matteo.

But there was more. Guilt still dug its claws into her flesh at the memory of how she'd wronged him. She'd been responsible for the wasteland that was the year they'd spent apart.

He'd forgiven her. This kiss proved it.

But how could she forgive herself?

Chapter Ten

ANGELA WAS FIRE AND RIPE femininity, flame and seduction in his arms. Even the hitch of her breath when he nipped her earlobe ratcheted up his hunger to desperate levels. And the way she kissed…

As if she too had felt starved this last year.

As if she never wanted to release him.

As if—

'Put me down,' she murmured against his lips.

It took a while to register the words. It was only as she reared back, her hands on his shoulders, that his eyes opened and belatedly he understood.

His immediate response was denial. 'No. You stay here.' Here being in his arms. He blinked and realised they hadn't moved beyond the entry of the bedroom suite.

Angela smiled, her lipstick smeared and her lips plump from kissing.

Who'd have thought her smile could make him harder? Yet it did. He wrapped one arm low around her buttocks and ground his pelvis against her soft belly. Her eyelids flickered and sagged and Matteo was calculating how many steps to a bed when she spoke again.

'Please, Matteo. Let me stand.'

He surveyed her features, the blush of arousal, the

half-lidded eyes, and knew she wasn't leaving him.

That had been his nightmare for too long. They'd be kissing, more than kissing, their clothes stripping away with the ease found in dreams, and suddenly Angela would make some excuse to withdraw. Then, once she was out of his arms she'd disappear and no matter how hard he searched, he failed to find her. He'd lost count of the nights he'd woken, aroused and filled with an aching sense of loss.

Reluctantly he let her slide down till her toes touched the floor. That in itself was an exercise in torture, feeling every centimetre of that lithely curved body traverse his own. Only the sight of Angela's closed eyes, pearly teeth biting her lower lip, lessened his regret. In this they were totally matched.

She swayed for a moment when she reached the floor and Matteo tightened his grip, holding her close.

'Now what?' His voice was guttural, the words slurred, and they were unnecessary, he realised as Angela stroked her hands down his torso, past his juddering heart, straight to his trousers.

Matteo sucked in a great gulp of oxygen as she undid his dress trousers. Yet as she tugged the zip down, the air escaped before he could fill his lungs.

Seconds later, warm, firm hands tugged his underwear down, releasing his monumental erection, then skimming the fabric down thighs that twitched at the brush of her fingers.

Matteo's head rocked back against the wall, his eyes closing, his shallow breathing a hiss of mingled delight and desperation. Eyes shut, he let her work his clothes off, lift one foot at a time and strip away shoes, socks, trousers and underwear.

Small hands stroked his legs. Every muscle turned to solid rock, his hands clenched into fists at his sides to stop him reaching for her.

Then he felt her warm breath across his groin and his eyes snapped open.

He looked down.

Ma che cavolo! She was going to kill him!

Before him, kneeling in a pool of scarlet silk, her hair like spun gold, was Angela. Her breasts heaved as if she found breathing every bit as difficult as he did, and that drew his attention to her décolletage, which, from this angle, was spectacular.

She moved closer, a pink tongue slicking that ruby mouth and a jolt of anticipation shot through Matteo, so strong he couldn't tell if it were pleasure or pain.

'Angela.' Her name was an incomprehensible croak, but it made her look up, her golden brown eyes locking on his.

She was going to be the death of him. The anticipation, the glory of her there, before him, was more than any mortal could stand. Because Matteo was so primed a mere touch would be too much.

Eyes holding his, she smiled and leaned in.

Warmth teased him, the moist luxury of her swirling tongue, then her mouth enclosed him and he saw stars. The world eclipsed into darkness and bright fiery lights that wheeled through his head. He began to shake and—

'No!' He clutched Angela's shoulders and pushed her back, groaning out loud at the wrench of sensation as her slick mouth left his body. An enormous shudder ripped through him, so strong that for a second he thought he was too late, that he'd spill before her.

Matteo stood, fingers tight on her shoulders, head bowed and thighs trembling, trying to think of anything but Angela kneeling before him, taking him as if he were some delicacy she longed to savour.

Hell! That wasn't helping. Every muscle knotted at the effort not to move, not to come.

'Matteo? What's wrong? You like—'

'I like too much.' It was a groan, rough and low. 'That's the problem.'

Just thinking about it weakened him. He heaved in a breath, the movement of his lungs so hard it felt like knives slashing his chest.

'Please.'

At the sound of that one soft word he opened his eyes. She was more beautiful than she'd ever been, and it was nothing to do with the sexy dress. It was the look in those glowing eyes. She looked like a woman in love. Like the woman he'd fallen for.

'I want you,' he ground out.

He shouldn't have said it, because it made her smile soften and once more he teetered on the brink of control. He'd never wanted a woman more. He was desperate for his wife.

'And you can have me. Later. First I want to start making up for what I did. It was all my fault that—'

With one swift movement Matteo bent and swept her up high, wincing as his erection collided with her softness, wrapping his arms around her as he leaned back against the wall.

'You don't have to pay me back in that way.' The idea had a sordid quality at odds with his potent arousal. The image of Angela kneeling before him was hard to resist, and the sensations... 'I don't want sex just because you feel guilty.' His throat closed on a rush of emotion.

Here he was, so hard one more move could have him losing it, yet talking himself out of what would, he knew, be pure rapture.

Because he didn't just want sex from Angela.

'It's not like that.' Her hands cupped his face and he forced his eyes open. They were so close it was easy to read her dismay. 'I love you, Matteo. I've never stopped loving you or wanting you.'

At her words the last defence around his heart shattered and fell. She meant every word, he heard it in her voice.

'But I feel guilty too, and I want to make this good for you.' Flame crept up her throat and seared her cheeks and a grim smile tugged at his mouth. Angela had been eager to go down on him but blushed at talking about it? His wife was a delightful conundrum.

'It will be good, *tesoro*. It always is between us. Yes?'

Slowly, she nodded.

'As for fault. Maybe I should have supported you more. I swept you into an unfamiliar world and expected you to adapt. But I was busy and—'

'Don't.' Her index finger closed his lips.

'You're right. This isn't the time.'

Matteo had done his best, shown heroic restraint, but there was only so much a man could do. He was, after all, flesh and blood, pressed up against the one woman in the world who could drive him to the point of ecstasy, or insanity, in seconds.

He stepped out from the wall, gripping her tight, then swung round and stepped forward so Angela's back was against the wall instead. He felt her gasp of surprise at the impact, or perhaps as his grip shifted as he propped her up against him with one thigh while he scrabbled at the long dress.

He swore under his breath, seeming to make no headway in the slippery fabric with hands that suddenly seemed uncoordinated. Then he felt slim fingers brush his as Angela reefed the material high.

Abruptly his palm met sheer stockings and above that bare flesh.

Matteo squeezed his eyes shut. It was too much. Too much and simultaneously nowhere near enough.

Then Angela relinquished her hold on the dress so it flowed over his hand and grabbed his shoulders instead. A second later she hoisted herself higher, first one leg, then the other wrapping round his waist, locking behind him.

'Angela.' He opened his eyes on her beautiful face and knew he was the luckiest man alive. Then she squirmed against him, tilting her hips high and thought fled.

His hand brushed damp silk, his fingers hooking her panties aside so he felt her soft curls against his knuckles. She shivered.

'I can't…' The words wouldn't come. Even thinking was beyond him, yet he managed to hold back, needing to know she was ready. Foreplay was impossible. There would be no finesse, no gentle teasing.

'I want you, Matteo. *Now.*'

Her mouth still formed the word when he surged

forward, parting slick folds and driving sure and hard right to the heart of her. It was so easy, so true.

There was a gasp of shock. His? Hers?

He met her wide stare with one of his own.

Had it ever been this impossibly good before? If so how could he have survived a whole year without her?

Matteo felt right for the first time since she'd walked out. Whole.

Then his mouth was on hers, stroking, tangling, taking and receiving. He half withdrew then plunged deep in a move he mimicked with his tongue.

Instantly he felt the tremors ripple through her. Her hands clutched him like claws, as if she held on for dear life, and her pelvis rocked his as the tremors grew stronger. So strong that an answering judder started at the base of his spine, curling round his body till suddenly there was no him and her. They were one being, utterly consumed by the fiery power that ripped through them like a bolt of lightning.

Except instead of obliterating them, this fire kept burning and burning as new waves of sensation burst upon them. He heard her high, keening cry, drowned by the sound of him bellowing her name, and then, an age later, there was only exhausted bliss, and the pair of them, clinging like the sole survivors in a world blasted clean and bare.

Chapter Eleven

THE FIRST GLIMMER OF DAWN blushed the sky beyond the window as Angela floated back down to earth, her heart still thrumming and her soul singing.

She lay, clasped in Matteo's arms, her head on his chest rising and falling with each shuddering breath he snatched.

Neither she nor Matteo had slept. They'd spent the night making love, and still they were no nearer quenching their need for each other. Angela suspected not even time would do that. He was her soulmate, the one man to make her feel like the woman she wanted to be.

She still couldn't quite believe they were here, together, sharing the aftermath of ecstasy.

In between making love they'd talked, sharing confidences, hopes and the heartbreak of the past twelve months apart.

'What are you thinking?' Matteo's voice, a rasp of deep pleasure across her senses, created a curl of wellbeing deep within.

'About how stupid I've been. You deserved better than a wife who ran at the first sign of trouble.'

'I thought as much.' He pulled her closer, so her slick body nestled even tighter against his. 'It's in the past, *tesoro*. Leave it there.'

Angela squeezed her eyes shut, emotion overwhelming her anew. 'Not many men would take that attitude. You're a remarkable man, Matteo De Laurentis.'

'I'm glad you think so.' There was a burr of humour in his tone. 'I want you to remember always how remarkable I am — intelligent, handsome, and a sex god too.' His hand slid down her flank, brushing her hip. 'But the blame for what happened isn't yours alone. I should have been more supportive, less wrapped up in the film I was making, more aware that you felt…out of place. The transition from self-absorbed bachelor to good husband takes a while.'

Angela turned, propping herself up above him, hot flesh to hot flesh, heart to heart. She felt like she'd come home.

The wonder of it still rocked her.

Matteo's spare, sculpted features were more than handsome in the dim light. But it wasn't his good looks that made emotion heave through her, it was the man beneath. She was sure she didn't deserve him but there was no way she could give him up.

She lifted one unsteady hand and traced the proud line of his brow. 'I should have had the courage to fight for you. I let my insecurities blind me to what I had.' Angela swallowed hard. 'I'd spent most of my life being told by my father that I'd never amount to anything, that my place was in the house, looking after him. Even though I thought I'd moved on from that mindset, when crisis hit, something inside convinced me what we'd shared had been an illusion. It was almost as if I'd been *expecting* to find you'd tired of me.'

'Never.' His large hand cupped her face. 'I fell in love with you just the way you are. Complex, talented and vibrant. We all have self-doubts. It's just a matter of learning to manage them.'

His touch against her smile felt good. 'That's what I've been doing. When I was in Australia I lived with my sister, Sonia. We hadn't been really close since our parents split and separated us. But we clicked instantly and she helped me look at my life.'

While Angela had grown more introverted and shy under their father's domineering presence, Sonia, growing up with their warm, supportive mother, was far more confident and willing to take risks.

'She helped make me over. And convinced me to see a counsellor about my self-esteem issues.' She paused. 'It's an ongoing project but I feel stronger.'

Matteo framed her face with both hands, his gaze intent. '*Tesoro mio*, I applaud you wanting to improve yourself. I can think of some areas I need to improve too, like my impatience, and my tunnel vision when I get engrossed in a project. But don't ever think I need a made-over version. I just want *you*.'

Angela drew an audible sigh, hearing his unmistakeable sincerity. No-one had ever made her so happy.

'Just so long as you know my image change is still pretty fragile. I'm not suddenly going to become an extrovert who loves parading on the red carpet, but I'll give it my best shot.'

Angela tilted her chin, facing down the insidious little voice that sounded so like her father's, telling her Matteo had only made love to her because of her glamorous makeover. That he'd fallen for her new look, not the real her.

She hated that voice and one day she'd banish it totally. Meanwhile she refused to let the doubts take hold. She'd never again let anything come between herself and the man she loved.

'*Angelo mio.' My angel.* Matteo lifted his head, his lips brushing hers in a delicate caress that sent a pang straight to her heart. 'This is about *us*, not the outside world.' His lips tilted up in a smile that was a blast of pure sexual allure. She felt it in every secret, sated place. 'I'll be very happy to spend lots of nights at home, enjoying private pleasures.'

'I like the sound of that.'

'So do I.' His kiss was full of promise. When he ended it he pulled her head down to his shoulder and wrapped both arms around her so they lay sprawled together, touching down the full length of their bodies. 'Now, it's time to sleep.' His voice blurred on a huge yawn. 'I haven't slept properly since you arrived. I've been living on caffeine and frustration.'

Angela snuggled closer, her pulse aligning to the steady thud of his heart beneath her.

'And when we wake,' he murmured, 'I'll convince you once and for all, that I want you just as you are.'

Even dazed with love and sexual gratification, Angela heard the erotic promise in his words. She doubted either of them would have the stamina to move for a week, but as sleep closed over her, she was smiling in anticipation.

The sun was high when she woke. Blearily she squinted at the sliver of sky visible between the almost-closed curtains. The first blue sky in a week. It felt like a sign. Probably because Matteo lay stretched beside her, an arm over her waist. The possessive gesture, even in sleep, made her heart quicken with pleasure.

Carefully, so as not to disturb him, Angela lifted her wrist, peering at the watch she'd forgotten to take off last night. Noon! She'd never slept so late.

For a second she panicked, thinking they were both appallingly late, till she recalled there was no filming today. Matteo had had the foresight last night, as he'd swept her into the hotel and past the manager's desk, to ask that a hold be put on their calls. Which meant they wouldn't be disturbed.

Beside her Matteo shifted in his sleep, mumbling something she couldn't catch. In the daylight she saw the lines of weariness around his mouth and recalled him saying he hadn't been sleeping. Had he lost weight too? His features, while still ridiculously attractive, looked more spare than she remembered.

Which meant Angela should *not* wake him up and suggest they shower together. No matter how tempting the thought.

But now it had surfaced the idea of a shower was irresistible. She'd fallen into bed still wearing makeup. She'd feel fresher, and more attractive, after a shower.

Gingerly she moved Matteo's arm, sliding out from beneath it. It took a while to locate and gather up her dress and discarded shoes. She smiled as she found one shoe nestled under his jacket where it had been discarded last night. Minutes later she tiptoed out the door and back to her own room.

Matteo groaned as he rolled over. He was torn between wanting to sleep for ever and needing the reassurance of his wife in his arms. If it weren't for his body telling him what a phenomenal night he'd had with Angela, he might have believed it a dream created by months of longing.

But it was no dream. He grinned, recalling what they'd done, and his blood pumped faster. They'd been even better together than before, something he hadn't thought possible.

But better even than the sex, was knowing she was here, *his* again. He'd make damned sure she never left him again.

Lying on his back, he reached for her.

His eyes snapped open.

No Angela. The bed was cold.

He jack-knifed up, scanning the room.

No sound from the bathroom. No spill of scarlet on the floor where he'd tossed her dress. Her scandalously provocative sandals had disappeared too.

Matteo ripped the sheet away and strode, naked, to the closed bathroom door. Inclining his head, he knocked and listened for her answer.

Nothing.

Heart filling his chest and gut swirling with foreboding, he opened the door.

Empty.

Matteo blinked at the bright sunlight streaming

into the bathroom, making the vast expanse of marble gleam.

It was late. Of course she was gone. No doubt she was in her own room, showering and dressing, too considerate to wash here where she might wake him.

Relief shot through him, easing his tense frame.

Once he'd finally let himself relax, his abused body clock had caught up with him, punishing him for so many days with too few hours' rest. Nothing, short of Venice sinking into the sea, or his wife deliberately waking him, could have wrenched him out of that deep sleep.

Yet, even as he told himself everything was fine, that Angela was in the next room, not on the other side of the world, Matteo felt rattled.

He stalked across to the dress trousers draped where they'd landed last night on a gilded chair. Not bothering with boxers, he shoved his legs in and hauled them up. He'd go commando and shirtless if it meant seeing Angela sooner.

In fact, he decided as he zipped up his trousers, he might tempt her into sharing a bath. Perhaps he'd ring room service and—

He was reaching for the house phone when he saw his own phone on the chair where it had dropped from his trousers. It was switched to silent but there was a call coming in. Angela?

'Hello?'

'Matteo? At last. I've been calling half the day. I thought you'd fallen in a canal or something.' It was the distinctive voice of the publicist working on the film project.

Matteo raked his hand through his hair. He

wasn't ready to deal with work.

'I'm sorry but I don't have time—'

'I'm afraid you're going to have to make time.' Her tone, usually sultry, with a hint of invitation when she spoke to him, was clipped. 'We have to decide what approach to take to those photos. That story will definitely feed public hunger for gossip about you but it's counterproductive to—'

'What photos? What story?'

There was a moment's silence in which Matteo found time to note how alone he felt without Angela wrapped in his arms.

'The photos of you and Gina Moretti. The story that you were having a red hot affair with her till your wife arrived in Venice and interrupted you.'

Minutes later, after a truncated conversation, Matteo trawled through the photos that were splashed across social media and several newspapers.

Damn it! Didn't the press have anything better to do than create stories without getting the facts?

He snorted at the thought. He wasn't so naïve. This sort of piece was grist to the mill for many. A few snaps showing what might be something compromising, an article, or in this case a dozen or so, full of innuendo and speculation plus quotes from anonymous sources 'close to Matteo and Gina'. Hey presto, you had a piece of fiction created solely to grab public attention.

If he weren't married, he mightn't even mind so much. But he was.

To a woman who'd already deserted him once for imagined infidelity.

His stomach plunged towards his bare feet.

Surely Angela wouldn't be sucked in by these lies.

Then he looked again at the screen before him. He and Gina were holding hands, looking about a breath away from a hot, heavy kiss, and as the reporter said, they weren't on the film set. They were on the balcony of Gina's hotel room.

Matteo ground his teeth. It was about the only thing the reporter had got right.

Matteo cleared the screen and called Angela. He could just walk down the corridor and knock on her door but that would take precious minutes. He needed to hear her voice *now*, saying she didn't believe any of this trash.

The call went straight to message bank.

Matteo spun on his bare foot and strode to the door, his pace picking up as he loped towards Angela's room.

She didn't answer the first knock. Or the second. He paused, hauling in air to oxygen-depleted lungs and forcing himself to wait.

Maybe she was in the bathroom. He checked his messages. Scores of them, mainly from the publicist but some from his family, one from Niccolo and another from Gina.

Gina! Belatedly his brain clicked into gear and he realised she wouldn't welcome this any more than he did. He dialled her number, rapping again on Angela's door, but that call went to voice mail too.

Great! His wife and the woman he was supposed to be having an affair with were both incommunicado.

'Angela? Are you in there? We need to talk.'

Utter silence met his words. Which meant either

his wife was out, or she refused to see him.

He leaned his head against the solid door, feeling abruptly as if he'd been sucker-punched in the belly.

After all they'd been through. After the soul-searching and blaming, after last night...

Matteo shook his head. He couldn't believe Angela would turn her back on him after last night. But then he hadn't believed she'd left him the first time either.

Just as well he was leaning against the door. He needed something to hold him up as his world shattered around him.

Chapter Twelve

'WHAT?' GINA RAISED A PERFECT-LY-SHAPED eyebrow. 'You said to wear something eye-catching.'

Angela shook her head and bit back a smile as she surveyed the actress. She shouldn't be amused, not with this press tornado threatening to engulf them all. Who knew what damage it would do to their reputations and the success of the film on which they were working so hard?

'Eye-catching, I said. Not something to give every man in the vicinity heart palpitations.'

For Gina had taken Angela at her word, arriving in a dress of candy pink and white polka dots that should clash with her hair but instead made her look sexily seductive. The fifties-inspired dress, with its figure-hugging fit and straight skirt with a slit up the back, showed off her luxurious curves to perfection. Add in killer shoes in candy pink, pouting lips painted the same colour and designer sunglasses that screamed 'movie star', and it was no surprise men were not just looking, but actually crossing San Marco Square to get closer.

Gina laughed, the sound husky and attractive. A waiter threading his way through the outdoor tables almost lost a tray of drinks at the sound.

Just as well Angela knew she had no reason to be

jealous of the actress. She really was stunning.

'You should talk. Though I shouldn't be surprised after seeing you in that scarlet dress last night.' Gina led the way to a table at the front of the outdoor café, in full view of the busy square. 'You're looking eye-popping yourself.'

Angela resisted the urge to twitch at her new dress as she subsided into a chair across the table from Gina. The dress, in a greeny gold that her sister claimed did wonders for her eyes, wasn't what Angela would usually wear out for coffee. The skirt floated in soft folds above her knees and the neckline plunged into a wide V, exactly matched by another V that felt like it bared half her back.

She settled into her seat and her pretty new gold and green bracelet of Venetian glass beads tinkled and caught the light. She'd bought it days ago, as if buying fripperies might distract her from the heartbreak of losing her husband.

But now she didn't have to worry. Matteo was hers. And she was determined to fight for him, no matter what stories the paparazzi concocted.

'Smile, *bella*,' Gina whispered. 'You're looking fierce. That's *not* what we're aiming for.'

'Sorry.' Angela smoothed her brow and focused on her companion, trying to block out the buzz of attention they were receiving. 'You're so much better at this than I am.'

The other woman shrugged, a movement that somehow highlighted her voluptuous curves. It struck Angela that if she *had* believed the scandalous story in the press this morning, she'd be jealous as hell of this gorgeous screen siren.

'Practice, *bella*. Just focus on something nice.

Like what you and Matteo did after he abducted
you from last night's party.' Her smile widened
as Angela felt warmth flood her cheeks. Not in
embarrassment but remembered pleasure. 'There.
That did the trick. You look like a woman who's
been thoroughly loved.'

Angela leaned back in her seat, acknowledging
the satisfied glow. 'That's because I am.'

'You need to calm down, Matteo,' Niccolo
advised under his breath. 'You're scaring the tourists.'

Matteo gritted his teeth and clattered down the
steps of another arched pedestrian bridge, shoul-
dering his way through a mob of people milling
around a tour guide holding a furled umbrella like
a flag. A couple recognised him and Niccolo, excit-
edly raising their cameras to snap them before they
disappeared.

'Calm?' he growled. 'If I could get my hands on
the paparazzo who took those photos, or whoever
made up that story about me and Gina—'

'You wouldn't touch them. Murder is still illegal
in Italy.' His friend strode beside him as they hurried down a long alley that snaked towards Venice's
main square.

'You're sure they were at San Marco?'

Angela still had her phone switched off but
Niccolo, arriving at the hotel just as Matteo left,
brought news that she and Gina Moretti had been
seen out together, their photos making a splash on
social media. Apparently speculation was rife about
his wife and supposed lover meeting the same day

the story of his alleged infidelity broke.

Though why the women would choose the busiest piazza in the whole of Venice to meet, he had no idea. If Angela really believed that story...

Matteo's heart sank. It was the worst possible timing. He and Angela had reconciled but their reunion was so new and fragile. He knew she wanted to trust him but those photos had looked all too convincing. Unless you knew they'd been discussing a difficult scene and Gina had suggested a new approach they could try the next day.

If only they'd waited till they got to the set to test out her suggestion!

If only—

'As if I'd get a detail like that wrong. I know the place like the back of my hand. I remember...' Niccolo dredged up a reminiscence about some PR event he'd attended there, surrounded by hordes of screaming fans and a particularly ineffectual MC.

Dimly Matteo noted the irony of choosing Venice, a city with canals instead of roads, to celebrate Niccolo's racing success. But he didn't really care. All he cared about was finding his wife. His friend was trying to distract him from the acid churning through his belly, and the fear, so real its weight was heavy on his shoulders. This time there'd be no second chance.

No! He refused to think that way. Angela was his. He'd fight for her, no matter what it took to convince her of the truth. He couldn't bear the thought of losing her again.

'Here.' His stride lengthened as the passage met the covered portico that ran round three sides of the piazza. Ahead, in the sun, were tourists, pigeons and a small sea of café tables.

Matteo's pulse tripped. He narrowed his eyes, surveying the vast expanse. For an instant he saw nothing but crowds. Then his brain made sense of the scene before him and he realised that despite the picturesque cathedral and palace at the far end of the piazza, and the towering campanile, there was yet another focus for the milling tourists' attention.

'This way.' He strode down and into the sunlight, Niccolo at his shoulder.

Gina's rich red hair would draw most people's attention, but it was the pale gold silk swirling around Angela's bare arms that snared his gaze. His stomach contracted on a wave of reaction. He didn't take time to find a name for the emotions soaring through him.

She looked fabulous, relaxed and sexy in a stunning green dress. Her arms were bare as if to catch the sun and she wore the locket that drew attention to the perfection of her slender throat. A smile lit her face as she chatted with Gina and his heart juddered from the impact even at this distance.

Derisive amusement twisted Matteo's gut. Angela could wear a sack, or neck to knee raincoat, and he'd still think she looked fabulous.

She was under his skin, in his heart, and always would be.

'Matteo, are you sure you want to do this here?'

He slowed his pace, casting a sharp glance at his friend. 'I need to see her. To explain.'

Abruptly Niccolo nodded, following as Matteo took the lead towards the table at the centre of so much attention.

'Matteo! Darling!' Gina's professionally modulated tones rose above the surrounding chatter. Was it imagination or did that chatter hush? 'And Niccolo Marchesi too. Aren't we lucky, Angela?'

Matteo slammed to a stop before his wife, the blood pounding too fast in his arteries, his breath unsteady as she looked up at him.

Yet instead of doubt or recrimination, he read nothing but pleasure in her eyes.

Could it be?

Dimly he was aware of Niccolo saying something to Gina and of Gina rising to join him, turning away as if to admire the view of the piazza. But his attention was focused on Angela.

'Darling, you came.' The wattage of her smile made him blink. 'We wondered what kept you.'

She put out her hand to him and Matteo instantly clasped it in his, discovering the rushing pulse on the underside of her wrist. Angela was far from relaxed, despite the image she projected.

What in hell was going on?

'*Tesoro*.' He lifted her hand to his lips, kissing her palm, feeling her trembling response, and something like hope filtered through his brain.

He yanked a chair out from the table and sank into it, leaning in to kiss her lightly on the lips.

At least he intended it to be light, a statement of intent for anyone who cared to notice, but when her mouth clung to his, something shorted in his brain.

The taste of her, that delicious, familiar scent…

He cupped her chin with his free hand, savouring her warmth, the softness of her skin, and the reassuring solidity of her, here, where he needed her. Slim fingers cupped the back of his scalp and relief racked him.

'Angela.' The words were a mere vibration against her lips as he made himself pull back, belatedly recalling their public venue.

Yet the magic didn't end, for her toffee brown eyes glowed brighter than he'd ever seen.

'Thank you for coming.'

He stroked his thumb over her bottom lip and watched, with mesmerised satisfaction as her eyelids fluttered. 'Of course I came. Why didn't you contact me?'

'You needed your sleep. I decided Gina and I could handle this. Our phones are off right now anyway. Too many people trying to call us and get a scoop.'

'You didn't believe...?' He didn't bother completing the question when Angela shook her head so emphatically.

'Not for a second. I knew there'd be an explanation. I rang Gina and she said it was an impromptu rehearsal.'

Matteo read the truth in his wife's eyes. She really *had* believed in him. It hadn't been a matter of Gina needing to explain.

'I knew I had to do something to scotch the story. So I suggested to Gina that we have a girls' day out together, drawing as much attention as possible. I figured, once people saw we were friends it might stop the other story, or at least cast some doubt.' Angela shrugged. 'You and Niccolo turning up here was a bonus. It almost looks like a double date.'

'I don't give a damn about the story. I only care

about you and what *you* believe.'

'Darling.' Her low voice was like a stroke of gentle fingers across his bare flesh. '*I* care. I care about you and your reputation, and Gina's for that matter. I care about our film too. And I'm ready to fight for what I believe in.'

Matteo leaned in and kissed her, a mere brush of the lips against hers. Yet it was the sweetest caress, a gift and a promise.

'I love you, Angela. I don't have the words to tell you how much.'

If he thought she'd glowed before, she was positively incandescent now.

'I love you too,' she whispered. 'I don't have enough words either and I'm the screenwriter in the family.'

Family. That word alone was magic. It gave solidity to everything he felt for this one, special woman.

And there was love too. Angela loved him. He felt the power of that with every breath he took.

For long moments they were lost in each other, till the shrill squeals of an excited child somewhere in the vicinity penetrated.

Matteo sat back, gradually taking in their surroundings. Sure enough, they were being watched discreetly and not-so-discreetly by everyone in the vicinity, though no-one sat close enough to hear their murmured conversation.

And Niccolo, being an excellent friend, was giving them privacy. He was currently halfway across the piazza, apparently showing Gina the sights as if she'd never been to Venice before.

'They look good together.' Angela murmured. 'That will keep the photographers busy and it helps our cause if they think they're a pair.'

'They'd make quite a couple.'

'Yes, but it won't go anywhere. I suspect there's already someone special in Niccolo's life.'

That jerked Matteo's gaze around to his wife. Niccolo was happily single, spectacularly so. 'Not that I heard.'

But Matteo found he had no interest in Niccolo's love life. A smile broke free as he drank in Angela's radiant beauty.

His eyes dropped to the pretty locket she wore and he remembered the jealousy that had skewered him, wondering if she carried some man's photo there.

'You want to see inside it?' She'd caught his look.

Matteo shook his head. 'Only if you want me to.' He guessed it was a photo of her mother.

For answer she leaned close, inviting him to open it. Her eyes never left his and what he felt now was stronger even than the zap and crackle of sexual attraction. This powerful emotion ran deeper, stronger, with the force of an ocean tide.

His fingers were unsteady as he slipped his hand between the gold and her warm flesh, working the catch.

It sprang open and sure enough, there was her mother, a pretty woman with a vivacious smile. But what made his heart hammer was the photo on the second side. A photo of him, hair rumpled and chest bare, laughing.

He remembered that photo. Angela had snapped it on their honeymoon. Seconds later he'd lunged across the bed and dragged her back down onto it so they could make love again.

That day had been filled with laughter and passion and a happiness so deep-seated it had changed him forever. He'd understood then that his life would only ever feel whole with his bright, shining angel in it.

Matteo cleared his throat and still the words came out husky. 'I never thought you'd keep this.'

Angela placed her hand along his jaw, pulling his head up till he met her loving gaze.

'I couldn't throw it away. Even when I thought the worst. You're a part of me.'

This time their kiss was feather-light, a gentle brush of lips, a trembling promise. Yet the power of what they shared left Matteo awed. It would take a lifetime with Angela to express fully how he felt about her.

'You know I adore you.' It was a small start.

Her smile was wondrous, filling all the dark shadows their separation had created. 'And I adore you.'

'For a woman who doesn't like the limelight you've coped wonderfully with being kissed in front of half the world.' Satisfaction filled him. And possessiveness. Angela was unequivocally his. She hadn't doubted him but instead had acted to protect him. The knowledge made his chest swell. 'You do realise there'll be people posting photos of us everywhere now?'

'Let them. We've got nothing to be ashamed of.' Her fingers gripped his tighter and a pulse of heat charged up from her grasp, igniting arousal.

'Excellent.' He stood, pulling her up with him. She came breathlessly, her smile dazzling.

Matteo tossed some money onto the table to cover the coffees, nodded to the hovering waiter, and led Angela away from the café.

'Where are we going?' She sounded excited, so happy she all but fizzed with it.

Matteo knew the feeling. The very blood in his veins was effervescent. There was a spring in his step and surely the sun shone more brightly than it had an hour ago.

He released her hand, instead slipping his arm around her, holding her close. 'We're going to expand upon your clever strategy by taking a very public, very romantic gondola ride. Do you think you'd mind being seen kissing in every canal in Venice?'

Angela's dreamy smile became a sexy grin that almost undid him. 'I look forward to it. Though it would take longer than an afternoon to get to every canal.'

Matteo led her past the Palace of the Doges towards the water and a row of gently swaying gondolas. 'Good. That gives us a goal to work towards.'

The sound of his wife's laughter filled his soul.

Who would have believed life could ever be this good?

AT THE
Italian's Bidding

Book 5, Hot Italian Nights

Prologue

*C*OME AND SPEND THE WEEKEND *with me, Lia. I need you.*

Lia reread the message in disbelief.

Niccolo Marchesi wanted *her* to spend the weekend with him?

Her heartbeat kicked from normal to frantic, revving just like the engine of Niccolo's latest race car.

She darted a look around the elegant hotel lobby, still empty of guests needing her assistance, then stared at her phone.

Niccolo never messaged her. Oh, they talked. Whenever he visited her family home for some celebration or when she caught up with her brother Matteo in Rome, Niccolo was often there. Niccolo and Matteo were still close after all these years, and Niccolo treated her as a little sister to be teased and indulged.

But he never went out of his way to seek her company.

Who could blame him? He knew full well about that teenage crush she'd had on him years ago.

The memory of his kindness then, his understanding, sent heat washing through her. No woman, not even a half-grown one, wanted pity instead of passion. And at seventeen it had been passion she'd desperately yearned for.

Thank goodness, at twenty-two, she was over him. She was busy with her own career, her own life. And if she took extra care to look good whenever she knew she was going to meet him? Well, who wouldn't? Niccolo Marchesi wasn't just a celebrated, phenomenally successful international race driver. He was handsome and sexy, always with at least one pretty girl in tow. Pretty? Make that gorgeous.

Lia frowned at her phone. Had he meant to send this message to Matteo? But no, he mentioned her by name.

How did he have her number, anyway?

The answer was easy. Any of her older brothers would have provided it. They treated him as one of their own.

Matteo had brought him into their home years ago. Niccolo had worked a season at the prestigious, historic hotel in the Italian Alps owned by his ultra-wealthy family. He'd been sent to learn the value of hard work. Lia's brother Matteo had worked there part time and the teenagers had hit it off instantly. After that Niccolo had spent all his spare time in the De Laurentis home.

Being addicted to speed and thrills like all Lia's brothers, Niccolo had returned every winter, since their mountain provided challenging slopes and perfect powder snow.

I need you.

Lia could imagine him saying it, an earnest look in his extraordinary dark eyes. His voice rich and deep and just a little husky as he reached out to her.

She blinked and thrust the fantasy aside.

As if! One thing she'd learnt about Niccolo – he might be a nice guy beneath those movie-star looks, he might even take it upon himself to be kind to a skinny, smitten kid, but he was *not* attracted to her.

In the years since she'd grown into a woman, he'd not once looked at her with anything approaching male interest.

To him she was the little sister he'd never had. So if he needed her it wasn't because he'd suddenly discovered he'd been pining for her all this time.

Lia settled back in her leather chair behind the reception desk and again surveyed the hotel foyer. Through the window sunlight shone on the cobblestones and tourists clustered to take photos of picturesque Bergamo, the quaint hill town with its small but ultra-luxurious boutique hotel owned by her brother Luca. She was even a part owner of the enterprise along with the other staff, due to Luca's innovative profit-sharing scheme.

Right now there were no guests needing attention. Nothing urgent to do. She turned back to her phone.

How could Niccolo possibly need her? At twenty-nine he was at the peak of his career, with so many wins under his belt the press were lauding him as a once-in-a-century sportsman. In addition to the millions he'd made from racing and sponsorship, he came from a well-heeled family. As for his love-life — he had the pick of women. It was well documented by the press and her brothers ribbed him about it all the time.

Need me for what?

She sent the message before she could have second thoughts.

Resolutely she put the phone aside and busied herself, double-checking bookings that had already been checked, and making a list of extra services that might be required. The American couple had spoken of a tour to Verona and—

A message pinged into her phone.

Need your help. Please?

Lia's heart fluttered. Niccolo needed her help?

The idea tugged at her conscience. Hadn't he come to her rescue when she needed him?

At seventeen, she'd been so fixated on him she'd almost convinced herself he reciprocated her feelings. When cornered by the other girls, taunting her about not having a date for the all-important local dance, she'd defiantly announced that Niccolo Marchesi, the newest, hottest star on the international racing circuit, would be her date.

It was a moment of insanity she regretted as soon as she'd spoken but then it was too late. The news spread like wildfire. Right to her brothers. And from there to Niccolo.

She remembered his solemn tone when he'd called to ask if it was true, and she'd stumbled, stricken, over her reply. The damning silence while he took it in. And the elation when, unbelievably, he'd promised to escort her, though it meant squeezing the visit into his already packed schedule.

She'd danced on air that night, radiant with happiness. Until he'd taken her home, gently kissed her on the forehead and made it clear that, while he cared for her like a sister, he had a girlfriend waiting for him elsewhere.

The fact was, she owed Niccolo. He'd stood by her and never reproached her for her foolishness. He'd saved her pride when it would have been far easier to let her face the consequences of her wishful lie.

More than that, he'd helped her family in so many ways it was impossible to count. Through knowing him, Luca, her eldest brother, had got valuable contacts who'd helped him as he developed his own chain of resorts. Because of that, Lia herself had a promising career in hotel management.

Another message arrived. This one promising an explanation on Friday afternoon, if she was willing to spend the weekend at his family's villa at Lake Como.

Lia chewed her lip.

Lake Como with Niccolo or spring cleaning her little flat?

Besides, there was that debt of honour. Niccolo *needed* her.

Lia ignored the flush of heat that thought evoked and told herself she was doing a favour for a friend. Whatever trouble Niccolo was in, she'd help him. Then she'd walk away, pleased to have helped and lighter for having cleared that ancient debt.

Chapter One

'YOUR *GIRLFRIEND*?' LIA'S VOICE ROSE half an octave and those remarkable eyes widened. Light brown, flecked with gold, they'd always drawn attention, even when she was a skinny kid with braces and a nervous habit of twisting her hair in her hand.

That shy, skinny girl was long gone.

He almost wished she wasn't. It had been far easier to deal with that Lia, his best friend's cute younger sister, than the dazzling woman she'd become.

'Temporarily.'

She planted her hands on her hips. 'How temporarily?'

'Just for the weekend.' He paused, wondering if, after all, this was a mistake.

But who else could he turn to? There was no other woman he trusted like Lia. Besides, she was perfect for the role. 'I promise to bring you back on Sunday night in plenty of time for work on Monday.'

He watched her pace across her neat lounge room, her movements all unconscious, sinuous grace, her slim body far, far too enticing. Desire punched straight to his gut.

Damn. That was a complication he didn't need.

Too often now he was aware of her as a desirable woman.

Shame sliced through him. Since she got over that painful bout of puppy love years ago, she'd made it clear she viewed him the same way she did her brothers. She was the only woman, apart from his grandmother, with whom he could totally relax. He could be himself, not the sporting hero or a walking advertisement for his team.

He valued that. Didn't want to lose it.

'Listen, if you're too uncomfortable——'

'It's okay.' She swung around, her long straight hair flaring around her shoulders like ebony silk.

Niccolo's fingers tingled. That hair of hers had taunted him far too long. Last time they'd met in Rome he'd laughed automatically at Matteo's jokes, all the time wondering whether Lia's hair would be as soft to the touch as he imagined. They'd crammed around a table in a cheap, cheerful trattoria that sold the best food, and Niccolo had basked in the sense of belonging the De Laurentis siblings always gave him.

Poor little rich boy! As if you haven't grown up with every advantage.

But her family had adopted him as one of their own, trusted him, and he couldn't betray that.

'So.' The word caught his wandering thoughts and yanked him back to the conversation. 'Are you going to tell me why you need a girlfriend for the weekend?'

He shrugged. 'My grandmother is celebrating her seventieth birthday and we're invited for the weekend.'

'*You*, not we.' She wasn't cutting him any slack.

So much for the little girl who'd once looked at him with stars in her eyes.

'Me and a friend.' He drew in a deep breath and crossed the room to stand at the window near her. From here the late sun highlighted her flawless complexion and the fascinating curves and hollows of her features.

Briskly, Niccolo looked away, out to the narrow street and a pair of guys strutting their stuff in jeans and leather jackets.

'You know my parents died when I was young and that I have no siblings.'

From the corner of his vision he saw her nod.

'My grandmother brought me up and she's always felt I…' Damn, but it was hard to share such personal stuff. 'That my life would have been better with a family.'

His gaze cut to Lia's and he saw the sympathetic warmth in her golden gaze.

He didn't need sympathy. He was perfectly fine as he was. Yet a tiny part of him revelled in the knowledge Lia cared.

How bizarre was that? It wasn't as if he'd had a terrible childhood. On the contrary, he'd had opportunities denied to most people. He might have been orphaned young, but his memories of his parents were hazy at best, and otherwise life had been generous.

'She conveniently ignores the fact I've got a host of cousins plus the whole De Laurentis family who've more or less adopted me.'

Lia nodded, but still she looked sombre. Strange how important it felt to wipe that serious look off her face and make her smile again.

'She's an imperious old lady but I love her. She doesn't nag but I know it disappoints her that I haven't found the right woman.'

As if there was any rush! He enjoyed being young and vigorous and pursued by gorgeous women. Okay, not all the time. Not when pursuit became stalking, or when he could barely hear himself think for the press of adoring fans.

'So you want us to lie to her?' Lia's mouth turned down in a sulky pout that sent heat unravelling through his veins. Since when had Lia's mouth looked quite so seductive? He scowled and saw her stiffen.

'Not exactly *lie*.' Not technically. 'The truth is I'd forgotten she'd asked me to bring someone special to her birthday celebration. It was only when we spoke earlier this week that she reminded me. Frankly I didn't have the heart to disappoint her. Besides,' he added with a winning smile, 'you *are* special.'

Lia tilted her head in that solemn, questioning way of hers. So too had she looked at him years ago across the scrubbed kitchen table of the De Laurentis home when he'd occasionally let slip some detail of his life away from the mountains. A world where the Marchesi name was synonymous with wealth, privilege and success.

'Surely you know plenty of women who'd be eager to fill the role.' Her tone wasn't exactly disapproving but there was a definite chill.

Slowly Niccolo nodded. Yes, he knew plenty of women. Beautiful women who'd be pleased to spend a weekend at the gracious old villa renowned even now for the parties his grandmother had hosted there in her heyday.

And excited to play your long-term girlfriend.

He flattened his mouth, remembering the recent paternity claim against him, made by a woman he'd never even met. It was hard to tell these days which women were interested in him, as opposed to his money or his public profile. There were some attracted, he knew, by the dangers of his profession, as if sleeping with a guy who regularly risked his neck on the track added extra spice. Or maybe they fancied themselves in the role of grieving widow with a stack of cash to sweeten the pain.

He shoved a hand through his hair. Since when had he become such a cynic?

'Niccolo? What's wrong? You look—'

He met Lia's serious gaze and smiled, watching the frown clear from her brow. But she didn't smile back. Maybe he was losing his touch!

'That's the thing. When my grandmother reminded me of my promise to bring someone I realised there was no-one I could take with me.' He put up his hand when Lia opened her mouth as if to argue. 'No-one who wouldn't get the wrong message if I invited them to meet my family, even if I explained the situation.'

Not that he could imagine sharing so much private stuff with any woman other than Lia.

He really was lucky to have her to fall back on, he realised. And how rare to know a beautiful, single woman who wasn't scheming to get herself into his bed or her hand into his bank account!

'You're afraid they'd read too much into the invitation?'

Niccolo nodded, watching as Lia processed that.

It was like waiting for a judge to pronounce sentence. She'd always been serious, her quiet nature a counterpoint to her brothers' volatility. But her smiles when they came, were worth waiting for. Even as a withdrawn teenager she'd lit up from within when happy.

He remembered her at seventeen, on the cusp of womanhood, yet so blatantly innocent and sweet it had pained him to think of her growing up and being hurt by some boy. He'd been protective as hell over her, ridiculously honoured that he'd been her first, innocent crush. Even when his manager had berated him for taking precious days off to fly back to Italy for her dance.

He saw her dubious stare and laughed. 'You think I'm caught up in my own reputation? Maybe. But there's no other woman I know purely as a *friend*, that I'd trust not to read too much into the invitation.' He didn't explain that most of the women he met saw only what they thought they could gouge from him. Or tell her about the sordid paternity case his lawyers were dealing with. Or the many and varied ways women, total strangers, had inveigled their way into his hotel room and other places they knew he'd be.

He spread his hands. 'You'll have to trust me on this, Lia. *Nonna* will be disappointed if I turn up alone. It won't completely wreck her party but I'd rather make her happy.' Especially as, just lately, he'd been forced to notice that his grandmother, despite her iron will, was showing surprising signs of frailty. 'It's just for a weekend. There'll be no talk of anything long term and I'll introduce you simply as a friend. No lies, but hopefully, a pleasant weekend for us all.'

Lia looked doubtful. 'And later, when she asks about us?'

'I'll tell her the truth. That we see each other from time to time but we weren't meant to be together.'

Was that relief or something else in Lia's bright gaze?

'And what will you tell Matteo and the others?'

Niccolo hadn't even thought of that. But Matteo was wrapped up in his own life at the moment, so patently happy to be reunited with his wife, Angela, that he barely seemed to take in anything else.

Hopefully it wouldn't ever come up. Because even knowing this was a sham solely to please his grandmother, Niccolo felt a furtive little ripple of masculine pleasure at the prospect of having Lia by his side all weekend. Lia looking cool and delectable and all too sexy.

'If it comes up I'll tell them the truth. I have nothing to hide.'

Except that when he looked at Lia he felt things he shouldn't feel for his best friend's little sister.

For the longest time she surveyed him. Her scrutiny was more intense than when his team watched the replay of his races, looking for ways to shave another few seconds of the records.

'What about clothes? I don't have couture dresses or expensive jewellery.'

Warmth spilled through his chest. Relief. She'd as good as agreed, if she was thinking about her wardrobe.

'You don't need haute couture.' It was on the tip of his tongue to say she'd look stunning in whatever she wore, but he caught himself in time. 'Just be yourself. No-one expects you to be anything else.'

Her lips pouted mutinously and Niccolo had the sudden urge to lean in and nip those luscious lips with his teeth. Warning sirens wailed in his brain and he shoved his hands into the pockets of his trousers.

'Be myself but pretend to be your girlfriend?' She didn't sound pleased about it but nor did she refuse. Finally she nodded and turned away. 'Just give me time to pack something for a party. I assume it's formal?'

Niccolo nodded, strangely humbled by her acquiescence.

'Thank you, Lia. I appreciate this.'

'Save your thanks for later, Niccolo. *If* we manage to get through the weekend okay.'

Chapter Two

*T*HIS WAS A MISTAKE. THE jittery feeling down Lia's spine was testament to that.

Despite the custom-designed luxury of Niccolo's car, she couldn't relax in the soft leather seat or concentrate on the blurring scenery as they passed.

Even though she was no longer a starry-eyed teenager who saw Niccolo as some sort of demigod, the idea of spending the weekend with him unsettled her.

Besides, she hated being part of a deception.

So why agree?

Was it really out of obligation because he'd salvaged her pride all those years ago? He'd gone far beyond what anyone else would have done in the circumstances. Plus he'd never uttered one word of reproach for the fact that *she'd* lied, spinning her pathetic fantasies in public.

Or was it because, when all was said and done, she *wanted* to be with him?

The idea was so unsettling her thoughts skittered away.

'Tell me the truth. Why lie to your grandmother? Just because she invited you to bring a friend doesn't mean you *must*.' The Niccolo she knew was honest to the core, just like her brothers. Or so she'd always believed.

She turned and looked at his profile, then wished she hadn't. Her gaze traced his straight nose, full, sensuous lips and high cheekbones. A squiggle of sensation stirred deep down inside her, an unsettling awareness.

His jaw tightened. 'She's been…unwell lately.' A swift sideways glance sent a fizz of heat spiralling through Lia and she shifted in her ergonomically luxurious seat. 'Though she wouldn't want anyone to know that.'

'I won't mention it.'

Niccolo nodded and turned back to the road. 'I know that.'

The simple words with their quiet certainty meant a lot. She'd never be more than a friend to Niccolo, but that, in itself, was special.

'She's not ill now. At least, she's slowly recuperating. But…' He shrugged and pulled out to pass a slow moving truck. 'Her illness was a wake-up call to all of us that she's not getting any younger. She has her heart set on seeing me happy, which I am, but her definition of happy is hearts and flowers and a woman by my side.'

The way he said it, with an almost cynical curl of his lips, made Lia wonder what he had against romance. Surely, amongst all those gorgeous blondes he dated, he'd found some he liked?

Of course he has. He just doesn't want to settle for one! He's having too much fun playing the field.

'Surely it's better to be honest with her and say you're just not ready for that?'

His smile was tight. 'I've been doing that for years. She *knows*. But she caught me out this week, assuming I was bringing a friend as she'd requested.' He laughed but there was no humour in it. 'She didn't sound her usual self, she sounded...' He shrugged. '*Nonna* is the least needy person I know. She's strong, iron-willed in fact, and she doesn't cling, but the other day...' He shook his head. 'Let's just say that for once I didn't want to disappoint her on this as I usually do.'

Slowly Lia nodded. Her own grandparents were hale and hearty now but just last year, when her own *nonna* had fallen and fractured her hip, it had struck home how vulnerable they were as they aged.

'Don't fret, Lia. It's just a weekend. Relax and enjoy the party. *Nonna* still throws the best ones, you know. There'll be plenty of interesting people and my cousins are good company.'

Lia tried to do as he said and relax. It shouldn't have been difficult. Driving with Niccolo was a pleasure. She'd wondered if, given his love of speed and his racing experience, he'd treat the road like a speed circuit. But though his mastery of the sleek, powerful vehicle was there in his effortless manoeuvring and quick acceleration, he drove within the speed limit. He never took chances that made her nervous.

With him she felt safe.

Her nostrils flared in a huff of self-derision. She'd always felt safe with Niccolo. The problem wasn't him, it was *her*. For there was a tiny, self-destructive part of her that still wondered what it would be like *not* to feel safe with him. To feel the thrill, the dangerous excitement of mutual desire.

She was destined never to find out.

'Did you say something?'

Lia shook her head. 'Not a thing.' Yet her thoughts kept whirring, her mind too wired to rest, though there was nothing to do but sit back and let Niccolo drive.

And try to ignore the deeply appealing, earthy scent that tingled in her nostrils. She'd know it anywhere. It hinted at cool, dark forests and warm male skin and it was innate to Niccolo. Years ago she'd thought it was some carefully balanced aftershave, but now she knew it was simply essence of Niccolo, unadulterated and headily delicious.

It was still her favourite fragrance.

What did that say about her? She shuddered to think.

The Villa Marchesi was unlike anything Lia had ever seen. Oh, she'd visited several of her brother Luca's famously elegant, exclusive hotels, even worked in one. Plus her brothers, all successful in their own careers, had lovely homes. But this was something different again, hidden deep within hectares of the most gorgeous gardens. Sweet wisteria scented the early evening air and she glimpsed colonnades dripping with delicate, white cascades of it. There were hedges and flower beds, tall, spreading trees and lawns so immaculate they looked like someone had unrolled an emerald carpet.

And beyond the beauty of the grounds was the lake, darkening to ink blue this late in the day. There were white sails out there still, skimming the water, and beyond that, a smattering of houses on the far side, then the steep rise of mountains beyond.

'It's fantastic,' she breathed, as Niccolo took the car around the gravelled curves of the drive at a snail's pace, wary, he'd said, of playing children.

Another swoop, this time past a small amphitheatre where classical statues vied with a froth of spring flowers, and she saw a small castle down by the lake.

'Is that it?' She frowned. Despite its grandiose style it was small.

Niccolo laughed, the sound like warm butterscotch lapping at her senses. 'That gothic monstrosity is the boathouse. Built by my great, great grandfather. See, there's a private pier.'

Sure enough, there it was, a long finger pointing out into the lake. An enormous motorboat rocked gently beside it and she could hear shouts and laughter coming from the family aboard it.

Then the car rounded a final curve and Lia stifled a gasp. Niccolo stopped the car while she looked her fill.

'You approve?' His voice held a lazy note, as if he already knew the answer but he turned in his seat as if curious to see her reaction.

'It's gorgeous,' she whispered.

Delight warred with horror. What had she walked into? She'd known his was a different world but this...

The neoclassical villa was square and imposing. Its warm, sand coloured walls were punctuated with huge French doors, framed by shutters in dark green. Traditional terracotta tiles covered the roof and there were balconies aplenty, all, she guessed, with lake views. Directly ahead were glossy double entry doors topped by a huge fanlight window.

It was grand and imposing, yet at the same time it was the prettiest house she'd ever seen.

A nervous laugh reached Lia's lips.

'What is it?'

She turned to find him closer than she'd expected, leaning towards her. Dark eyes held hers and her breath snared.

Lia forced herself to look away, back to the villa. 'It's the sort of mansion you see in magazines about the rich and famous.'

Niccolo's world was light years away from hers. She'd known him so long she'd almost forgotten he came from a family that had made and kept its wealth for generation upon generation while her own family had begun as farmers, tied to the soil and at the mercy of the weather, the markets and the banks.

Niccolo had fitted in so perfectly to the De Laurentis family, only his accent hinting he was different. Yet now Lia realised what an enormous chasm there was between them.

Warm fingers captured her jaw and gently he turned her to face him. Lia told herself it was the shock of seeing Niccolo's family wealth, not his touch, that made her so breathless. She wished she believed it.

Either way she was in trouble.

'It doesn't make a difference.' His brow crinkled in a frown, his straight eyebrows slanting down in a V. 'I'm still the same Niccolo.'

Lia looked into those sombre dark eyes and wondered why he cared what she thought. After all, they were only friends because of her brothers. She was the add on, the little sister they'd taunted and protected and let tag along. But sitting here, enveloped by his warmth, reading his serious expression, Lia felt...

No, she was imagining things.

Annoyed with herself, she stiffened. Hadn't she learned years ago, not to let her imagination run away with her?

'Of course you are,' she said briskly, pulling back till his hand dropped away. 'It's just that I never think of you like that...' Lia waved a hand towards the villa. 'Rich, I mean.'

'Thank God for that,' he murmured and switched on the engine.

Lia frowned. What did that mean? That he was pursued by mercenary women? It wouldn't surprise her. But surely there were others too, women who saw him for the decent, caring man he was. A man who—

No! She wasn't going there again. Lia distracted herself by straightening her clothes and fussing over her hair.

'You look fine.'

'Sure.' He was just like her brothers. 'You didn't even look.'

'I looked.' His deep voice hit a strangely gruff note that made her hands still. 'Believe me, you look terrific. You always do.'

And that was enough to set her pulse skittering. One casual compliment from Niccolo and she was all aflutter. Lia set her jaw. This was *not* going to happen again. They were friends, that's all. She was doing him a favour. End of story.

Nevertheless, she felt woefully nervous when he pulled up before the entrance. Surreptitiously she checked her lipstick when he got out of the car. Then he was at her door, holding it open with an old-fashioned courtesy that made her silly heart dip. Or maybe that was because of the winning smile on his handsome features.

'Welcome to the Villa Marchesi, Lia.'

She was just returning his smile when another voice spoke. 'Yes, welcome to my home.'

Lia twisted on her heel to see a small lady, beautifully dressed in a dark green suit that had the subtle sheen of silk. She wore shoes that exactly matched the suit — were they silk too? — and a choker necklace of luminous pearls. Her hair, pure silver, was cut perfectly in a chic, short style.

Niccolo placed his hand at the small of Lia's back and she was grateful for the warmth of his touch as he urged her forward. Before this exquisite little woman she felt rumpled and gangly.

'*Nonna*, allow me to present my friend, Lia De Laurentis. And Lia, this is my grandmother, Signora Marchesi.'

'I'm so pleased to meet you.' Niccolo's grand-mother stepped forward and clasped both of Lia's hands. 'I've heard so much about you.' At Lia's blink of surprise she continued. 'I've met two of your brothers, Matteo and Luca. And of course Niccolo talks about you too.'

Lia turned but Niccolo's attention was fixed on his grandmother. What on earth had he found to tell his grandmother about her?

'It's lovely to meet you, Signora Marchesi. And so kind of you to invite me here for your birthday celebration.'

The old lady squeezed her hands. 'The pleasure

is all mine, believe me. Now,' she turned to Niccolo, 'you can unpack while Lia and I get better acquainted.' She smiled, an unmistakeable glint in her eyes.

'And just to prove I'm not an old fogey, despite my advancing years, I've had the blue suite prepared for you both.' She leaned in and whispered to Lia. 'It wasn't done in my day, of course, sharing a bed before marriage, but I'm trying to move with the times.' She beamed and looked at Niccolo who stood statue-still beside them.

Lia's heart crashed against her sternum. Share a room? Her skin prickled all over as if each fine hair stood on end. A rush of blood warmed her cheeks. Now she really did feel as gauche and embarrassed as the schoolgirl she'd once been, sighing her heart out over Niccolo.

Slowly Lia turned, waiting for him to say something, anything to untangle the situation.

A pulse throbbed hard at the base of his neck and a frown furrowed his brow. Clearly this was a surprise for him too. Yet still he didn't speak.

Lia swiped her tongue across suddenly dry lips. 'I don't—'

'No, no, don't thank me,' Signora Marchesi said. 'It's the least I can do. I can't tell you how thrilled I am that Niccolo has brought you here. Besides,' she moved closer and Lia caught a waft of delicate designer perfume, 'the villa is full to the rafters and there are no spare rooms so it's worked out well.'

The old lady hooked her hand in the crook of Lia's elbow and turned into the house. That was when, suddenly, Lia became aware of how frail she was, despite her immaculate appearance and wide smiles. There was a tremor in that old hand and she really did need support.

Now wasn't the time to argue over what Niccolo's grandmother had planned as a generous gesture.

Lia darted one quick glance to Niccolo, but his expression gave nothing away. Was he as horrified as she? Any lingering idea that one day he'd be attracted to her died then, when she saw his grim expression. Clearly he was *not* happy.

Whipping her head round, she managed a smile. 'You have the most beautiful home, Signora Marchesi.'

Her mind was racing so much she barely heard the other woman's response.

Coming here with Niccolo had been a mistake. She shivered as a potent cocktail of emotions swirled through her.

Lia just hoped she'd get through this weekend without revealing her attraction to him. Oh, yes, she'd told herself so often that was a thing of the past, that she was well over Niccolo Marchesi. But just a couple of hours in his company and she knew she'd lied to herself.

He was just as dangerously attractive as ever.

And now they were stuck sharing a room!

Chapter Three

'I APOLOGISE, LIA. I HAD NO idea she'd planned to give us this room.' Niccolo kept his voice even, despite the strange, tight feeling that had gripped him since his *nonna* made her devastating announcement.

He'd been torn between reluctant humour at the timing of her foray into modern mores and something more tangled and complex. There'd been embarrassment for Lia, forced into this ludicrous situation simply because she'd agreed to help him. And a skein of something far darker and more urgent. Something that even now throbbed through his belly to the base of his spine and danced along his skin.

Excitement.

Desire.

Anticipation.

He clenched his teeth, locking his jaw tight as if somehow that could miraculously counter all the dangerous emotions simmering inside.

For the woman before him, the woman he'd spent the evening with, wasn't the kid he'd once known. He'd been aware of her transformation over the years but had battered down his fascination as best he could by seeing her only with her family, ensuring there were plenty of distractions.

There were no distractions now.

Her soft brown eyes surveyed him carefully from across the bedroom. She'd been like that all evening, careful. As if one false move might disrupt her equilibrium.

Did she sense his reaction to her? Did she fear he was going to jump her now they were alone?

Hell! The idea of Lia scared of him… He swung round and paced to the balcony, opening the full-length windows and letting in some air.

'I know you didn't.' Her voice was cool. 'But I hoped you'd have a solution. You didn't say anything at all.'

Niccolo swung round at the accusation in her voice. 'What was there to say without revealing the truth about us? Besides, you heard her. She's invited all my relatives plus a host of old friends. The villa is huge, I grant you, but it's fully packed.'

Lia sat down abruptly, not on the wide bed, he noticed, but on a damask-covered chair. She rubbed her fingers over her forehead and instantly Niccolo felt ashamed. She looked exhausted, and not surprising. They'd spent the evening with his extended family. Lia had held her own beautifully, chatting with cousins and aunts, cooing over a couple of babies, and, of course, entrancing all the men.

In four strides he crossed to where she sat and hunkered down before her. Instantly she froze and regret stabbed. Was she really so wary of him?

Gently he took her hand, rubbing his thumb over her smooth skin, noticing again the soft, exotic lily scent he'd always associated with her. Either she still used the same perfume or the entrancing fragrance was entirely natural.

'It's a ridiculous situation, Lia, but I promise you we'll get through it.' This close her doubtful gaze was like sunlight, golden and alluring. 'As for not disabusing my grandmother on the spot...' He shrugged and again felt the weight of his recent fears for the old lady.

'You saw yourself how frail she is. She puts on a good front but she's still recuperating from major surgery.' That scare had been the catalyst that had made him rethink his life.

Lia's fingers turned and gripped his. 'Will she be all right?' Concern laced her beautiful, dulcet voice and darkened her eyes. It was a phenomenon he'd seen before with Lia and still it fascinated him, the way strong emotion changed the colour of her eyes.

'The doctors believe so. With luck and care she'll be around for a long time yet.' At least he hoped so. 'But, in the circumstances, I didn't want to make a fuss when we can sort this out ourselves. Besides, giving us the suite is a huge concession and I didn't want to embarrass her in front of someone she'd just met by throwing the gesture in her face.'

Lia held his gaze steadily. 'It's nice to see how you care for her, but I don't see how we can *sort this out*. Unless you're proposing to climb out the window and sleep in the boatshed?'

Niccolo shook his head. Actually, that was an option, but only as a last resort. 'I'd have to be up before the crack of dawn. The kids usually race down there as soon as it's light. Plus I heard my cousin, Giancarlo, promise to take them out on his boat. No, my option is simpler. We share the suite but not the bed.'

He paused, watching her intently. 'If you trust me.'

Still her brow knitted. 'Where would you sleep?'

He gestured to the chaise longue on the other side of the room. It was a decorative antique and probably not much softer than the floor but it would have to do.

Lia's fingers stirred in his. Did she realise he still held them? He *liked* touching her. He enjoyed the differences between them, her hand slender and soft, his broad and callused. More, there was a scintillating shiver of…something that burred under his skin whenever they came in contact. Even now, when she was clearly distracted, thinking about his words rather than him.

Maybe this attraction he felt was totally one-sided!

Niccolo didn't know whether to be relieved at the idea or horrified. It lacerated his pride. He was used to women responding to him. He'd never had to work hard for a woman's attention in his life.

But you don't want that from Lia, do you?

She's your best friend's little sister.

You're supposed to protect her, not seduce her.

Abruptly, Niccolo pulled back, dropping her hand and shot to his feet.

She tilted her neck and looked up at him and he felt a powerful surge of possessiveness swamp him. He wanted to—

'Okay.'

'Okay?' He frowned, still lost in urgent thoughts of how he'd like to get up close and very, very personal with Lia, the elegant, mesmerising woman he'd known since she was in braces.

It didn't matter how often he reminded himself
of their shared history, the trust between him and
her brothers. Nothing could squash the rising tide
of lust he strove so hard to hide.

'We'll share the suite, but not the bed.'

She got to her feet, her hands going to her neat
chignon. Seconds later her hair cascaded around
her shoulders, glossy and inviting.

Reflexively Niccolo took another step back,
needing distance to counter the urge to grab a
fistful of that lustrous hair and run it through his
fingers.

'I'm tired.' She didn't meet his eyes but turned to
her suitcase and removed a few handfuls of bright
silk. 'I'll take the bathroom first if that's okay.'

'Of course.'

But it wasn't okay. Because no matter how he
tried to distract himself, Niccolo was supremely
aware of the fact that just beyond the bathroom
door, under the shower he could just hear, was Lia,
naked and all too alluring.

Niccolo turned and strode out onto the balcony.
He'd busied himself arranging a couple of pillows
on the chaise longue, pulling a T shirt and boxers
from his bag. They'd keep him decent tonight. He
wouldn't shock Lia by sleeping in the buff as he
usually did.

That took a whole two minutes. So finally, reluctantly, he turned his phone back on. Sure enough,
there were half a dozen messages from his manager.
Reluctantly he hit speed dial. Enrico answered at

once and was soon in full flood.

His manager knew he had things on his mind, decisions to make, and he was determined to convince Niccolo to make the *right* decision by his team, his fans around the globe, and of course, Enrico.

Niccolo sighed and scraped his palm around the back of his neck. He really was becoming negative!

Since racing had ceased to be about freedom and fun and turned into a pressure cooker of everyone else's expectations.

Oh, he could handle the pressure. And he still loved the speed. But the truth was he no longer loved racing the way he once had. Was it boredom after so many wins? No, surely he wasn't so conceited. Yet increasingly he was dissatisfied with the life he led, and the world he inhabited. Put on a pedestal simply because he was gifted with good reflexes and a talent for speed.

Increasingly he found himself hankering after other challenges.

A sound from the room behind him made him swing round.

Instantly his tension notched to breaking point. The muscles of his neck and shoulders drew taut and he lost the thread of the phone conversation as Enrico's voice quacked down the line.

Madonna mia! If this was a test he was doomed to fail. Even with the length of the room and the balcony between him and Lia as she emerged from the bathroom, Niccolo felt his blood rush to his groin so fast he almost reeled.

She wore a silk negligee the colour of mountain violets, dark and rich. She'd tied it tight at her waist, as if to cover herself as much as possible. But that only drew the fabric taut against her curves. Fascinated, Niccolo traced her delectable figure with his gaze. She was slim but rounded everywhere a man could want.

His blood beat hard and fast, as if he were on the track, waiting for the starter's signal.

Lia turned and the light from the hand-blown chandelier spilled in caressing waves across her hips and high breasts, her exquisite profile and the dark gloss of her hair. His mouth turned arid. He'd known, oh, how he'd known, that Lia was sexy and beautiful. But the intimacy of seeing her like this undid something vital within him.

She reached towards the dressing table and her long hair hid her face.

'Niccolo?' Enrico barked in his ear. 'Did you hear me? We need a definite commitment this coming week.'

Niccolo expelled the breath he hadn't known he'd held and forked his hand through his hair. Now wasn't the time for this discussion, not when he couldn't focus on anything but the woman pulling back the bedcovers.

In one swift, almost furtive movement, she slipped off her negligee to reveal a lace-edged nightgown. He had an impression of bare arms and a narrow back, pale as the creamy camellias blooming in the garden below, of a neatly rounded bottom outlined in dark silk, and then she was in the bed, hauling the covers high.

'Niccolo?'

He swung round to stare across the lake to the sprinkle of lights on the far side. 'I heard you,

Enrico, and all the points you raised. But I need time. I'll call you after the weekend.'

He waited a full five minutes, just standing, staring into the night, waiting for his erection to subside.

He scraped a hand across his jaw. He could not, absolutely *not* go in there while he was still aroused. Lia trusted him. Her *family* trusted him to look after her.

Another five minutes, then another five. Finally, when the roar of desire was a mere hum in his veins, he swung round and walked into the room.

She'd turned off the overhead light but that only made the atmosphere more— No, he wasn't going there. He kept his eyes off her as he grabbed what he needed and headed to the bathroom for a long, cold shower.

'Goodnight, Niccolo.' Her voice sounded different. Small, as if muffled by the vast four-poster bed.

He slammed to a halt but didn't turn. 'Goodnight, Lia. Sleep well.'

It was going to be a hell of a long night.

Chapter Four

THE BED WAS AS COMFORTABLE as a cloud yet Lia lay on her side and stared at the view through the window. The dark mountain rose on the far side of the lake, and closer, the tops of the trees shivered in the moonlit garden. She'd forgotten to draw the curtains, too caught up in the need to get to bed and out of Niccolo's sight as soon as possible.

If she'd known she'd be sharing a room with him she'd have brought long pyjamas that buttoned to the neck, not the new silk nightdress she'd bought with her recent performance bonus from work.

Not that she'd needed to worry about him seeing her half undressed. He hadn't even looked at the bed when he came in from the balcony, or when he returned from the bathroom.

If she'd needed any proof that he didn't find her attractive, that was it.

Why should he? He was used to famous models and beautiful socialites draping themselves over him. Lia, like everyone else in Italy, and the world for that matter, had seen the photos. Everywhere Niccolo went there was a gorgeous woman glued to his side. Usually blonde, usually looking as if she couldn't wait to get him naked.

Lia's breath caught on a rip of pain.

It shouldn't hurt that he didn't see her like that. She didn't *want* him to think of her as just another convenient woman to warm his bed.

And yet…

It was no good. No matter how she tried she couldn't evade the fact she wanted him in *her* bed. And more, in her life, not just as a family friend. She wanted him as a woman wants a man. It was a deep-seated ache, a gnawing hunger, a heady excitement, and at the same time a tenderness, a concern that nothing could shift.

Why else had she scurried to do his bidding when he'd put forward his outrageous proposal?

What had begun as a schoolgirl crush had bloomed into something far more elemental. Niccolo was the reason she'd never been with a man. No man she'd dated ever made her feel like *this*, so alive it was as if sparks showered her every time their eyes locked.

On the far side of the room the chaise longue squeaked as Niccolo rolled over again. For the longest time he'd lain unmoving, but as the moonlight had shifted across the floor, he'd turned more often. Not surprising, since the seat was shorter than him and for all its elegance, probably not particularly comfortable.

Lia stared wide-eyed into the night and faced the truth. She…cared for Niccolo. Cared too much. But this was no romantic film where the gorgeous hero suddenly realised the girl he'd known forever had grown up. He'd never love her. Never view her as anything more than a friend. He'd be horrified to know she'd saved herself for him. Not deliberately, but because no other man had measured up to *him*.

Her heart sank and she pressed her lips so hard together that pain radiated along her jaw.

Even if he did notice her, or want her the way she craved him, they came from completely different worlds. Visiting his grandmother's villa had shown her exactly how far apart those worlds were.

The plain fact was he liked her, but would never see her the way she wanted him to. Never care the way she wanted. As for viewing her with lust…!

Another series of noises as Niccolo tried to get comfortable in his makeshift bed.

On a surge of energy, fuelled by anger at her own stupid imaginings, Lia pulled back the covers and stood. Even from here, in the half dark, she could see how uncomfortable Niccolo was. His head was cricked up at an angle and his feet dangled off the end.

Lia looked back at the four-poster. It was enormous. Far too big for one person.

'Niccolo.'

Instantly his head jerked up and his eyes met hers. Strange how, even in the gloom she imagined she felt the impact of his dark-eyed stare.

A tiny tremor passed through her and Lia wrapped her arms around herself, impatient at her body's instant response.

'Don't torture yourself any longer. The bed's big enough for two.'

'Sorry?' He sat up. Pale light washed his broad shoulders and solid chest, emphasising the fierce, honed strength of him. Lia's pulse skittered abruptly to a faster beat.

His hair was rumpled, his powerful legs long and

bare. Even those feet, now planted apart on the floor, looked… strong.

Something, a primitive voice of warning, clamoured that she was making a mistake. Stripped to just a T shirt and boxers, Niccolo looked more elemental, more *masculine* than ever.

More dangerous.

Nonsense. He'd only be dangerous if he was attracted, which clearly he wasn't. He was a friend, a platonic friend. Damn him!

Furious, with herself and him, Lia spun round and stalked back to the bed.

'Don't worry, Niccolo. I don't expect you to make love to me if we share a bed. You might as well get some sleep so you can enjoy the celebrations tomorrow.'

Pride dictated that at least one of them emerged tomorrow looking as if they'd slept. It was bad enough that Niccolo's family thought they were having sex half the night.

For some reason the idea only stoked her anger. She flipped her hair back over her shoulder, wondering for the thousandth time why she hadn't cut it. She was tired of it, tired of everything. Her skin felt taut, her body stiff and uncoordinated. Even the lace of her lovely new nightgown scratched. Why had she packed this for a weekend away with Niccolo? Because she'd hoped he might come to her room and—

'I don't want to disturb you.'

Even his voice, deep and so deliciously warm it settled on her like a blanket, made her grit her teeth. She was too close to doing something she'd regret, like telling him how she felt. Like imploring him to take her in his arms.

'What do you think you've been doing for the past couple of hours?' Her voice was waspish and she didn't care. 'Take the other side of the bed and sleep. Maybe then I can too.'

Niccolo frowned. It was rare to hear Lia grumpy. She had a sunny disposition, not a brooding one. But there was a definite snap to her voice. Had he really kept her awake?

He was on his feet, heading for the bed, even as she got in the far side. It was only as she settled against the pillows that he realised what he was doing. How readily he was following.

Niccolo paused and surveyed the bed. In normal circumstances he'd say it was plenty big enough for two. But this wasn't normal. This was Lia. And just thinking about lying on that broad mattress with her made his body stiffen. Could he do it? Sleep with her and not turn into a heat-seeking missile, homing in on her unsuspecting body?

'Niccolo.' Abruptly she sat up, dark hair spilling around her. 'I'm sorry. I'm grumpy because I'm tired and stressed.'

Yes, he heard it in her voice. His conscience told him he was the cause of her stress. He'd been the one to cajole her into this charade.

'Please come to bed. We'll both sleep better and that will make tomorrow easier.'

And tomorrow would be difficult for her. Why hadn't he thought before about exactly how tough it would be? Tonight she'd been swamped by a horde of relatives and friends. Tomorrow the villa would be filled to the brim for his *nonna's* birthday dinner. Lia would be wary about putting a foot wrong and betraying the fact they weren't as close as everyone believed.

He lifted the bedding and slipped between the cool sheets, telling himself he did this for Lia. She'd relax now and sleep and he…well, he had a decision to make about his future. He'd concentrate on that.

Yet, as the minutes ticked by into hours it wasn't his racing future that captured his thoughts, it was the woman lying on the other side of the mattress, her breathing finally easing into a deep, slow rhythm, her hair splaying across the pillow in lustrous invitation.

Lia woke to the sound of children laughing and the slap of feet on a paved path somewhere below the balcony. Blearily she opened her eyes and saw the gold and peach flush of early morning wash the room.

She smiled sleepily and snuggled down into the bed. It had taken ages but finally, when she'd just about given up, she must have drifted into a deep, dreamless sleep. Now she didn't want to move. She felt relaxed, cosier than she'd ever felt even in her own bed.

Stifling a yawn, she shifted towards the beckoning warmth behind her. And froze.

She blinked. Once, twice. A sudden roaring in her ears coincided with her heart jumping high against her throat. After a single deep, indrawn breath her lungs froze.

But her senses didn't.

The rich, deeply appealing scent of warm male and cool forest glades filled her nostrils. Her lips grazed her warm pillow and the fragrance intensified, transforming into taste. She blinked again, focusing not on the distant window but the pillow in front of her eyes. It wasn't snowy white linen but the dark gold of Niccolo's arm. Her head rested on the curve of his shoulder, her lips touching his biceps.

Lia had an almost overpowering urge to slick her tongue along that beckoning curve of muscle.

Another breath, this time a shuddery intake of shock as she realised she lay, not on her own side of the bed, but on his! Worse, she was cocooned against him. That tantalising heat at her back was his broad chest. And lower she'd pressed her backside right up against what felt like an erection of massive proportions.

She'd heard of morning arousal but hadn't dreamt it would be quite so...

Thought dried and crumbled as he moved, murmuring something she couldn't catch. His breath fanned her hair and tiny pin pricks of sensation rippled across her flesh.

Behind her, powerful thighs tucked up against the back of hers and she realised the heavy weight at her waist wasn't the bedding, but the drape of Niccolo's arm.

He was asleep with her in his arms.

And clearly, given where they were in the bed, he hadn't crossed the mattress to her. She'd been the one to crawl over and cuddle up against him.

Fire danced in her belly. Between her legs she

seemed to liquefy as that bold shaft nestled against her buttocks hardened still further.

Her nightdress was up around her thighs and she supposed she was lucky it hadn't hitched even higher.

She tried to feel relief but instead it was regret she had to master as she stared wide-eyed into the dawn light. Regret and frustration. And a great, big dollop of shame.

Was she so needy she couldn't keep away from Niccolo even in her sleep?

For a moment she considered drastic action. She could turn in his arms and kiss him full on the mouth, run her fingers through his hair and kiss him till he forgot she was his friend's little sister. Make him think of her as a sexy woman.

Or maybe she could simply drag her nightdress a little higher and press her bare flesh to his till he accepted her unspoken invitation.

Flames flickered and flared low down in her body where that aching emptiness had set up. It would be so simple.

Her mouth tightened. Simple to seduce a man from sleep into sex before he had time to consider? Wasn't that cheating?

No, what she wanted was Niccolo, wide awake and fully aware, looking at her with desire in those gorgeous dark eyes and reaching out to—

With a ruthlessness born of desperation Lia sliced off that train of thought.

The man was asleep. His erection had nothing to do with her, other than that she was female. He didn't want *her*. He never had. Never would. If he had then he'd never have simply turned his back on her last night and dropped off to sleep almost as soon as his head hit the pillow in this vast bed.

Setting her jaw, Lia took his wrist in her hand and gently, carefully, lifted his hand over her hip and put it behind her. Holding her breath, thankful that this magnificent bed was too plush to squeak, she edged slowly forward till they were no longer touching.

Still Niccolo breathed deeply and evenly. He had no idea how close they'd been and never would. If she had to sleep on the chaise longue tonight, so be it. Anything to avoid a repeat of this...torture.

Except, a little voice in her head piped up, it was wonderful too. Part of her had wanted to lie there as long as she could, and maybe convince Niccolo into a little early morning pleasure.

Except he's not attracted to you. Remember?

Surreptitiously Lia slipped out of bed and gathered some clothes. Minutes later the bathroom door closed behind her.

It was only when the door snicked shut that Niccolo expelled the air caught in his lungs.

He'd thought for sure she'd realise he was awake.

But the way she'd stiffened in horror as she realised where she was, where *he* was — his shaft pressed right up against the inviting groove between her buttocks — proved she didn't want anything to do with him. Not sexually.

Another deep breath, dragging oxygen into lungs that had frozen. His jaw ached from clamping it too hard. Ditto the muscles in his thighs and arms.

He'd wanted to lash her to him, nuzzle that fragrant, soft hair that teased his flesh every time she shifted. He'd wanted to kiss her till she was senseless and abandoned and begging for him. But most of all he'd wanted to power into her with a carnal urgency that scared him. Scared him because he'd only clung to sanity by a thread. Another minute, another wiggle of that curvy backside against his crotch and his good intentions would have been history.

Niccolo rolled onto his back and stared up at the embroidered hangings over the bed.

Doing the decent thing had never been so hard.

His lips curved in a mirthless smile. Hard was definitely the operative word.

He'd spent the whole night awake, even though he'd feigned sleep well enough that Lia had finally relaxed into slumber herself. Initially her tension had been palpable.

And later… He sighed and scrubbed his bleary eyes. Later, soft and sexy, warm and impossibly tempting, she'd gravitated to him, and maybe he'd pulled her closer too. Which meant Niccolo had spent the night hard as a rock and hardly daring to breathe.

But he'd done it. He'd respected Lia as she should be respected.

So why the hell did he feel defeated?

Chapter Five

GUESTS CROWDED THE LARGE SALON, glasses raised as Niccolo led the toast. 'To *Nonna,* and to many more happy years.'

'To Signora Marchesi.'

'To Giovanna.'

Satisfaction filled Niccolo at seeing the old lady so happy. Only a few months before he'd wondered if she'd make this birthday. Now he had every hope she'd be around for years to come.

There was laughter and applause as she cut the enormous cake with the help of some of the youngest Marchesis. Then the guests pressed close, each wanting to talk with her.

Niccolo took the opportunity to cross to Lia, standing near the open doors to the garden.

There'd been a constraint between them all day he couldn't explain. After all, he'd behaved impeccably. Even now he couldn't quite believe he'd managed to spend a night in her bed and not make a move on her.

Oh, she'd smiled and laughed today and stayed at his side, making an effort to appear the perfect companion. But even if no-one else sensed that it *was* an effort, he did.

'You look fantastic.'

Huge eyes of golden brown lifted to his but she

didn't smile. 'You said that earlier.'

'It bears repeating.' He let his gaze rove the long black dress in some silky, stretchy fabric. It clasped her beautiful curves the way his hands wanted to. Its narrow halter-neck strap left her shoulders bare and its severity, its only decoration being the lines of sequins along that strap, drew attention to the purity of her features.

She looked like a sexy Madonna.

She'd even left her hair down in a sleek, inky fall that accentuated her pale skin.

Even from across the room, giving the congratulatory speech for his grandmother, Niccolo had had to fight not to stare at Lia.

Especially since she'd been surrounded by men. The sight of them crowding close made his hackles rise. He hated knowing each one wanted to try their chance with her.

His own cousins, Pietro, Giancarlo and Dante, had lingered nearby. All day they'd made their appreciation obvious. Giancarlo had even told Lia over lunch that she was dating the wrong Marchesi. Fortunately for Giancarlo's pretty face, Lia had laughed off his flirting before Niccolo's unaccustomed anger got the better of him.

Even now they vied for her attention, until he warned them off with a possessive glare.

'You brush up well too, Niccolo.' Lia's gaze skated his dinner jacket and bow tie before meshing with his. Again he felt that jolt of energy, as if he touched a live wire. It was a sensation he'd become familiar with lately, but in the past two days it had grown so strong it took an effort to appear impassive.

Niccolo took a long sip of his drink, hoping the

fiery burn might assuage his restlessness.

Lia looked away and smiled at Paolo Calderone, the playboy media star who'd been ogling her all evening.

Niccolo's blood reached boiling point as he turned his shoulder on the leering layabout. 'Come.' He took Lia's arm, ready to propel her out onto the terrace.

But the touch of her soft, bare flesh shorted his brain. In an instant he was back in that wide four-poster bed, holding her close, her breath warm and humid on his arm, her cheek trustingly nestled beneath his shoulder. Her—

'I'd rather stay here.' Lia's voice was low but there was no mistaking the mutinous line of her pouting lower lip.

Niccolo frowned. Here? With a mob of slavering men?

If he didn't know Lia, and the fact she never played the field, never indulged in teasing, flirtatious games, he'd think she *wanted* to be at the centre of these hungry male eyes.

But there was no teasing light in her expression. Instead there were shadows in her eyes and her smile seemed forced as she answered some question from Calderone, who stepped closer.

What was wrong? Had something happened to her? Someone hurt her?

As far as he knew everyone had loved her. She'd charmed his relatives and the other guests, her quiet assurance and warm manner as engaging as ever.

Niccolo watched as Lia and Calderone exchanged small talk. His patience wore thin at the way Calderone's gaze kept dropping to her pert breasts.

Niccolo's hand tightened on her arm till she shifted, wincing, and he realised he held her too tight. Instantly he released her arm and instead swept her close to his side, revelling in the press of her exquisite body against him. His arm was around her back, his hand clamping possessively on one warm hip. She was so smooth beneath the thin fabric, he wondered if she wore underwear and had to stop himself sliding his hand lower to check.

He felt her swift intake of breath at his embrace, then a shuddery exhale, but she kept up the chit chat with Calderone.

Short of dragging Lia against her will from the room, there was nothing he could reasonably do.

Even if he did get her alone he doubted she'd tell him why she was so ill at ease today. It was more than the masquerade. Gut instinct told him it was far more. She'd played the part to perfection. But it was as if the woman he knew so well had become someone else. Someone determined to keep him at a distance mentally and emotionally, even if not physically.

He couldn't stand it.

The realisation had him knocking back the rest of his drink and snagging another from a passing waiter.

'So, Niccolo.' Calderone drew himself up straighter as if trying to match Niccolo's height. 'What's this rumour that you might take a break from the racing circuit?'

Lia's head swung up, her eyes meeting his. He read shock there, and enquiry, but she said nothing, merely smiled slightly. Just as if she really was his girlfriend, leaving it up to him to share his news or not.

He shrugged and fixed the other man with a lazy smile that he hoped Calderone found annoying. If he decided to change career, he wouldn't be giving this slimy Casanova the scoop.

'Is there a rumour? I hadn't heard it. But you know there are always rumours. Didn't I hear something about you and that very young singer from Calabria? The one your current girlfriend introduced you to?'

Calderone's inquisitive expression froze, his smile so brittle it looked like his whiter-than-white teeth might just shatter.

'You're right,' he murmured. 'There's always the most outrageous gossip.' He looked past Niccolo. 'If you'll excuse me, there's someone I need to see.'

'That wasn't very nice,' Lia said softly when he'd gone.

Again Niccolo lifted his shoulders. He felt better already without that shark circling Lia. '*He's* not very nice.' He paused. 'Come outside for a little.'

Lia looked up into that sculpted, familiar, beautiful face and knew something was wrong.

She didn't want to be alone with him out in the soft evening. She didn't want to share the beauty of the exquisite garden with Niccolo. It had been tough enough playing the role of happy girlfriend during the day without being alone with him now.

For alone with him was when the *real* acting began. Then she had to pretend, for the sake of her pride and their future friendship, not to be affected by him.

But there was something on his mind. Something holding his strong frame taut and corrugating his wide brow. And the truth was she *did* care for him. Too much.

'Just for a little.' She put down her glass on a side table and let him lead her out the door, preternaturally conscious of his athletic body against hers, that long thigh, the jut of his hipbone, the warm, close clamp of his hand.

As soon as they were into the garden she broke from his hold, telling herself it was relief she felt to be away from him, not loss.

By mutual consent their steps turned towards the water. Lia surveyed the lake, taking in the deep indigo velvet of its surface, wishing she felt half as calm.

'Why did you want to come—?'

'Lia, what's wro—?'

They stopped, facing each other. It felt as if something punched the air between them. A force, a reverberation. Something that drummed to the beat of the blood coursing hard through her body.

'You first,' he said.

He lifted his hand as if to touch her, before his arm fell to his side. Had he sensed the way her every muscle froze in anticipation of his touch?

Did he know that if he *did* touch her she was in danger of unravelling? Of spilling the secret of how she felt about him?

Had he any idea how close she was to the edge?

The idea appalled. Surely she hadn't betrayed her feelings. She had to distract him, quickly.

'Why did you want to come out here? Aren't

you enjoying the party?'

Lia watched his mouth turn down, grim lines bracketing his lips. 'Of course. It's wonderful to see *Nonna* so happy. But I'd had enough of Calderone and his like. Who invited him here, I haven't a clue.'

He paused then asked, 'Is everything okay? You don't seem yourself.'

A bubble of humourless laughter rose in her throat but she squashed it. 'Of course I'm not myself. I'm pretending to be your girlfriend.'

More than that, she was pretending to Niccolo she was heart-whole and totally unaffected by him. The strain was just about killing her.

'Is that so difficult?' She didn't recognise his voice. It sounded stretched. Almost the way she felt, tugged by opposing forces and barely able to keep up the pretence that all was well. But this was Niccolo. The man who took everything in his stride, from press hordes to breakneck speeds that would terrify anyone else.

'I'm not good at lying.' She breathed deep of the garden's sweet-scented air. 'I feel so guilty pretending to your grandmother, and to the rest of your family that I'm someone...special.'

His hand gripped hers. 'You are special, Lia.'

Sudden fury blindsided her. How could he be blithely unaware of how difficult this was? She tugged her hand free and took a few steps towards the pier jutting out into the still lake.

'Don't. Just...don't.'

'Lia?' His voice came from over her shoulder and she knew he was only a pace away. She felt the warmth of his body reaching out to her, smelled his scent even though it should be masked by the riot of sweet perfumes from the nearby blooms.

She wrapped her arms around herself and lifted her chin. 'It's nothing, Niccolo. Nothing you need to worry about.' Because tomorrow she'd go back to Bergamo and her real life, and there'd be no more wishes or hopes or dreams about Niccolo. She wouldn't allow it.

'Have I done something, said something to upset you? You're not yourself. You seem…unhappy.' His voice was soft as a curl of smoke, wrapping itself around her.

Yet she sensed he stood solid and unmoving behind her, ready to deal with whatever ailed her.

Her mouth twisted. As if! This was her problem and hers alone. Deep down it wasn't the charade they played that upset her but that he'd slept beside her and hadn't felt what she had. She wanted him to care for her not only as a friend but as a lover.

She wanted him with every tortured fibre of her aroused body.

And she could never tell him. If she did she knew she'd never see him again.

'Tell me.' She swung round and met his stare. 'What Paolo Calderone said back there, is it true? Are you taking a break from racing?'

Those straight shoulders rose in a fluid shrug. 'I'm not sure. Maybe.'

He paused and Lia realised she was prying. Maybe playing the role of girlfriend had gone to her head. His grim expression confirmed she'd overstepped the mark. They were friends, but Niccolo didn't share stuff like that with her.

'Sorry, it's none of my business.' She made to walk past him, back to the house, till his hand slid through her elbow, calluses grazing her skin and bringing it to tingling life.

'Don't.'

She stopped, looking up into dark eyes she could barely read in the gloom. 'Don't what?'

Niccolo shook his head. 'You really want to know?'

Slowly Lia nodded. 'Of course.' She wanted to know everything about him. Even now, hurting at the realisation they could never be more than friends, she wanted to help him through whatever it was that bothered him. She wasn't used to seeing Niccolo as he was tonight.

'I'm thinking of giving up racing.'

She frowned. 'But you love racing.'

'Used to. These days it's more about the media circus and the sponsorship than the actual racing, and even that...' He spread his hands, palm up. 'Maybe I've grown out of the need to hurtle around a racetrack at top speed.'

Lia nodded. 'That French driver's accident would have an impact on anyone.' It had been sudden, dreadful and left the man unable to walk.

Niccolo shook his head. 'It's not that, though I suppose it's made me stop to think about *why* I'm racing. I haven't lost my nerve so much as my interest.' He laughed, the sound anything but amused. 'I feel like there's more I can do, more challenges I can face, instead of spending my life doing the same thing again and again. I entertain people but I don't do anything really useful.'

He dropped her hand and paced down to the lake, shoving his hands in his trouser pockets. His broad shoulders hunched and for the first time in all her memories of Niccolo, he looked…troubled.

'Is it so bad, entertaining people?' Personally she hated his career. She couldn't watch his races, for fear of an accident like the Frenchman's. But she'd always thought he enjoyed it.

His slanting smile caught her breath. 'I know. I've got nothing to complain about. And I've made a fortune at racing, quite separate from what I've inherited.'

He bent to pick up a pebble then skimmed it far out across the water.

'I still love speed. I'll never give up recreational skiing or racing, but there's a difference between making it your career and *achieving* something.'

'You want to achieve something meaningful?'

He slanted a look her way. 'I knew you'd understand, Lia.'

Those simple words made the sun burst warm and glowing inside her. Her own woes faded as Niccolo smiled at her.

A voice in her head said she was beyond redemption. She needed to get away from him now and keep a healthy distance between them. But it was drowned by the need to support him.

Niccolo was always strong, definite, controlled. He'd never once needed anything from her before this weekend. She liked the idea of helping, even if it was just to lend an ear.

'Have you decided what you want to do?'

He nodded. 'The Marchesi family holdings include a company, a rather neglected company that provides training opportunities for unemployed kids. It provides education, life skills and professional training for those who would otherwise struggle. It does fine work but it could do more. With an injection of funds and a higher public profile. With a little more organisation and better networking with industry employers—'

'The sort of contacts you could provide,' she said, thinking of the people he knew, not just in the automotive industry but in the media, promotions and so many other areas.

'You're not going to tell me I haven't a clue what I'm doing?' His mouth tipped up at the corner in a devastating smile.

Lia shook her head. 'You're clever and resourceful and I've never known anyone more determined.' In that he was on a par with her brothers. They all knew what they wanted and went straight for it.

He nodded. 'It would be something...worthwhile. The previous CEO achieved in the beginning but became satisfied with the same goals, year after year. I see so many opportunities.' He paused. 'And it would be good to take on a company that my father founded and see it shine.'

'You'd do a brilliant job. You'd be a role model to a lot of those kids too.' Apart from his keen brain and his refusal to give up once he'd decided on something, Niccolo had empathy. He listened to the needs of others. Like that night all those years ago when he'd gone out of his way not to disappoint a starry-eyed girl.

He laughed and her heart danced. 'I expected you to tell me I didn't have the training for it. Almost everyone else has.'

'You'll learn. Besides, one thing I know about you, Niccolo. You thrive on challenge.'

Chapter Six

THRIVE ON CHALLENGE!

Niccolo gritted his teeth and wished to hell he faced a simpler challenge tonight than sharing a bed with Lia. Like breaking the land speed record, or abolishing youth unemployment.

After their discussion by the lake he'd felt closer to her than ever before, as if they were attuned. She'd been so understanding, readily accepting the massive change he wanted in his life when so many others urged him to continue as he was, making them money. Unlike them, Lia cared for Niccolo the man, rather than Niccolo the walking headline and source of income.

That closeness only made his desire for her stronger, gave it depth and an authenticity lacking in his previous affairs.

But he and Lia weren't having an affair, were they? She looked on him as a brother.

Hell and damnation!

He should run a mile. Yet here he was, accompanying her to their room.

Each step up the marble stairs felt like a step closer to disaster. The tension across his shoulders was surely enough to crack his bones.

He'd aimed to stay downstairs as long as possible, farewelling guests and overseeing the clean up.

Anything to delay entering the bedroom. But seeing Lia's pale face and the smudges under her eyes made him change his mind. She looked fragile yet she'd stayed with him, playing the role of girlfriend so well it was harder and harder to remember this was make-believe.

It needled him that he still hadn't got to the bottom of what worried her. Lia wasn't a good liar and he sensed it was more than her charade in front of his family that bothered her.

They reached the top of the stairs and she stumbled. Instantly his hand snapped out to support her but she shrank away as if afraid of his touch.

A scowl settled on Niccolo's brow and an ache in his belly. She was really worrying him.

He let his hand drop to his side as they walked together, in aching silence, down the long corridor. The only sounds were the beat of his blood and the swish of her long dress, like a whisper inviting him to reach out and touch.

His hand fisted as they reached their suite and he opened the door for her. Despite his best efforts his gaze traced her bare shoulders, the creamy skin of her upper back revealed by the dress as she passed. His gut clenched.

He wanted to sprint back down the stairs, jump into his sports car and work off this tension driving hard and fast.

The alternative, driving himself to oblivion, hard and fast inside Lia, was just too tempting.

Heat rocketed through him, desire for her saturating every part of him. His nostrils flared as the tantalising, rich scent of lilies reached him. Maybe it was something she washed her hair in. He leaned closer before he could stop himself, then made himself pause on the threshold, gathering some shreds of control.

She flinched as the door shut behind him, but she didn't turn around as she took out the pretty drop earrings and put them on the dressing table.

In the mirror before her he saw Lia's mouth bunched tight as if with pain. Surely her hands were shaking too.

In a couple of strides Niccolo crossed the room.

'Lia?' Her head was downcast. She didn't realise he could see her reflected expression as her beautiful lips twisted.

Gently, because he sensed she was hurting in some way he'd yet to uncover, Niccolo took her arm. Again that tiny flinch, though his touch was light. Slowly he pulled her round until she faced him.

For the first time since he'd known her she refused to look at him. That killed him.

He couldn't bear to think of her so distressed yet believing she couldn't share her problem with him. Surely she trusted him that much?

He wanted to take away her pain.

He wanted to give her pleasure instead. The very thought was a blast of agony to the back of his skull as he struggled to do the decent thing.

'Look at me, Lia.'

She swallowed and nodded but then froze. He saw her pulse flutter hard and fast at the base of her long, fragile-looking throat. He wanted to lean in and taste her there, kiss his way up to the classically sculpted line of her chin and from there to those lips, glossy and enticing. He wanted—

'*Dannazione!*' He hauled her against him before second thoughts could prevent him. He had to do something to ease the hurt engraved on her beautiful face.

Heart pounding, he lashed one arm around her, holding her tight, willing her to relax against him and let the pain go. His other hand lifted to her hair. A shiver rocketed through him when his hand touched that softness, as exquisite as the finest silk, but he ignored it, focusing on *her*, not the prickle of heat and hunger filling his belly.

'It's okay, *tesoro*. Whatever it is, I'll make it okay. I promise.' He pressed her face against his shirt, willing her to relax, but she was rigid against him.

Seeing her in such distress tore at something deep within. It was as if a fissure opened up inside him, raw and aching.

He heard a muffled sound. A laugh? A cry of distress?

Niccolo slipped his hand under her chin and lifted her face. Still she avoided him, keeping her eyes closed.

Something like panic stirred. Niccolo faced danger and the spectre of death every time he raced, but he'd never felt so helpless as he did now, watching Lia grapple with whatever it was that turned her from vivacious and happy to distraught.

'I'm fine, Niccolo.' As if that husky, ghost of a voice convinced him. 'There's nothing you can do.'

'There must be. Tell me, Lia.'

A mighty shudder rippled through her. A moment later she straightened, pushing her shoulders back. Her jaw angled up and her eyes snapped open. Her pupils were huge in a blaze of shimmering golden brown and to his horror Niccolo realised he'd never seen her so close to tears.

'Ah, don't cry. Whatever it is, we'll make it better.'

She shook her head, almost violently, her long hair flaring and slipping over his hand.

'No.' Her voice was stronger now, with a whiplash undercurrent of bitterness. 'This isn't something you can kiss and make better.'

Niccolo almost groaned, wishing the words undone. His attention dropped instantly to her lips, finely cut and lushly inviting.

There was a roaring in his ears, a shaking in his belly and his hands tightened on her, one at her back, one sliding round to cup her head. He couldn't let go. Couldn't force himself to step away. His feet were cemented to the floor.

She tempted him beyond endurance and she didn't even realise.

'Why not?' His grating voice was unrecognisable.

He told himself it would be fine to touch her mouth. A tiny kiss from a friend, over as soon as it began. A demonstration that he cared for her, was here for her. That whatever her problem was, he'd help.

A brotherly kiss!

Except when he leaned in to touch his lips to her cheek she moved, no doubt startled. He felt the shock in her straining body.

Then somehow, surely without intending to, his lips grazed hers. Grazed and clung.

Because to withdraw was utterly impossible.

Lia's lips were so soft, so perfect, fitting to his as if made for that very purpose. Niccolo froze. Amazing as it was to admit, he'd never felt so undone by a woman. Yet all he did was touch her lips!

They tasted like honey. Honey and Lia, the most beautiful woman he'd ever known.

Niccolo inhaled sharply, strengthening his resolve to draw back. Except now he dragged in air warm from her flesh, scented with the lily and woman perfume of Lia. There was no turning back. Not yet. He stood unmoving, one hand cupping her skull, the other splayed over the sinuous indentation of her waist.

Until, shocking him to the core, he felt the slick of her tongue along his mouth. And a warm vibration, like a soundless hum of pleasure, resonate through her.

Niccolo tried to summon the will to move, to break the embrace. Then it came again, tentative but real, her tongue sliding across his bottom lip.

A man was only human after all.

He'd done his best, tried to be strong, but there was a limit to endurance.

Angling his head, pressing closer, he opened his mouth and sucked her questing tongue into his mouth. Sucked hard, drawing his own tongue against it in a duel that was all invitation and pleasure.

Niccolo's hands trembled as they never did at the wheel of a racing vehicle. He felt as if he held sunlight and innocence in his arms and was torn between protectiveness and the need to possess.

He moved his hand, changed his grip to angle her head for easier access and, instead of stiffening in rejection, Lia melted in his arms, her curves sliding against him, her head bowing back under the pressure of his, and again that wordless vibration of pleasure. He tasted it, swallowed it, then plunged deep into her mouth, demanding more.

It was like admiring a daisy and discovering it was a lush, sensual rose in disguise.

Her mouth was rich velvet, tempting and seductive. Her body undulated against him in blatant, needy invitation, and Niccolo found himself backing her up against the dressing table. He crowded her between his thighs, his erection instant and powerful, jammed up against her belly.

Somewhere, in the back of his brain, his conscience commanded he pull back. But then Lia's hands crept up his chest, over his shoulders and she wrapped her fingers around his neck, pulling him down towards her as if she too couldn't get enough.

It was bliss.

It was torture.

Devastatingly fantastic yet not nearly enough. Already his hand was roving her body, down over the ripe curve of her buttocks, then digging in through the thin fabric till she gasped and rocked her pelvis into him, her head falling back.

Niccolo had never seen anything more alluring than Lia, her kiss-swollen lips open as she gasped for air, a flush of arousal tinting her throat and cheeks and her eyes glowing gold. They were a siren's eyes, luring him on, inviting him to forget restrictions and taboos and take her. Here, now.

His breath came in harsh gulps that couldn't quite fill his lungs. His skin was tight and uncomfortable and he needed to rip off his clothes.

But more than that, he needed to have Lia. The pain of not tearing himself free of his trousers and taking her right here was making him dizzy.

'We should—' He'd been about to say something about stopping, except Lia tilted her hips in a sinuous move that brought her pelvis high against him.

His conscience disintegrated in a ripple of lust that began at the base of his spine and raced straight round to his groin.

Lia knew what she was doing. She wasn't *that* innocent.

Her heavy-lidded stare invited and challenged.

With a growl of triumph, Niccolo swept his mouth back down to hers, possessing her with a bruising thoroughness that still couldn't allay the need thrumming in his veins. He hungered for Lia, for all of her, writhing and gasping beneath him as he took them both to heaven.

He slid his hand from her face, down past her collarbone to her breast. His hand trembled as he cupped her fullness in his fingers. Was it because she fitted him so perfectly or because this was Lia, the woman who'd been secretly driving him crazy for so long? Whatever the reason, she made him want to slide to his knees and worship her. To give her everything he had. And to please her as no man had ever pleased her before.

He smiled as her eyes fluttered closed and she arched up high into his touch, a tiny sound of delight falling from her open lips.

It was then that Niccolo knew he was utterly lost.

Chapter Seven

LIA CLUNG TO THE DARKNESS, knowing that this had to be a dream, the sort of dream that had kept her from sleep too many nights.

Besides, she'd read Niccolo's shock, his attempt to hold back, and she didn't want to watch him when he finally withdrew from her.

For withdraw he would, as soon as his brain engaged and reminded him this was ordinary old Lia in his arms, not some bountiful blonde model. Not at all his usual type.

She'd wanted to scream at him that *she* was his type, if only he'd give her a chance. And now, somehow, a miracle had happened and he was kissing her. Not just kissing. His touch, his tone, the fine tremor in his big, powerful frame all made it clear he wanted her as fervently as she did him.

The things he did with his mouth and hands...

The sensations aroused her and scared her too, just a little. Because all this was new. New and wonderful and she didn't want him to stop.

She'd loved Niccolo so long, craved him. His touch, his hunger, smashed every inhibition, every constraint she'd placed on herself. Lia could no more pretend indifference than she could fly to the moon.

Her heart leapt sky high as his roughened hand

tightened around her breast. Instantly a dart of heat shot straight to that achy spot between her thighs that felt swollen and needy.

Lia pressed her hand over the back of his, pushing her breast further into his cupped hand, and heard Niccolo swear under his breath. Or maybe it was a prayer.

She, at least, was beyond help. The only one who could help her now was Niccolo.

'More,' she pleaded, groping for his other hand and planting it hard on her other breast. She'd waited so long for his touch.

Exquisite sensations pierced her. And deep within, a rolling wave of liquid warmth rose and spilled. She was damp between the legs and desperate for more.

Relief flooded when Niccolo pushed her back hard against the dressing table, the solid length of his erection crowding her.

'Yes.' The little hiss of pleasure escaped on a sigh that ended when his mouth slammed into hers. He ripped one hand away to hold her head where he wanted and kissed her with fierce, devastating precision. She'd thought their first kiss spectacular. This one sparked fire in her blood and incinerated thought.

Lia clung to him, meeting the savage intensity of his mouth with a need that had been too long contained. He'd lit a fuse and she was combusting, burning up in heat and hunger. That initial tiny frisson of anxiety incinerated to ashes at the glorious reality of Niccolo caressing her, *wanting* her.

He didn't break the kiss as he lifted her onto the dressing table and with one smooth movement, slid his hands up her thighs, bunching the jersey fabric higher and higher. When the hem was at her knees he shoved that up too, and air wafted across her bare skin. She felt daring, wanton.

He pulled back from her mouth. 'You're wearing stockings.'

Lia frowned at the interruption to that luscious kiss, pausing as he uncovered her. But something about his husky voice made her open heavy lids.

He looked...

Her heart crashed against her ribs. She'd never seen Niccolo look like that. Taut, as if teetering on the very edge of control.

His head snapped up and midnight dark eyes possessed her.

'You don't like stockings?' Uncertainty flickered. His mouth twisted in a grimace, as if he hurt.

'You're joking. What's not to like?' Deliberately he drew one long finger from the top of her stocking up her inner thigh towards the wet strip of silk at her core. Did he like thongs too?

But the question dissolved as he stroked her there and she shuddered. The feel of him where she most wanted him, it was too much and far, far too little.

Lia wanted more. She wanted everything.

Clamping her thighs around his hand, she pulled his head down and kissed him so hard on the mouth their teeth clashed. Desperation rose at the idea he might, even now, pull away from her.

'Easy,' he whispered, stroking her cheek. But it was too late for easy. Lia was now officially desperate. Nothing could assuage this terrible clamour inside but Niccolo. As he returned her kiss she tugged at his belt, slipping it open as easily as if she'd done it thousands of times.

Only in her dreams.

But the catch on his trousers proved too difficult and with a grunt he pushed her hand aside to take care of it himself.

It was really happening. Her and Niccolo!

The enormity of the moment was enough to inject a flash of common sense. Yet even as she drew breath to ask, Niccolo tugged out his wallet and withdrew a small, square package.

By the time he shoved his trousers down he'd sheathed himself and Lia's heart pounded fit to burst from watching his deft, urgent movements. From seeing him aroused and proud. She licked her lips, her mouth suddenly parched as anticipation soared to breaking point.

Lia shifted restlessly, waiting for him to move back so she could strip off the thong that was all the underwear she wore. Instead she felt a long finger loop under the fabric and wrench it aside. She was still rigid with shock at his touch there, when suddenly he was against her, demanding entrance.

Niccolo was hot, so hot. For a moment Lia stiffened, aware of the boundary they crossed. She felt exposed and suddenly wary. Then he feathered a caress along her jaw, up into her hair, easing her tension.

When she softened against him he gently lifted her leg with his other hand, twining it around his hip, stroking her thigh with his palm, crooning words of approval.

Now Lia no longer felt uncertain. His tenderness and the sensation of flesh pressing flesh banished her momentary hesitation. She wrapped her other leg round Niccolo, chaining him to her.

'*Tesoro.*' His words blurred in a hot cascade of endearments that melded with the throb of her heartbeat.

Still he surged into her, slow and sure, and Lia gasped at the unfamiliar stretch, the exquisite sensation of male hardness against slick feminine softness. It was shocking, wondrous. Impossible! She'd anticipated a sting of pain but there was none, just a fullness that she relished, despite its strangeness.

Finally Niccolo came to rest right at her heart and her breath escaped in a shuddering sigh.

He possessed all of her, that's how it felt. As if he'd taken her body, but gave back far more.

Lia held her breath in wonder, till she realised he'd stopped moving. She opened her eyes and found him watching her, his eyes fathoms deep and rich in sensual secrets.

'Lia.' He'd never said her name like that before. As if it was both question and answer to something vast and eternal. His mouth hooked up in a smile. 'Look at us together.'

Following his lead she bent her head, just as he withdrew from her. Her immediate sense of loss was tempered by awe and sheer carnal excitement at the sight of his shaft, so long and powerful, sliding almost free, then pushing home with an urgency that stole her breath and sent stars of rapture whirling.

She'd never experienced anything so erotic in her life. She'd expected that with Niccolo, sex would be great. Though she'd shied from admitting it, that was probably why she'd never taken a lover before.

But this... This was beyond her imaginings.

Lia tightened her grip around his waist and held on to Niccolo's shoulders. He was moving again, easy and measured, but once more, his return thrust sent her flying closer to delight.

She didn't want measured. She wanted Niccolo as *she* was, shivering on the brink of losing herself. She pulled his head down and kissed him with all the pent-up passion of years of wanting. At the same time she circled her hips, trying to accommodate even more of him. Trying to assuage the yearning for *more*. For everything.

A huge shudder ran through him and he growled, deep in the back of his throat, making the fine hairs on her arms stand to attention.

Then, suddenly, he let go. Those carefully measured movements became a rapid, urgent bucking. He tore his mouth from her and instead nipped the flesh at the base of her neck, creating an erotic current that arced from her throat to her nipples and down to her pelvis. One hard hand squeezed her breast and suddenly, out of nowhere, her climax struck. It filled her, tossing her high as the stars, then shattered her, just as Niccolo rasped her name and drove into her, spilling his vital heat right at her core.

It took forever for the vibrations to die down, leaving her to float back to reality on a cloud of bliss.

Vaguely she was aware of Niccolo cradling her close, of his heart running out of control, or maybe that was her heart. They were so completely joined it felt like there was no beginning or end, no separate beings. That they were one.

Niccolo rested his forehead against Lia's. He had no words to describe his feelings. His brain was thick with pleasure. But when fragments of thought were possible he realised he felt greater than the man he'd been. Like some immortal walking in glory.

He kissed her neck and traced lazy circles on her back. Instantly she shivered and her inner muscles tightened around him.

Niccolo froze. Was it possible? Even after that monumental climax? He stroked her and she moved, this time arching languorously against him, and sure enough, again that secret embrace as her muscles clamped him. And, yes, instead of withdrawing from her, he found himself thickening, halfway to another erection.

In a couple of urgent moves he'd shucked off his shoes and dress trousers. Still Lia clung, as if she too, needed this closeness.

He'd never been like this with any woman. Never believed it possible.

He grinned, facial muscles pulling taut as he scooped his hands under her bottom and lifted her off the dressing table.

Lia gasped but clung on, her legs, shaking now, still wrapped about him.

'Easy, *cara*, easy.' A couple of steps took them to the bed and he sat with her astride him. Lamplight cast shadows across her fine features and made the sequins on her dress sparkle. The coverlet was cool beneath his bare buttocks but he was overheated, still wearing his jacket and tie.

'Undress me.' His voice was hoarse, as if he'd been shouting his exultation. As he said it he explored the side zip of her dress, tugging it open. He watched as her brilliant eyes slowly focused again and her lips curved up.

He waited till she'd stripped the bowtie from him and shoved his jacket from his shoulders before he lifted the slippery fabric of her dress. Obediently she raised her arms so that slowly, oh so slowly the evening dress rose, revealing lithe hips, a pale belly and narrow waist, slender ribcage and full breasts tipped with dark raspberry nipples. The sight of her caught at something in his chest and a different kind of heat saturated him from his skeleton to his pores.

Niccolo hauled the dress over her head and onto the floor. His hands shook and his mouth was dry and that promising erection grew by the second. She felt it too. How could she not? Her eyes widened as suddenly Niccolo's patience tore. He wrenched at his shirt buttons, tearing them open in one decisive tug. The cufflinks took longer but soon they were both naked.

'Now,' he murmured and rolled back on the bed, holding her against him so she reared above him, high breasts tantalising. But not this time. He moved again and she was beneath him, and around him, her hair like a fan of silk on the pillows.

A sliver of regret hit him as he watched her beautiful eyes widen. The shredded remnants of his conscience clawed for attention, urging him to stop, give her time. But then Lia smiled. Slow and wide and utterly, incomparably beautiful.

'Make love to me again, Niccolo.'
So of course, he did, long, long into the night.

Chapter Eight

NICCOLO CAME AWAKE IN AN instant, his senses alert to the sweet perfume tickling his nostrils and the warm woman gathered close in his arms.

His eyes snapped open, his body tensing as he took in Lia snuggled up against him. The sun was already high, spilling over her glorious raven hair and camellia-pale skin.

And the rumpled swathe of sheets barely covering them.

His body tightened with the instant recall of last night. Of how spectacular the sex had been. How out of control she'd made him.

Niccolo's pulse thrummed hard, each beat a hammer at his conscience.

No, Lia hadn't *made* him do anything. He'd been driven, had felt his control shatter completely and irrevocably, but it wasn't Lia's fault. It was his. He'd been the one to touch her, to want her, to lead her into sex.

He'd been responsible.

The fact it had been sublime was no excuse. Guilt dragged at his belly as he thought of facing Lia's family, knowing he'd betrayed their trust this way. And Lia too. Last night she hadn't been herself. She'd hurt in ways he didn't understand.

He'd taken advantage of her.

He was the one with all the experience. Despite her enthusiasm it was obvious she'd had little experience of intimacy. Her look of sheer wonder as they'd scaled the heights of ecstasy was emblazoned on his brain. At one point he'd even wondered, just for a millisecond, if she was a virgin.

But that was ridiculous. Lia was beautiful and passionate. She had her choice of men. Besides, if she'd saved herself, why give herself to him on the spur of the moment?

He couldn't think with Lia in his arms. He didn't want to think. He wanted to wake her with his body and take her again to that pinnacle of bliss where she'd cried out his name.

Already his erection was solid proof that, conscience or not, what he wanted most of all was to stay here with her for the rest of the day.

His gaze dropped to the upper slope of her breasts and he flinched. Instead of smooth, creamy skin there were reddened marks. Beard rash. He scraped a hand over his jaw.

Curiously it was the realisation he'd marked her in his passion, rather than the promptings of his scruples, that made him pull back. What did that say about him?

Grimly, he eased his arm from beneath Lia's head and extricated himself, inch by slow inch. She rolled closer, as if following his body warmth, her arm outflung across his pillow as he got out of bed.

For a full minute he stood, looking down at her, telling himself to go. Hoping she'd wake and look at him with that wonder in her eyes, begging—

No! It had been wrong last night and it was

wrong today.

The sex had been stupendous. But what he'd done...

He spun on his foot and strode across the room, collecting clothes and heading for the bathroom and a long, cold shower.

'You don't have to tiptoe across the room. I'm awake.' Lia smiled at the sound of Niccolo's approach. She felt a little achy in places she'd never ached before and she wasn't sure she had the strength to move. But the bright sunshine flooding the room was nothing to the radiance she felt inside. It was as if she'd swallowed the sun.

For so many years she'd been in love with Niccolo. Hopelessly, she'd once thought. But it had been far more than a schoolgirl crush. It had lasted this long, grown stronger if anything, and now, after last night, she realised he finally saw her for the woman she was. Lia wasn't naïve enough to believe that a night of sex meant Niccolo loved her back, but one step at a time.

She snuggled down into the pillow in anticipation, waiting for him to walk around the bed. She hoped he hadn't dressed. Surely they'd have time before breakfast to...

Lia's brow twitched into a frown when she saw Niccolo. He looked magnificent. He'd even shaved, revealing the strong angle of his jaw she so admired. His damp hair was slicked back and he wore a casual jacket over a white T shirt and jeans.

But his eyes... They weren't the eyes of the man who'd made love to her last night.

Lia sat up, her heart jerking into a painful rhythm. 'What's happened? What's wrong?'

His gaze dropped and instantly her nipples puckered, the skin of her breasts drawing tight at the heat in his stare. She reached down and grabbed the sheet, tucking it under her arms, warmth rising under her skin. Ridiculous but even after last night she wasn't used to being naked with Niccolo. At least not naked with him at a distance.

'Is it your grandmother?'

'Sorry?' He lifted his eyes to hers. 'What about my grandmother?'

A sliver of something very like satisfaction spiralled down through Lia's insides. She was disappointed Niccolo had showered and dressed without her, that he clearly wasn't intending to come back to bed, but there was no mistaking his fascination with her nudity. It made her feel a little less self-conscious.

Despite his fervour last night, Lia was all too aware she wasn't as pretty as his usual girlfriends, nor as experienced. Spending the weekend playing a pretend lover, knowing she was nowhere as glamorous or sophisticated as the women he was accustomed to, had been hard.

'Is your grandmother all right? I can see something's wrong. I thought maybe…'

'As far as I know she's in perfect health. Though I suspect she'll sleep late today.' Yet the frown lingered, knotting his forehead and his dark eyes looked wary rather than welcoming.

Lia's skin prickled, starting at her nape and spreading in chill waves over her shoulders and arms then racing down her spine.

'I'll bring you up a tray so you can breakfast in bed.' His tone was short, almost curt.

Lia stared up into his handsome face, trying and failing to guess what was wrong.

'It would be nice to eat together. Maybe on the balcony.' She'd been going to suggest breakfast in bed, but his brooding expression stopped her.

'No, I won't have time.' He paused, shoving his hands in the pockets of his jeans.

Lia frowned. Niccolo looked ill at ease. His stance, his movements seemed cramped. Usually he had an aura of athletic strength and confidence but now it was sorely missing.

'I have to go out. On an errand for my grandmother.'

'I'll come with you.'

But Niccolo was already shaking his head. 'No. Stay here. You can rest.'

'Niccolo? What's wrong?' A horrible thought occurred. 'Is it something I did? Something I said?' Whatever had happened, the ardent lover of last night had morphed into a man who was clearly uncomfortable with her.

A vast weight plummeted through her, like a rock, cracking through her joy and tentative excitement.

Lia tightened her hold on the sheet over her breasts.

'I'm sorry, Lia.' Just that, with his eyes so dark and blank it was like looking into some vast, empty cavern. 'Last night should never have happened.'

Everything inside her stilled. Even her breathing stopped. Lia had a sudden, dreadful feeling that when it started again, the pain would be unbearable.

Then Niccolo was sitting on the bed near her thigh and he had her hand in his. She exhaled in relief. He must have qualms about making love to her under his grandmother's roof. Or maybe because in the beginning he'd been urgent rather than careful.

But she'd revelled in his passion! His later tenderness had been exquisite, but his raw, possessive carnality as he'd taken her that first time had merely added another dimension to her long-standing love for him.

She'd loved him forever but now she'd tasted his ardour, everything was magnified. How could any woman *not* be in thrall to a man who needed her so desperately? Who gave her such bliss?

'It's all right, Niccolo.'

She put her hand onto his cheek, cupping the hard edge of his jaw and loving the intimacy of skin on skin. Had he shaved for her? The idea bubbled out of nowhere, banishing her doubts.

Lia breathed deep, inhaling the forest mountain scent of him, mixed with the earthy tones she'd learned last night signalled arousal. A smile tickled her lips, till he caught her hand and drew it away from his face.

'It's not all right, Lia. It was a mistake.' This close she couldn't miss the dull certainty in his eyes. Gone was the vibrant man she'd known so long, replaced with a stern, merciless stranger.

'A mistake?' Her hand shook in his but she couldn't help it. Nor could she form any new words. That single one — mistake — rang like a tolling bell in her brain.

'It wasn't a mistake. It was beautiful.' Lia willed

him to agree. To tell her it had been as life-altering for him as it was for her.

But of course it wasn't. What was she thinking? He'd had countless lovers, probably vastly more experienced and…inventive than her. Her skin shrank back against her bones and she tried to pull her hand free but he wouldn't release it.

She met his eyes, ignoring the voice of pride that told her to shut up. For she had to know. 'I see. That was just me, then. Obviously it wasn't any-thing special for you.'

Part of her, the desperate, yearning part, wanted to beg him to teach her the skills she so obviously lacked. But the words wouldn't come. It was all she could do to keep her head up, even as her hopes crumbled to ashes in her mouth and her vision blurred.

'Lia! How can you say that? Of course it was beautiful.' His fingers tightened around hers and he lifted his other hand as if to caress her face. Only to drop it and frown.

'Then what? I don't understand.' Was he trying to protect her feelings? Of course Niccolo wouldn't want to come straight out and say she was no good at sex.

Yet even as she thought it, confusion rose. He'd climaxed too, several times.

So what had she done wrong?

He stroked her hand and tiny shivers rippled under her skin. He only had to touch her… Not even that. Just a look and she went up in flames.

But right now his look wasn't that of a lover. It was set, determined, passionless. And it sent a shard of ice straight to her heart.

'I did wrong last night, Lia. You weren't yourself and I took advantage of you. It was unforgiveable.'

Lia stared, aghast at both his expression and the harsh regret she heard.

'You didn't take advantage. I kissed you, remember?'

He shook his head. 'You were tired and then there was the wine you'd drunk. If any other man had made a move on you last night I'd have knocked him out. Instead I…' He shrugged, those broad shoulders lifting stiffly. 'You're family and—'

'Hold it right there!' Lia dragged her hand from his. 'We're *not* family.'

'As good as. You've grown up with me in the house, hanging out with your brothers. What would your relatives say if they knew we'd had sex? Your brothers? They expect me to look after you, just like they do.'

A hollow feeling ripped at her stomach, widening as a chasm tore open within her.

'This has nothing to do with my family. This is to do with you and me. My brothers don't tell me about their sex lives and I don't expect to tell them about mine.'

Niccolo scraped a hand across his gorgeous, taut face as if trying to wipe away the memory of last night.

'This is different and you know it, Lia. I've always been like a brother to you.'

She shook her head, her hair swirling about her shoulders. This was turning into a nightmare.

'I've never thought of you like that, Niccolo. Ever.' She let those words sink in. 'I treated you as a friend but never a brother.' Now was not the time to announce she'd secretly nursed a passion for him from afar. That what had begun as a teenage crush had never truly been conquered, but had instead morphed into true, deep affection.

'You're not my protector. I don't need one. I'm not a kid any more, Niccolo. I'm an adult.'

'You're inexperienced. I realised that last night and I should have stopped but I didn't.' His face looked chiselled from stone, as if every word cost him. 'I had an obligation to protect you. Instead I—'

'Tell me the truth, Niccolo.' She folded her arms across her chest, holding in her jumping heart and trying to keep the hurt in too. Even so, she knew her voice shook. 'Is all this old-fashioned stuff because I was a virgin? Is that why you're tying yourself in knots?'

If she'd slapped him she couldn't have got a stronger reaction. His face paled and his eyes bulged in unmistakeable horror.

Too late Lia realised her mistake.

'You were a *virgin*?' His lips twisted and he swore under his breath. He dropped her hand, instead palming the back of his neck. 'I wondered but I wasn't sure.' He shook his head. 'Who do I think I'm kidding? I didn't *want* to be sure. Because I didn't want to stop.'

Suddenly he was on his feet, striding across the room, thrusting open the door to the balcony and heading out to lean over the edge, hands clamped on the balustrade and head bent as if he had trouble sucking in enough oxygen.

Stunned, Lia stared. He hadn't wanted to stop. Of course he'd enjoyed last night. She'd known that before he confused her with his apologies.

She waited for him to turn around and come back to her, but he stayed where he was. A man apparently battling demons.

Lia frowned. They were demons of his own making.

With a soft curse she flung aside the sheet and stood. She glanced around, looking for her robe but couldn't see it. Just then Niccolo whipped round and their eyes met.

Instantly currents of electricity coursed through her as if she'd touched a live wire. From her lips, her breasts, between her thighs. Even running from the backs of her knees to her heels and round her waist.

The look in his eyes told her he found her desirable. More — he *wanted* her. But his grip on the railing, arms splayed out on either side as if to anchor himself, told her he wasn't going to come to her.

Lia swallowed. No man had ever seen her naked, except Niccolo. She felt self-conscious and at the same time strong and powerful. She refused to cover herself or buy into his guilt trip because they'd shared themselves.

It had been utterly glorious.

Lifting her chin to counteract the lump in her throat, Lia crossed to the door. She paused, letting him look his fill. Every inch of her hummed with energy, with want and anticipation.

But she wouldn't beg.

'First, this isn't about my family, this is about me and you, Niccolo. I won't let you use that as an excuse.'

'It's not an excuse. It's about honour and obligation. About doing the right thing.'

Men! Suddenly fury outweighed caution. 'I'm not an obligation, Niccolo. I'm a woman. And as for honour...' She breathed deep and saw his gaze fix on her breasts as they rose. The sight both delighted and infuriated her. 'Your honour isn't affected by the fact I chose to have sex with you. Surely you don't carry on like this when any of those other women,' she waved one hand disparagingly, 'elect to sleep with you.'

'But you're not one of them. You're deliberately misunderstanding.'

'Am I?' Her hands went to her hips. 'Rubbish. You're tying yourself in knots because the truth is your friendship with my family means more to you than any relationship *we* might have.' Lia's words stalled as the truth struck. It was true. And it would always be true. Matteo was his best friend. And Niccolo regularly caught up with Luca and Gennaro, even Aurelio on occasion.

A great weight crushed her chest as she tried to breathe, making her words emerge raw and husky. 'I had sex with you because I care for you, Niccolo. I wanted to share that with you. I still do. And as for my virginity,' she couldn't believe she had to spell this out, 'ending that was *my* decision, not yours.'

Suddenly she'd had enough. Standing here, naked both physically and emotionally, was too hard, when all she wanted was for him to fold his arms around her and tell her this wasn't an end but a beginning.

She choked down a ball of hot emotion. 'If you

can ever get past your…scruples,' she spat the word, 'then let me know.'

Then she spun on her foot and marched to the bathroom. Once inside she snicked the lock shut and stumbled to the plush chair beside the bath. She couldn't drag in enough air and her legs wobbled as if they were made of overused elastic.

But worse, far worse, was the knowledge her night of rapture, and her fragile belief in a relationship with Niccolo, were over. Last night as he'd shared his hopes for the future, she'd felt so close to him, honoured to hear his secret plans. And later…

Lia slammed her mind shut on what had come later.

There was nothing more for her with this man. After years of dreaming and hoping finally, surely, this would cure her of her pointless yearning.

Niccolo wasn't for her. He never had been and never would be. For just now he'd met her gaze with eyes that were dead.

The memory slithered through her, as cold and killing as any deadly reptile.

Whatever had motivated him last night — lust, possibly tinged with curiosity and lubricated by the fine wine that had flowed at the party — it was finished now.

Niccolo had rejected her. Worse, he regretted what they'd done. There could be no going back.

Chapter Nine

'IT'S SUCH A SHAME LIA had to leave early. I was looking forward to spending the day getting to know her better. She's such a lovely girl, Niccolo. Far more genuine than some of the women you and your cousins have dated.'

Niccolo froze in the act of passing his grandmother a cool drink.

Leave? His nape prickled and his skin grew tight. His heart rammed hard into his ribs then lurched into an unfamiliar rhythm.

'Niccolo? What's wrong? You've gone an awful colour. Don't tell me it's food poisoning! No-one else is ill this morning.'

Dazed, he looked down into his grandmother's concerned face. He'd felt appalling all morning, tense and restless and... *Dannazione*! He didn't have a word for the sickening brew of emotions, guilt and lust, honour and protectiveness. But the idea of Lia leaving without talking with him —

'I'm fine, *Nonna*. Not sick at all.' He ignored the nausea swirling in his gut. 'Here, have your drink.' He passed it to her and subsided into the chair beside her, positioned to catch the view over the gardens to the lake. In the distance he heard kids laughing and his cousin Giancarlo's speedboat revving as it left the private pier.

'It's Lia, isn't it?' Shrewd eyes surveyed him.

Niccolo sipped his own drink and wished it was alcohol. Anything to numb the feeling that everything that had been so simple was now completely out of control.

'As you say, it's disappointing she had to leave so early but—'

But what? What excuse had she used to explain her departure? And how had she left? He suspected public transport to Bergamo on a Sunday would be painfully slow. *If* she'd returned to her apartment there and not headed for her family home.

She'd been so distraught, so worked up, who knew where she'd gone?

Again guilt smote, swift and lethal, shredding what was left of his conscience. And more than guilt. Fear. Fear for the damage he'd done. He'd hurt her when he'd tried, too late, to protect her.

'I thought it odd that she left when you were ferrying your aunt and uncle across the lake.' The old lady paused. Piercing dark eyes skewered him where he sat. 'What happened, Niccolo? She seemed happy yesterday.'

He thought of prevaricating. Of pretending everything was fine. But he didn't have the heart for it. He'd never felt so wrong inside.

Niccolo slumped back into the cushioned seat and raked his fingers through his hair, mildly astonished to discover his hand shook. He, whose iron nerves and steady hands were legend on the racing circuit.

He'd handled it all wrong.

'She *was* happy.' He thought of the tender interest on her face when they'd talked down by the lake, her smiles as she'd chatted with his family. Her beautiful eyes wide with wonder and delight as he'd taken her to ecstasy. Last night she'd glowed, positively incandescent and he hadn't been able to drag his eyes off her.

How had he wrecked all that?

He swung round. 'How did she go? Did you see?' Pride be damned. He was more concerned about whether Lia was all right than admitting a fault before his *nonna.*

'One of our guests offered her a lift.'

The sick feeling in Niccolo's belly intensified, bile rising to his throat, threatening to make him gag.

Please, not Paolo Calderone.

The thought of Lia with that slimy playboy made him want to punch something, preferably Calderone's smarmy face.

Surely, even if she was upset, Lia wouldn't have turned to *him* for help?

'Who was it?' He could barely get the words past his gritted teeth. 'Calderone?'

'Of course not. I didn't invite him to stay the night. It was my friend Marco from Padua. He had to leave early and— Niccolo? Where are you going?'

He was already on his feet, bending to kiss her on the cheek. 'Thank you, *Nonna.* I promise to explain later.' Though not everything. 'I'm sorry I can't stay, but I have to see Lia.'

The astonishment faded from his grandmother's face, replaced by a cat-that-got-the-cream smile as she took his hand in hers. 'I'm glad. I like her very much, Niccolo.' She paused, squeezing his fingers.

'I just hope she forgives you.'

Niccolo didn't question her assumption he was the one in the wrong. He was too busy wondering if Lia would even talk to him.

He'd never been so terrified in his life.

Lia tightened the belt of her robe with determined fingers. It wasn't the silk robe she'd bought to match her pretty new nightdress – the one she'd worn when she'd shared a bed with Niccolo. She didn't think she'd ever wear those again. No, this was crisp cotton, serviceable and fresh.

She couldn't bear the touch of silk against her skin. It reminded her of last night. And of Niccolo.

Don't go there. Not now.

The first thing she'd done on returning to her apartment was have a long shower, her second for today. As if she could wash Niccolo Marchesi from her mind and body as easily as she washed her hair.

But she feared nothing would erase the memory of him, standing there in the bright sunlight, as handsome as a young god, telling her what they'd shared had been a mistake.

A *mistake*!

Fury seared through her and she welcomed it. For it incinerated, even if only for a moment, the hurt. He'd enjoyed himself but not enough to outweigh his precious scruples. *She* was less important to him than her family.

She'd always known it but had hoped this weekend he'd changed.

As if!

She brushed her hand down her bright red robe,

telling herself she'd been bold and strong, just like this red. She had nothing to regret, apart from the fact she'd spent so long pining for a man who'd never appreciate her.

Her mouth threatened to crumple but she wouldn't let it, despite the terrible crushed feeling inside, as if something was irretrievably broken. Instead she picked up her comb and began to untangle her wet hair.

She'd put on her prettiest dress, and a whole lot of makeup, then go out. She'd ring one of her friends, maybe make up a party for a meal out. She'd—

There was a knock at the door and Lia froze. Instantly, unstoppably, her mind went to Niccolo. Niccolo finding out she'd left and following her.

Her heart was pounding fit to burst and the woman in the mirror had bright colour in her cheeks where before there'd been none.

She dropped the comb with a clatter and grabbed the edge of the bathroom basin.

She would *not* do this to herself. It couldn't be him. He'd be counting his lucky stars she'd left after that awful scene at the villa. No doubt he'd find excuses to avoid her in future.

It was her brother Gennaro's engagement party next weekend and Luca was bringing someone special to meet the family too. Matteo and Angela, newly reunited, would be there and even Aurelio had hinted he might bring a friend. For a little while Lia had fantasised about Niccolo attending as her date, not just as a family friend.

But Niccolo would probably find himself with sudden urgent business on another continent.

Her heart squeezed.

Face it, Lia. You won't be seeing him for a long time.

If Niccolo didn't find reasons to avoid the De Laurentis family gatherings in future, she would. She'd all but told him she loved him and all he could think about was what other people would say! She deserved better.

The knock came again, longer this time.

Lia swung round and headed for the front door. It would be one of the neighbours. Nevertheless, she had to take a deep breath before she cracked the door open.

'Lia. Thank God!' Dark eyes held hers, sending her belly into a desperate loop the loop. Her heart pulsed so fast she felt sick.

Instinctively she pushed the door. She refused to face Niccolo. Not yet. Not before she had a grip on her emotions.

But it stuck. She shoved with all her strength but couldn't shut it. Then she looked down and saw one large, hand-made leather shoe wedged in the gap. Inexorably the gap widened, the door pushing back towards her despite her desperate grip.

'I don't want to see you, Niccolo. There's nothing more to say.'

'The hell there isn't.'

Suddenly he was there, crowding her entry with his big shoulders and his magnetic personality. She could almost feel her nerves zapping at the energy he radiated.

Lia stepped back, one hand closing the collar of her robe, the other hugging her waist tight, as if that would suppress the terrible anguish inside.

Her head snapped up. 'I told you, I don't want you here.'

'Too bad. I need to see you.' His mouth was grim as he closed the door, then had the temerity to lock it.

A shiver ran through her. Indignation, surely. Not anticipation. No, she had too much pride for that. No way was she going to fall into this man's bed again.

Not that he wanted her there.

Not that they'd even made it to the bed that first time.

The memory swamped her, making a mockery of her outrage. For despite her fury and hurt, there was longing too.

She still wanted him.

Still loved him. That was the worst part of it. How much easier if it had been a one night stand with a stranger instead of the culmination of years of yearning.

Niccolo folded his arms, planting his feet wide, as if challenging her to eject him.

But suddenly Lia didn't have the energy. Heart pummelling and limbs stiff, she turned and crossed to her big, overstuffed armchair. It was old-fashioned and worn but it was like sinking into a sustaining embrace. She hooked a cushion to her stomach and wrapped her arms tight around it, tucking her feet beneath her. Hoping she had the stamina for this confrontation.

Niccolo stared down at Lia and swallowed. Beautiful, feisty, gorgeous, Lia looked damp and angry but somehow smaller than when she'd tried to push him back onto the street. She had such a big, generous personality he tended to forget how little she was. Right now she looked as if a stiff breeze would blow her over, despite the determined set of her chin.

Because of him.

He'd rehearsed what he'd say all the way from the villa. He'd planned explanations and counter arguments. But the sight of her, so fragile and defiant, cut through his carefully formulated words.

Was he too late?

Was the damage irretrievable?

With a thud he hit the floor with his knees, ripping the cushion from her grasp and tossing it over his shoulder. He took her cold hands in his and held tight. She didn't resist, didn't react at all. That, more than anything, terrified him.

'I'm sorry, Lia. I didn't mean to hurt you.'

It wasn't enough, he knew. But it was the truth.

She didn't meet his eyes, just stared down at his hands clutching hers.

'Do we have to do this?' Her voice was cool, and if he didn't know her so well he might have missed the tell-tale tremor. She was still hurting.

That knowledge pierced him like a stiletto blade through the belly. Desperately he hoped he could fix this.

'You know we do. I owe you—'

'You don't owe me anything! I'd rather you just left.' Her gaze collided with his and fierce heat shot through him, knotting his belly and igniting dormant fire. His hands tightened.

He wasn't leaving. Not yet. He pushed aside a rising tide of fear, refusing to give in to it.

'I owe you so much, Lia.'

She swung her head from side to side, wet hair

flying wide. 'If you dare to thank me for giving you my virginity I'll… I'll…'

'What? Slap me?' How he preferred her volatile and furious to meek and vulnerable.

She tried to pull her hands free of his but he wouldn't let her. It was a bullying tactic, using his superior physical strength, but he'd use anything he could to make her listen.

'The gift of your virginity is something I'm never going to forget, Lia, whether you like it or not.' Last night was seared into his brain, burnt into his very being. He met her glare head on, refusing to back down. 'But I was going to say I owed you for what you did, helping to make my grandmother's weekend so special. She likes you very much, you know.'

Lia's tension eased just a little and her forehead wrinkled. 'Oh.' She lifted her shoulders. 'I like her too. I can see why she's so special to you.'

He nodded. 'And I have to thank you as well, for letting me ramble on about my future options. Most people think I should settle for what I've got. Build on what I've already achieved in racing. It's rare to have someone actually encourage me to follow a new dream.' Words couldn't convey how much that had meant. How precious Lia's support was. With her he felt he could be totally honest, and he valued her opinion.

'I'm sure your grandmother is supportive too.' Lia's tone was tight, as if she didn't have enough breath.

Niccolo lifted stiff shoulders. 'My grandmother is a rare woman.' Lia was another.

His heart throbbed up high in his throat as if

trying to burst free. Her face was set and tense. No sign of softening. He had to lay his cards on the table, convince her of his feelings.

'I want to thank you for last night, Lia.'

He hadn't thought it possible for her to grow more rigid but she did. The tension in her almost crackled.

'You're thanking me for the sex?' She said it as if it was something distasteful, and part of him mourned. Last night she'd been so open and passionate. Had he completely ruined that between them? She shook her head. 'I should be thanking *you*. Your expertise made all the difference. All those women you've had in your bed have taught you a lot.'

Niccolo found himself so angry he almost wanted to shake her. Except this was *his* fault.

Besides, Lia had been an innocent. How could she possibly know? She had nothing with which to compare last night.

He thought of her inexperience, the fact he was the only man who'd brought her such pleasure. He alone had felt the slick, tight welcome of her delectable body, and been gifted with the sight of her coming apart in rapture. All those things, and more, made him feel proud and protective and above all, blessed.

'You think it was that, Lia?' He stroked the backs of her hands with his thumbs and watched as she couldn't repress a shiver. Hope stirred. She wasn't as impervious to him as she pretended. 'You're wrong. Last night was wonderful, magnificent.' He watched her eyes widen. 'But not because of any sexual expertise on my part. I was functioning on sheer desperation. I *needed* you, Lia. I didn't have time for seductive techniques.'

He stopped and let that sink in. He'd never bared himself to a woman this way before. It made him edgy, vulnerable even, yet strangely elated. 'The reason it was so mind blowing was *us, tesoro*. The fact it was you and me together.' He *had* to make her understand.

'You're just saying that.'

'Why would I?'

'How should *I* know?' Her voice rose to a wobble that sent regret spearing through his middle. 'To get me back into bed maybe? To scratch an itch?'

'Ah, Lia. I may not be good with words, but even I know it's going to take a lot more than that to get you back in my bed.' He released a shuddering breath. 'And for what it's worth you're far more to me than an itch that needs scratching.' He felt his throat constrict on the words. How he'd hurt her!

But she didn't pick up on the raw emotion cramping his belly and making it hard to breathe.

She tossed her head. 'I know. I'm an obligation.' Her voice was sharp with sarcasm. 'A responsibility. A—'

Niccolo couldn't take any more. He yanked her forward, wrapping his arm around her slim waist and tugging her to the edge of the chair. Her face was against his, her hand splayed wide across his heart. He lifted his other hand to capture the back of her head, his grip merciless as he held her against him. When he spoke his lips were a mere kiss from hers.

'Okay. I was a prig and I deserve that. But no

matter how old-fashioned it may seem, you'll have to get used to the fact I *do* want to protect you.' He groaned, feeling his control unravel. 'Just as much as I want to make love with you again and again and again.'

Silence. He pulled back enough to see huge eyes, solemn and golden, staring back at him.

'You want sex? After what you said at the villa? You've got to be joking.'

He shook his head. His emotions were so tangled. No-one had ever messed with his head the way Lia did.

'Of course I want sex. But I want a whole lot more, Lia.' He drew in a deep breath, fortifying himself for the truth.

'You've always been special, Lia. When you were younger it was like having a little sister. No!' He pressed a finger to her lips when she would have spoken. 'Let me finish, please.'

Her eyes flashed fire but she said nothing.

'But for a long time now what I've felt for you has been…different.' He saw her eyes widen and nodded. 'I had no idea you felt it too and it haunted me that the girl I'd cared for like a sibling had grown into a woman I was attracted to. What I felt for you wasn't in the least brotherly and I felt guilty about that.'

Niccolo paused, trying to find the words. 'Men are simple creatures, Lia. We tend to see things in black and white. For so long you were off limits sexually as far as my head was concerned. The trouble was the rest of me has been spending a lot of time lusting after you.'

'You have?' She didn't sound angry now, but he

could only read shock and curiosity in her frown. Nothing to give him hope. Niccolo's stomach dived. But he refused to give up.

'I have. But that's not all.' He sat back on his heels so he could see her face more clearly. This was so important he needed to see her expression. 'I've been having erotic daydreams about you for ages now, but it's not just your body I want, Lia. I've done a lot of thinking since this morning. Or maybe I should say, facing up to truths I've been avoiding. I realised that all this time when I've found it so hard to commit long term to any lover it's because at the back of my mind there's a woman with golden eyes and a smile as bright as the sun. A gorgeous, vivacious woman who's honest and generous and all the things I've ever wished for.'

'If you're trying to make up for what you said this morning you're doing a good job.' She strove for a light tone but he couldn't miss the way her voice wobbled, or the fine tremors shaking her body. 'I never knew you could be so silver tongued.'

Still she didn't trust him completely. How could he blame her?

Niccolo pulled her close and discovered his hands were shaking. Could she feel that? Would she take pity on him?

She tilted her head back so their eyes met. Hers glistened and his heart turned over. He had to get this right, for both their sakes.

'I love you.' He said it slowly, letting her read the truth in his eyes, hoping to hell it was enough. Hoping she felt something similar for him. 'I've loved you a long time, Lia De Laurentis. Even when you were a teenager with pigtails. But I have a suspicion I've spent the last couple of years falling in love with the woman you've become.'

'A suspicion?' Her voice was husky.

He nodded, seeing the dawning brightness in those remarkable eyes. Emotion beat at his chest, rising hard in his throat.

'That's right. I've never been in love before, so I'm guessing that's what this feeling is. Like there's something huge and wonderful inside that's making my skin too tight and my heart too big.' He paused, his pulse racing. 'If you let me I'd like to investigate further.'

'To see if it really is love?' Her brow wrinkled and all he could think was how he wanted to kiss it smooth.

'Actually, I'm pretty sure it is.' There, it was easier to admit than he'd imagined. A smile tugged at his lips, but he wouldn't let it come. He still had a long way to go to convince her. 'I'm hoping that if you let me spend time with you, take you out—'

'Like a boyfriend?'

Niccolo couldn't read her thoughts and that scared him. She wasn't responding. 'Exactly like that.' He nodded. 'Then maybe you'll discover you feel the same way about me.'

Her beautiful face remained expressionless and Niccolo knew a sudden, desperate fear she was going to banish him for good. A chill engulfed him, so intense numbness threatened.

He couldn't imagine how he could go on without her now that he'd found her.

Then she smiled, the corners of her mouth tilting up in a slow, glorious curve that transformed her taut face into a beacon of beauty and more…

of happiness.

'You must be right about men being simple creatures.' There was a gurgle of laughter in her voice that felt like warm honey easing his frayed nerves. 'I've been in love with you as long as I can remember, Niccolo. I've just become very good at hiding it. So, yes, I'll go out with you and see where that leads.'

He stared, dumbfounded. He'd hoped but this… He shook his head, barely able to believe it. 'You mean it?' You'll forgive me?'

Had she really been in love all this time? How could he not have noticed?

Because you've been so busy trying not to notice anything about her, in case you broke all the rules and seduced her.

Lia's golden eyes danced and his pent-up breath eased out of cramped lungs. This was *real.*

'I could be persuaded, if you work at it.' Her lush mouth lifted at one corner in a smile that was like a glimpse of heaven after mortal fear. 'I might even,' she leaned in close and he felt the warm silk of her lips on his ear, 'let you sleep with me again. Just for the sake of your research.'

Convulsively, Niccolo tightened his arms around her, hugging her so close it was a wonder either of them could breathe.

She was his. Would always be his, he'd make sure of it. He was going to devote the rest of his life to making her happy.

Briefly Niccolo closed his eyes, fervently thanking whatever fates had brought them to this point.

'In that case, *tesoro*, I suggest we go somewhere a little more comfortable to discuss our first date.'

'Date? I'm not sure I can be bothered getting dressed.' She pouted so beautifully and so ostentatiously that he laughed, hugging her to him. 'What if I want to stay in?'

This woman would kill him yet. But in the most glorious way.

'See? Already we're on the same wavelength. I was thinking exactly the same thing.'

Niccolo rose to his feet, sweeping Lia high in his arms. The teasing light died from her eyes as he stared down into her expressive face, and he felt again that thump of emotion, like a sledge hammer to the solar plexus. Except instead of bringing pain, it filled him with pure joy.

'Be warned, Lia. I want you in my life, always.'

'Good.' Her soft palm stroked his cheek. 'I feel exactly the same.'

Then there was no more talking for a long, long time.

FALLING FOR THE
Brooding Italian

Book 6, Hot Italian Nights

*To all the readers who've enjoyed
my Hot Italian Nights Series and asked for more!
And once again, thank you to Guisy C!*

Chapter One

THE FIRST TIME AMBER MONCRIEFF met Aurelio De Laurentis he didn't speak to her, just nodded during the introductions, then proceeded to brood silently from the other side of the wide conference table.

Yet she'd felt his eyes bore into her through every stage of her presentation. His scrutiny sent trails of heat snaking through her body to all sorts of secret places. It made her feel nothing like a public relations professional but definitely all woman.

The second time they met, at a wine expo, she'd *felt* him before she'd seen him. Every nerve ending had gone onto high alert, the blood rushing faster in her arteries as she turned and found him surveying her across the room, while he talked with the American CEO of a huge multi-national beverage consortium. Amber discovered later that the CEO had tried and failed to acquire De Laurentis Wines.

The Italian's stare as it met hers had been unreadable. Yet it made her lower body soften and a hollow ache start up deep inside. She'd known, with the certainty of a woman used to male attention, that sooner or later Aurelio De Laurentis would cross the room and try to separate her from the group she was with.

She was still deciding whether she'd let him,

when she discovered she was completely wrong. He'd left the expo and didn't come back.

Amber had been left…unsettled, her body humming with tension as if she'd come too close to high voltage wires.

The third time their paths crossed, the evening began with them seated at the same table at a wine industry awards night and ended with them in bed together. It was a week before they parted and during that time they barely left the hotel.

Amber was determined the fourth time would be different.

It had to be. Too much rode on this.

She gripped the wheel of her small rental car tighter as she followed the autostrada north out of Rome, towards Aurelio's vineyard. She told herself determination made her tense. Yet there was a swell of nausea in her stomach too, a flare of nerves. For she'd proved herself far too vulnerable to Aurelio.

She'd thrown caution out the window in response to the invitation glittering in his dark eyes. He'd given her pleasure, so much pleasure! And excitement.

And he'd hurt her terribly when he'd walked away.

This time she wouldn't let herself be seduced by those black-as-night eyes and the earthy sensuality that seeped from every pore of his hard, masculine body.

This time she'd be careful. As careful as she'd always been, before Aurelio De Laurentis swept her off her feet and between his sheets.

This time she wouldn't be readily available for sex, or so easily ignored afterwards. It still stung, remembering how he'd left her without a back-ward glance. There'd been not even a text in the intervening six weeks. It was like those seven days sharing the most incredible intimacies and the most exquisite joy had never happened.

It more than stung. Amber had felt humiliated and confused. Worse, even now when anger fizzed in her blood, the pain of loss was constant.

Amber's mouth flattened in a tight line. She had no-one to blame but herself. He'd made no prom-ises. On the contrary, he'd made it absolutely clear he wanted a short affair, no strings, no ties.

It was exactly the sort of liaison Amber had always avoided. She didn't do one night stands or casual hook ups, preferring relationships based on more than sex. Yet she'd found herself agreeing, overwhelmed by her response to the laconic, char-ismatic man who only had to look at her with that intense stare for her to burn up with need. She'd flung aside all caution, letting herself give in to a visceral attraction she'd never before experienced.

A night had become two, become a week, and they'd shared so much. Aurelio had been open about his humble roots, his love of winemaking despite its challenges and his grand vision for his company. Amber had shared her own hopes for the future, her excitement about being in Italy, and rambled on about her family back home in Aus-tralia.

She'd felt she knew him, as he knew her. Despite his initial comment about a no-strings affair, the bond between them grew strong. She'd even believed it grew stronger than the fierce, ever-pres-ent sexual attraction between them.

She'd been wrong. He'd walked away and never thought of her again. Never once bothered to make contact. Her one call to his phone hadn't been answered, though she'd rung at a time she knew he'd be in the office, dealing with paperwork. He'd *chosen* not to answer or call back.

Amber's teeth ground in sheer indignation. No matter what the circumstances, he owed her the courtesy of responding. She refused to be fobbed off. She'd thought better of him. She'd never imagined Aurelio could stoop to such rudeness, such callous disregard of her dignity, let alone her feelings.

Her skin shrank back against her bones as she recalled how thoroughly and how easily he'd brushed her off. As if she, and what they'd shared, were nothing.

Amber knew it was what he'd stipulated that first night, but it rankled. For somewhere between that first cataclysmic joining, hard up against the door of the hotel room, and the morning she'd woken to find him dressed, packed and on his way home, her heart had got involved.

She firmed her jaw. Their fourth meeting would be different. This time they'd meet on her terms, not his.

Aurelio stared at the results of the latest stock-take. As he thought, they'd need more storage space soon. The issue was whether to expand here or further down the valley at the vineyard he'd just purchased. The vineyard that would allow him to increase yield and production to meet market demands, while ensuring quality remained high.

He refused to sacrifice his standards for easy money despite the pressure for more, more, more. The company had made the transition from well-respected wines to phenomenal success, and high quality was the key.

He sat back and rolled his shoulders, then stood to straighten stiff legs. The tiny room tucked in one corner of the winery was far too small for all the administrative work these days. Too small for a man as tall as he.

But he liked being down here, at the heart of the winery, rather than in the new offices he'd installed as the business expanded. He loved the scents of old wood and ripe fruit, the shadows and shapes of vats and barrels, the continuity between him and those before him who'd toiled over this earth for generations, making the wine for which the region was renowned.

He smiled, thinking of Paolo, the nuggetty, weathered man who'd been his boss and mentor, and was now his friend and partner. The old guy had worked hard for decades. He deserved the comfort of a padded seat and an endless supply of decent coffee while he took a break from vineyard work.

If only Aurelio could convince him to take it easy more often.

He glanced at his watch and grimaced. He was late for their meeting. Aurelio waved to one of the cellar hands, reminded him about a vat that needed cleaning, and strode out into the sunlight.

Instantly his gaze went, not to the new tasting room and administrative building, but to the nearest slope of grapes. The precious bunches were already forming. With luck it would be another good season.

Tempted as he was to detour to the vines, he headed for the building. Acquiring a new public relations and marketing consultant was critical. He and Paolo had narrowed the choice down to two front runners to win the contract. But since he was trying to get Paolo to slow down, not devote so much time to physical work, he'd left it to the old man, who had an instinct for people as well as vines, to make the final choice. That minor heart attack last year was a warning. If Paolo wouldn't heed it, Aurelio did. By hook or by crook, he'd get his partner to spend more time off his feet.

Paolo favoured the older, established firm. Not Aurelio's first choice, but he knew the company would do an excellent job. The alternative, an energetic one-woman dynamo, wasn't Paolo's style.

Aurelio's step faltered. That choice was too fraught to consider.

His thoughts slewed to Rome and the presentations he'd watched there.

To Amber Moncrieff.

His pace slowed even as his pulse picked up, his heart hammering an all-too familiar, needy rhythm against his ribs. Familiar because that's what happened whenever he thought of Amber.

She invaded his thoughts on a regular basis. Too regular.

Sighing, he raked his hand across his scalp.

He'd done the right thing, ending it.

He had no regrets. She'd known the score, and so had he.

Except it still felt like they had unfinished business. He'd left the city a month and a half ago and still he couldn't settle into routine. It had taken far more willpower than it should have not to answer her call.

Even as he'd known it was for the best, it hadn't felt right. He might prefer burying himself in the demands of his vineyard to socialising, but he'd never before stooped to avoiding a call.

As if he was worried he wouldn't be able to maintain his distance if he heard her voice, soft and beckoning in his ear!

Grimacing, Aurelio headed into the new building. He was torn between relief and disappointment that he wouldn't see her again.

If there'd been any chance that Amber would win the job, he'd never have slept with her. She'd known by then that she'd missed out on the contract, for he'd made no secret of the fact Paolo was in detailed discussions with the rival firm. Knowing Paolo, Aurelio had understood it was simply a matter of time before the larger company came on board. Which meant there'd been no conflict of interest between work and desire when he and Amber spent that week together.

In that time Amber hadn't once mentioned marketing. But then they'd both had other things on their minds.

It had been hard leaving her. Surprisingly even harder to sever all contact. But their break had to be absolute.

No ties, no emotional complications. That's how he needed it. It was the only way he could operate.

Aurelio marched into the building, feeling out of

sorts, only to slam to a halt as his nostrils caught an unexpected scent. Honeysuckle and sunshine.

He frowned, his senses going into overdrive.

He was imagining things, he had to be.

One of the office workers was trying out a new perfume, that's all. Except this wasn't just honeysuckle. There was added depth to the aroma. A depth that reminded him of summer but, he'd assumed, was something to do with the reaction of the scent on warm, female flesh. *Amber's* warm flesh to be precise.

Shaking his head, Aurelio strode down the corridor to the meeting room. The woman had even sabotaged his sense of smell — a vital tool for a winemaker!

Husky laughter caught his attention, the sound swirling like early morning mist around his tight chest. Heat flared, bright and powerful, in his belly, radiating through him, making him overwarm in the pullover he wore while working in the cool winery.

Yet the skin at his nape prickled. That laugh—

'That will teach you to use a satnav. Give me an old-fashioned map any day. It's a wonder you found us.' Paolo's gruff voice sounded indulgent.

Aurelio stepped into the room just as a woman spoke. 'Oh, there's nothing like a little adventure. You wouldn't like life to be too boring, would you?'

He froze, mid-step, head jerking round to the woman who stood with Paolo near the window, looking at the hillside vineyard.

Something sharp plunged through Aurelio, like a dagger slicing through his internal organs, leaving a terrible, yawning ache.

Amber!

What the hell had Paolo done?

Aurelio blinked but the vision before him stayed unchanged.

The woman with her back to him wore a sleeveless, white dress that should have looked plain but somehow appeared sophisticated and sexy. Maybe because of the way it hugged her slim curves, or perhaps because it ended so high on her thighs.

Aurelio swallowed jerkily. It felt like someone had sandpapered his throat.

His gaze tracked down endless, perfect legs to high heels that stirred something unwanted in his gut.

Desire.

But it wasn't just the sexy shoes. It was the dress, the curves, the legs. Hell, it was Amber. Everything about her was designed to drive a man into meltdown. Even the tender curve of her neck since she'd secured her glossy dark hair high. Aurelio recalled how her hair had felt, soft and silken against his skin, drifting around his thighs as she—

'He's late. I'm sorry. He loses track of time when he's in the winery.' Paolo sounded gruffer than ever.

'That's understandable.' Her voice was low, designed for seduction. 'It takes dedication to produce such superb wines.'

Aurelio must have moved, must have made a noise, because abruptly she swung round.

Something slammed into his chest. Something powerful enough to flatten his lungs and steal his breath.

Elegant bones. Ebony lashes and eyebrows that

were arresting when teemed with silvery grey eyes. Neat, even features, and a mouth, full and ripe, that almost made him groan aloud.

Amber's was a classic beauty that would make any man keep looking. But Aurelio knew so much more about her, all intriguing, all attractive. Her fiery passion, the exquisite sensitivity of her body, the intriguing mind that lay behind those cool looks…

He was scuppered, he realised with a sinking feeling.

In an instant all his certainties, all his control, teetered on the edge of smashing to smithereens.

Because there was only one certainty when he looked at this woman.

Want. Pure, simple want.

Chapter Two

AMBER'S STOMACH FELL ABRUPTLY, AS if she plunged from the very top of a massive rollercoaster to the bottom. At the same time her heart raced to a quicker beat, her breath stalling in her lungs then starting up again, rapid and shallow.

One look was all it took.

Every time it was like this.

She'd hoped that by now, after he walked out on her, she'd have some immunity. But even anger was no protection against this primal response.

Even if she could ignore the stark attractiveness of Aurelio's strong features or the powerful masculinity of his tall, rangy frame, there was the memory of his surprising tenderness as he caressed her with those big, callused hands. The unexpected gleam of humour in those liquid dark eyes. The sense, still unbroken, that they shared far more than sex.

Amber blinked. Even his hair, thick and dark, invited her touch. As for the hint of a cleft in each cheek, half hidden by stubble, she knew precisely how intriguing they became when he smiled. And that mouth…Aurelio's mouth was sensual and well-shaped. The mere sight of it sent memories rushing through her, of those warm lips kissing her into mindless ecstasy.

Shock, desire, longing smacked into her, rocking

her back on her heels. She felt her eyes widen, her pelvis soften, and that instantaneous, unstoppable response gave her the strength she needed to meet his stare and lift her chin a notch. She refused to be a pushover for this man. Instead she stiffened her knees, ignoring the fact her legs felt as weak as overcooked tagliatelle.

'Hello, Aurelio. It's good to see you again.' Her voice was rough-edged, but at least it was even.

She fixed a smile on her face, the sort of smile she used when dealing with difficult clients. Her emotions were too powerful and too complex for simple pleasure. All she could do was hope to keep them hidden by playing the calm businesswoman.

He stiffened, his brow twitching, and she widened her smile. Had he expected her to fall in a heap when she saw him? Or maybe run to him and throw herself into his arms?

She had more self-respect than that.

Yet she didn't walk around the table and offer to shake his hand. There was a limit to her courage. Physical contact would test her strength too much.

'Amber.' He inclined his head so infinitesimally she wondered if it actually hurt him to move. Or whether her presence meant so little that was the only greeting he could be bothered to give.

Pain scoured her heart. Pain and a horrible fear she faced defeat before she'd even begun. But she was no quitter. She met his stare with one of her own, lifting her eyebrows.

'This is…unexpected.' His deep voice eddied around her, making her insides curl.

Amber frowned. 'You didn't know I was coming?'

How could that be? Surely he'd been party to the final decision on who'd implement a new PR and marketing strategy for the winery. He and Paolo were partners but it was clear that Aurelio was the powerhouse behind the enterprise.

Paolo spoke up from beside her. 'The final decision on the contract was mine, Amber. It just took me a while to make up my mind. After your presentation in Rome, you were Aurelio's preferred choice, but I initially favoured a larger, longer established firm for the job. They came close to convincing me, but the more I thought on it, the more I realised you understood us and what we're doing here. Your proposal respects that.'

Amber swung round, staring into the weather-beaten face of the older man. For the first time that day the tension in her jaw and stiff shoulders unlocked a little. It meant so much that her vision was recognised. She'd known she was up against some big guns for this contract and had worked incredibly hard to win it.

'I'm glad you changed your mind.'

He beamed. 'So am I. You're a perfect match for our needs. A background in wine, a great track record, and a really clever campaign plan. Even an old guy like me can see we need to move with the times.'

'But maintain that connection with the winery's history and integrity. The fact that tradition and quality are valued as well as modern innovation.'

Paolo nodded. 'Exactly. A merger of old and new.' He turned to the man still standing stiff and silent just inside the door. 'You were right, Aurelio. She's just the woman we need.'

Which begged the question of why Paolo hadn't told his partner he'd awarded her the contract. Aurelio had made it clear in Rome that the contract was going to another company.

There were undercurrents here Amber didn't understand. Not least the fact Aurelio had left the final decision to Paolo.

Slowly, reluctantly, Amber turned towards the man watching them from the door. There it was again, that punch to the midriff that was her body's response to Aurelio. She just hoped she hid it from him.

He didn't look welcoming.

Forget welcoming, his stern stare grew close to a scowl.

There could only be one reason. He didn't want her here. Between the day of her presentation and now, they'd had a scorching affair. Presumably he didn't want a reminder of that.

Did he think she was going to beg him to take her back?

But then she'd never been his, had she? She'd merely been a partner for convenient sex. And if Aurelio could look at her like they'd never shared anything more tender, then she could reciprocate. Pride came to her aid, despite the piercing ache inside.

'I'm looking forward to exploring the vineyard.' She smiled at Paulo. 'It looks impossibly scenic but it's the soil and the grapes that really interest me. And the end product, of course.'

'Of course.' His smile was warm, a stark contrast to his partner's silence. Yet that didn't seem to bother Paolo. 'We'll bring in your luggage then start the tour.'

'Luggage?' Aurelio's tone was sharp.

'Of course. Amber is staying for a few days, getting an in depth knowledge of the place. That was what you wanted, someone who understands not just the business but the place and the ethos behind it.'

Amber watched Aurelio's mouth compress and realised he was biting back an objection. *Not* the start she'd hoped for. But she'd known this wasn't going to be easy.

A woman came to the door, calling Paolo away for a phone call. He excused himself, saying he'd return soon.

Leaving her alone with Aurelio.

After long, silent minutes that notched her tension even higher, he finally closed the door and stepped further into the room. Instantly it seemed to shrink, as if the walls crowded close, or some invisible presence sucked the oxygen from the air, leaving Amber's lungs cramped and overworked.

Aurelio raked his fingers back through midnight hair that fell back in place looking just a little rumpled. The sight made her recall how he'd looked naked in bed, his heavy-lidded eyes full of invitation and his tousled hair a reminder of the passion neither could get enough of.

Her traitorous heart lurched hard against her ribs, as if trying to get closer to him.

Amber curled her fingers tight and stood exactly where she was.

'It's no good.' He shook his head. 'This isn't going to work.'

'Sorry?' She blinked up at him as he stalked

around the table towards her. Fortunately he stopped more than an arm's length away.

Did he too feel this snapping spark of energy? Like electricity arcing between them?

Amber found herself arching back, resisting a force field that threatened to draw her off her feet and into his arms.

Self-disgust welled. She couldn't be that needy. The man was giving off keep-out vibes so strong it was a wonder they didn't light up the room.

'I'm sorry, Amber.' For the first time since he'd arrived she saw a flicker of something in his adamantine expression. She could almost imagine it was regret, till his jaw hardened, making him look more unyielding than ever. 'You can't stay here.'

For a long moment she digested his words. 'It's not convenient for me to stay at the vineyard? No problem. I'm sure I'll find accommodation in town. It's—'

'That's not what I mean.' He shrugged his wide shoulders as if releasing a muscle ache. 'I mean you can't work here. You can't take the job.'

Amber hadn't expected him to welcome her with open arms but nor had she expected such absolute rejection. A tiny part of her, the part that had hoped he'd longed for her just as she'd yearned for him, shrivelled up and died. In its place, indignation ignited.

'I'm afraid I already have.' She took a step forward so she could brace one hand on the conference table. Suddenly she needed the support, especially when she saw how he stiffened at her approach. If proof were needed that he was now immune to her, that was it. This man was obviously uncomfortable just being close to her.

He didn't want an ex-lover cramping his style.

Aurelio shook his head. 'It will be easier if you simply tell Paolo you've changed your mind. That you can't take the job.'

Slowly she tilted her head, surveying him from the obstinate jut of his jaw to the pulse thrumming at his temple. Taking in his absolute, unnatural stillness.

How had she ever imagined he might have missed her?

'Easier for whom? Not for Paolo. He's already put a lot of work into getting me here. Definitely not for me. I've rearranged my schedule to be here. I've committed to the job.'

'You know what I mean, Amber.' Aurelio's low voice grew harsh, a definite growl. 'We can't work together.'

Suddenly Amber found she didn't need the support of the sturdy table any longer. She straightened, firm on her feet, her hands anchoring on her hips.

'You mean it would be easier for *you* not to work with me. Why is that, Aurelio? You don't want to be reminded of past mistakes?'

Surely he viewed their brief liaison as a mistake. Otherwise why be so adamant that she couldn't stay?

'But you're wrong,' she continued before he could answer. '*I* can work here. I don't have to like or admire clients to work with them.' She paused, letting him digest that.

'Even when you're not wanted?'

His words were a blade to her breast, cutting away her breath. For a moment she only blinked, registering an uprush of pain. Had she really thought he might share her feelings? How naïve she'd been.

'Amber.' He took a step forward, his expression softening as his hand lifted towards her.

She burst into speech, needing to stop him before he touched her.

'You may not *want* me here, but you need me. That's clear from what I saw of your current marketing efforts. The quality of your wines is selling them for you but you need much more than that to succeed at the next level, especially now you've committed to such a large expansion.' She paused, hefting oxygen into too-tight lungs. 'But it won't be for long, Aurelio. I'll just be here a short time and then I'll work from Rome. I'm sure you can put up with me for a few days.'

He frowned and opened his mouth to shut her down, but Amber was ready for him. 'I've signed a contract with your company and I intend to honour that. I hope you do too. If not, I'll seek legal advice.'

'You wouldn't do that.' His voice was low and even but she caught the flare of surprise in his eyes.

Amber angled her jaw so high she stared straight into the dark gaze that was once more impenetrable. Had she imagined that flash of shock? He looked immovable and totally unshakeable.

'Wouldn't I? I'd love to hear you argue your case in court. What would the grounds be? Inability to work with me because I've seen you naked? Fear that I'll make a pass at you?' She shook her head. 'I'm simply here to do a job. Believe me, you have nothing to fear from me on that score.'

Chapter Three

AURELIO STARED AT THE WOMAN before him and felt the ground shift beneath his feet.

His response to her, the feeling of connection, grew stronger every time they were together. He'd told himself he could enjoy a quick affair with her then walk away and resume his normal life without a backward glance.

How wrong he'd been!

He'd known she was passionate, clever and sexy as hell. She intrigued him and her business savvy had been just one more element that added to the appealing mix. Even her fluent Italian with its Australian accent charmed rather than jarred.

But he'd never fully appreciated the sheer dynamism of her till now. She stood, slender arms akimbo, jaw tilted defiantly, her cool, crisp tone completely at odds with the storm sparking in her light eyes. It was like watching thunderclouds roll in over the mountain peaks, he decided, seeing the flare and sizzle of emotion beneath those long, lustrous lashes.

Her colour was high and her breasts rose and fell quickly, betraying her laboured breathing. But she didn't look cowed. She looked magnificent. Alluring. Beautiful. Even her patent disdain as she stared down that straight nose at him, did nothing to detract from her beauty.

He craved her.

The sight of her, the scent of her perfume, the knowledge he had only to stretch out one hand to feel the silkiness of her pale skin, were pure enticement.

Yet Aurelio stayed where he was, despite the urge to reach for her. He didn't trust himself. He knew how dangerously Amber weakened his determination to keep himself separate. For if there was one thing life had taught him, it was that he needed to be self-contained. He'd survived the last decade by cutting himself off from personal relationships, other than with family, and by devoting himself to work.

'You need this job so badly?' The impression he'd had was that they'd be lucky to get her working for them. There was no doubt she was in high demand.

Something flickered in Amber's eyes, something he tried and failed to decipher. Her gaze darted to the view outside of green vines with hills rising beyond.

'I agreed to take on the work and I turned down other projects because of that.' Her gaze slewed back to his, those gleaming eyes fixing him to the spot. 'Your company selected me after a rigorous selection process and I expect to be treated with courtesy and respect.' Her stare narrowed. 'Would you treat any other contractor the way you have me?'

Of course not. But then he'd never in the past come close to mixing work and pleasure.

She hit close to the bone with her talk of fairness.

His own success in the wine industry was built,

not just on talent and hard work, but the respect and encouragement of those who'd recognised and nurtured his talent. Success on merit was important to him.

Aurelio had never let his feelings compromise his standards before, but then he'd never felt anything like this bone-deep certainty that having Amber around would be catastrophic. Every nerve in his body was on high alert, screaming that she needed to go.

Either that or—

'As I thought. This is because we slept together.' Her mouth twisted in a moue of disapproval that only made him remember how those lush lips had felt beneath his. Heat exploded in his belly, and something else, a sensation that undermined his determination. He identified it as regret.

A defiant, rebel part of him even wanted to reach out and drag her up against his body, to remind her what they shared couldn't be so easily banished.

Aurelio drew a deep breath, shaky with the force of will needed to squash that impulse. He shoved his hands into the pockets of his jeans and kept them there.

Amber shook her head. 'But if you think that means I'm here to seduce you into my bed, you can think again. I can tell you,' disdain dripped from every syllable, 'I have zero interest in getting intimate with any man right now. That specifically includes you.' Her voice rang with a clarity that left no room for doubt. Her expression was contemptuous.

Strangely, instead of reassuring Aurelio, he felt something like disappointment.

He'd persuaded himself Amber was like him, happy to slake the overwhelming wave of lust that had engulfed them with a short affair. He'd made it clear he wanted nothing more.

Yet now, having her repudiate him and their week of intimacy as nothing, grazed his ego.

No, more than that. It actually hurt. Because on some level that week with Amber Moncrieff had stood out from the other time-limited affairs he'd had over the years. It had been brighter, better, on a scale nothing else matched.

That's why he'd cut all contact with her. Because he felt...different after being with her. Too restless. Too edgy. He'd known that what they shared teetered on a dangerous brink. That if he didn't protect them both by walking away, things would end in disaster. He wasn't cut out for anything long-term, much less permanent. The very idea filled him with horror.

'You regret Rome?' The words shot out before he could stop them. He couldn't even say why he needed to know. Yet now they were out, lying heavy in the thick air, Aurelio realised he needed her answer. The thought she regretted their time together hollowed his gut. His chest was too tight, his ribs seeming to contract around his lungs.

Her fine eyebrows shot high. 'I didn't think you were into post mortems.' One slim shoulder lifted in a nonchalant shrug. 'We had our time together and it was fun while it lasted. There's nothing more to be said.'

Fun! She thought it had been fun.

A deep channel of emotion carved through him at her words.

Aurelio wanted to accuse her of lying, of making light of what had been a stupendous experience. Not just for him but for her. He'd seen the stars in her eyes, read her little possessive gestures, and known he'd made a mistake, staying with her so long.

But she'd been impossible to resist. He'd let himself, just for a little, bask in her tenderness, in that heady sense of connection.

He should have known better!

Best to end the affair when they were merely friends with benefits than when one of them had begun to imagine a future together. Aurelio might be close to a recluse now with his utter devotion to work, but he knew when a woman was starting to weave romantic dreams.

It was the one thing in the world he avoided at all costs. For the price of loving was too high when it ended in blood and ashes.

'Aurelio? What's wrong?' Amber's voice had a husky edge and when he refocused he saw she was leaning forward, her brow crinkled in concern. It was enough to drag him from the miasma of memory.

'Nothing.' He stiffened, thrusting aside old hurts. The past was dead and gone.

He rolled his shoulders, spearing a hand through his hair. Was she serious about a lawsuit? That was the last thing they needed.

Business had been steadily growing since he'd taken over the vineyard. Recent awards and the company's reputation for only the finest quality wines meant income was excellent. But they'd just expanded with the purchase of a large vineyard further down the valley. Cash flow was tight and he resented the notion of spending it on lawyers.

Why couldn't Amber see sense? Despite her concern, there was no mistaking the martial light in her eyes. The woman was ready for a fight.

Because you rejected her. You were the one to end the relationship and you weren't subtle about it.

Because she'd begun to care and as soon as you realised, you dropped her so fast her head spun.

Not one of Aurelio's finer moments. Usually he was more subtle. Definitely more considerate. But for some reason being charming and considerate had always been much easier after a one or two night fling with a woman he essentially didn't care about.

With Amber something had happened. Something had jarred him into being less than smooth or gracious.

Oh, he'd said the words, but somehow they hadn't come out right. Instead of being likeable, witty and urbane, he'd sounded stilted, as if he lied when he told her the truth — that it was past time he returned here. That it had been wonderful but it had to end.

Obviously she held that against him.

'Is that why you took the job? Because you hold a grudge against me? You want to disrupt things here and make me pay?'

The hint of softness in her expression vanished. Her beautiful mouth thinned and her eyes narrowed to gleaming slits of glacial ice.

'You've got some ego, Aurelio De Laurentis, if you think this is all about *you!*' She crossed her arms and he had to fight not to let his gaze drop to where the white fabric of her dress hugged her breasts like a lover. Heat shimmered through his belly and he fought to focus.

'I applied for this contract before I'd met you. I did most of the negotiations with Paolo.' She shook her head, her expression pinched like a disapproving schoolmistress. 'I know you're a wunderkind in the winery, and that you've transformed a previously average vineyard into something special. But not everything in this world revolves around you.'

She drew a shaky breath. Was she trying to rein in fury? To his consternation, even angry she was far too appealing. And her huffiness proved how wrong he'd been in his suspicions.

'I have neither the time nor the inclination to bother sabotaging your business. *I've* got standards and a reputation to maintain. Associating with a failing business isn't in my five year plan.' Her gaze, scathing before, grew needle-sharp. 'I take pride in my work and I expect to succeed.'

Aurelio wanted to dislike her combative attitude. But how could he? She was right. He was treating her unfairly because he was uncomfortable with the idea of working with her.

Uncomfortable! The word did nothing to convey the gut-deep premonition of trouble looming in this woman's shadow.

He released a breath from tight lungs. He could force her hand. Surely she wouldn't pursue a legal option. But even if matters didn't go that far, he didn't want to taint the winery's reputation.

Besides, despite his instinctive recoil at the idea of working with her, Aurelio prided himself on being a fair man. She didn't deserve such treatment.

'Very well.' He dragged his hands from his pockets and crossed his arms over his chest, registering the quickened slam of his heart against his ribs. 'You can stay till the weekend. That will give you enough time to get a feel for the place and learn all you need to. After that you can call Paolo if you have queries.'

She nodded stiffly, no sign of either relief or pleasure on her face. Had he expected she'd smile and thank him for conceding what had already been agreed in her contract?

Aurelio told himself he wasn't that desperate to revel in this woman's smiles, to see her eyes soften as she looked at him.

'While you're here you'll deal with Paolo. I'll be busy with other things.' It was true, but to Aurelio's chagrin, it sounded like an excuse.

'That suits me perfectly.' Amber's eyes were diamond chips, glittering hard and cool. 'I'll make sure you don't even know I'm here.'

He nodded and turned away. 'Paolo will be back soon. He'll look after you.'

Amber waited till he'd left the room, then sank down onto a straight-backed chair, her knees quivering and her stomach churning. Her shoulders slumped forward, her arms crossing over her abdomen.

A flash of heat, a surge of protectiveness, welled.

She'd never felt so riled yet so impotent.

Or so despairing.

She'd had such high hopes. That she'd convince Aurelio they were meant to be together. Even now, with his brutal dismissal leaving a metallic taste on her tongue, and a mix of fury and hurt roiling through her, she couldn't break free of the conviction they *were* meant to be together.

Because she'd fallen in love with him.

She'd let herself be swept off her feet, despite knowing he wanted only a fling. Aurelio had never lied to her. Yet, despite all her caution, he'd somehow ensnared her heart. For she *knew* this aloof stranger wasn't the real Aurelio.

She just wished she knew what had happened to him to make him like this, so eager to see the back of her.

But that wasn't all of it. Things were far more complicated than that.

She was having his child.

Chapter Four

WON'T EVEN KNOW SHE'S THERE. Ha!
He'd thought of nothing else but Amber since she'd arrived.

Aurelio looked around the laboratory, where he'd been checking the sugar levels of a new white wine. He rolled his shoulders and sat back in his seat. At this early hour he was alone in the winery, but that didn't stop his thoughts straying to the slender, sassy brunette who'd taken over his world in the last two days.

She haunted him, making him stop in his tracks when he came across that light, lingering honeysuckle scent that told him she'd been nearby. She invaded his bedroom at night, a dream lover who kept him tossing and turning, waking even more disgruntled than when he'd tumbled, exhausted, into bed.

Aurelio couldn't get her out of his head. He'd excused himself from the evening meal he'd been invited to share with Paolo and Amber in Paolo's villa on the edge of the estate. He'd avoided the administrative building like the plague and, when Paolo had shown her the recently expanded winery, Aurelio had found business to occupy himself off site.

But he'd caught glimpses of her in the distance.

Heard her warm, throaty laugh, and something snagged in his chest as he recalled them laughing together in Rome.

Worse, he discovered it wasn't only desire she stirred, though he was in a state of semi-arousal a lot of the time, thinking of her. There was much more, and that was dangerous.

Aurelio found himself missing the warmth of her smiles and outgoing personality. He remembered her inquisitive mind, so quick and fascinating. How they'd spent hours in Rome talking, between bouts of sex so phenomenal, it was no wonder she'd imprinted herself on his brain.

They'd discovered common tastes and interests. Things as diverse as classical guitar music, detective thrillers, snowboarding and excellent coffee.

Plus she'd grown up on a vineyard in Australia, in the Riverina area where she learned his language from her Italian immigrant neighbours and friends. She understood his preoccupation with growing seasons and weather forecasts, with pests and pro-duction as well as blending, bottling and the fine balance of an excellent wine.

She'd fascinated him with talk of hot Australian summers, of endless sand beaches and lazy barbe-ques. Her easy-going acceptance of life and people contrasted with her driven, achievement-orien-tated attitude to work. But he admired both immensely.

Admired. Aurelio tried to tell himself that was all he felt.

It didn't work.

The trouble, he decided, was that they'd spent such a short time together, all of it spectacularly fantastic. She'd acquired the mystique of some perfect paragon of femininity. Sexy. Fun. Witty. Interested and interesting.

She appealed to his body and his mind in a way that hadn't happened in years, because he'd made sure not to let any woman so close.

He shot to his feet, tidying away the lab equipment. For the first time since Amber had arrived he felt better. A man with purpose, a man in charge again. Because he'd worked out a solution. It was so simple he was amazed he hadn't seen it before.

Spend time with Amber away from the rosy haze of sex.

Soon he'd discover those flaws that would reduce her from too appealing for his peace of mind, to ordinary. There'd be something he didn't like. Something that turned him off. That was usually the way with the women he met. It was just that with Amber he'd been too sideswiped by passion to notice her faults.

Once he discovered her feet of clay, those habits and character traits that he disliked, she'd bother him no more.

All he had to do was get to know her better, and at the same time keep his hands off her...

Amber planted her feet a little wider and angled her camera, getting a better shot of the golden morning sun across the vineyard, and in the foreground, the bright green grape leaf and a curled cluster of grapes.

She snapped another shot, and another, trying to get the effect she wanted.

The photographer she'd organised would do it better of course, but Amber was determined to capture the ideas she had in mind. That would make it easier to explain precisely what she was after for the new campaign.

Easier too, if she didn't have to return to the winery again to complete her work. Each hour she spent here, shunned by Aurelio, ate at her like acid. Any hope he'd regret his outrageous behaviour was futile.

He'd shown his true colours, demanding she leave, refusing to have anything to do with her, as if there was something *tainted* about her. Fury and hurt welled and she blinked hard.

Or was he afraid she'd cramp his style if another woman came along?

Talons clawed at her belly. For all she knew she'd been just one of scores of women he seduced and discarded.

She and her child deserved better than Aurelio. A man who clearly had no interest in long-term relationships. Who patently didn't care for her. Who, for all she knew, was so selfish he didn't have it in him to be a good father. Oh, he was sexy, charming and clever, a phenomenal winemaker, but they weren't the characteristics a child needed. A child thrived on stability and love.

As soon as she had what she needed she'd be on her way back to the city, where she'd try to figure out how to get over a broken heart. And how to be a single mother.

A ripple of apprehension shot through her, making her hands shake. This wasn't how she'd imagined having a child. She'd imagined a loving partner, a family.

But she'd cope. She'd have to.

Maybe she'd even return to Australia, to be close to family when the baby came. She adored life in Italy, having made it her home after a year's university student exchange and never leaving. But she'd need support.

Later on, when she didn't feel so lacerated by Aurelio's rejection, she'd tell him about the child. But not yet. Not when she was still absorbing the news herself.

She hadn't planned on telling him early anyway. Naïvely, she'd even thought he might unwillingly press her into a duty marriage for the sake of their child. She'd seen enough unhappy marriages to know she wanted true love or nothing. She suspected the pressure to marry for the sake of an unborn child might be stronger in Italy than Australia.

How ridiculous that fear had been!

Given Aurelio's attitude since she arrived, he'd probably accuse her of trying to trap him with her pregnancy! Amber huffed out an unamused laugh.

She'd wanted to see if it were possible to build a loving relationship, or failing that, a friendship that would help them parent together. Right now that seemed laughable. Aurelio made a point of never being around her.

But there was plenty of time, she assured herself. Surely, eventually, he'd come around, for their baby's sake. Their child deserved love from both parents.

For now it was best if she concentrated on caring for herself and the baby. She couldn't cope with the idea of sharing her news with a man who looked at her like she carried the plague.

Amber reached out, propping one hand on the end post of the row of vines. Suddenly she felt exhausted. Keeping up the pretence that all was well, when everything was such a mess, drained her. Maybe she should—

'Amber?'

For a second, her head bowed and dark hair swinging forward, hiding her surroundings, Amber wondered if the deep, concerned voice was a figment of her imagination. Some silly wishful thinking. For the voice sounded like Aurelio. Not Aurelio the man of thunder and ice who'd tried to eject her from this peaceful valley, but Aurelio the tender lover, the one who'd walked straight through all her feeble defences and stolen her heart.

She gasped as pain shafted through her chest. She couldn't take much more of his pointed aversion. Maybe she should leave today.

'Amber!' The voice was closer and definitely not just in her mind. She whipped her head up to see Aurelio before her, feet planted wide and hands shoved deep in his pockets. He looked… concerned.

Could it be? Yet even as she thought it his expression clouded to something unreadable. She sensed, even if she couldn't see, the chasm between them.

'Yes?' Her voice was brittle but that was the least of her worries. Amber felt heartsore and tired, almost ready to admit defeat. Their standoff drained even her formidable energy. Or maybe that was the pregnancy.

'Are you hurt? You look…' He shrugged, lifting

one hand from his pocket and spreading it wide.

Hurt? She ached from the effort of maintaining a façade of cool professionalism. The pain of rejection was like a knife wound clear through her middle. Then there was fear of the unknown, of everything she didn't know about being a mother. Sometimes that weighed so heavily it was all she could do to stifle panic.

Amber let her hand drop from the post and straightened. 'I was thinking.' It wasn't a lie, she assured herself.

'Thinking?' he said it slowly as if testing the word on his tongue.

'Yes, I do that sometimes.' The words had a waspish sting she didn't try to soften.

His eyebrows rose but instead of taking umbrage at her sarcasm, his mouth curled up at one corner, revealing a long dimple in his cheek that tugged at something deep inside. Amber stifled a groan. Even now, close to hating him, she couldn't blank out her attraction to him.

'What were you thinking about?' Did he move closer or was it just the effect of staring into those velvety dark eyes too long?

'Oh, the usual.'

How to fall out of love.

How to keep the career she'd been building and raise a child at the same time.

How to cure a broken heart.

Amber gestured with the camera towards the grapevines in their neat rows. 'I'm working on a few shots that will help me explain what I want to the photographer I've booked. But don't worry,' she tilted her chin higher, 'I won't be long. You'll have your privacy soon enough.'

Aurelio frowned, lifting a hand to rub the back of his neck. 'There's no need to rush.'

Amber hid her surprise. This was the man who changed direction so as to avoid her. He'd missed meals too, leaving poor Paolo at first chagrined then annoyed by his partner's behaviour. Now, if she didn't know better, she'd say Aurelio looked embarrassed.

She had to be imagining things.

'Oh, I wouldn't want to *intrude*. You've made it abundantly clear you don't want me anywhere near you.'

Deliberately Amber turned away and took her time setting up the next shot. She fiddled and adjusted her angle but it was useless. There was a tremor in her hands that hadn't been there before and she'd lost her train of thought. She tried to focus on her idea about capturing the vineyard at different times of the day, and about the early golden light on the vines, but couldn't concentrate.

Repressing a sigh of frustration she scooped up her bag and slung it over her shoulder then stepped away, further up the slope.

She'd only taken one step when she realised Aurelio moved too, shadowing her.

Amber pivoted around, eyes wide. 'What are you doing?'

'Following you. We need to talk.'

She felt her eyes boggle. 'I think you've said all you need to. I've got the message loud and clear that you want me gone as soon as possible.'

Again that dimple appeared in his cheek, though this time it wasn't caused by a smile but a grimace.

He rubbed his face and they were so close she heard the scrape of his hand across his unshaven chin. Amber remembered how she'd been fascinated by that soft abrasion and how Aurelio had insisted on shaving so as not to mark her skin with his bristles.

She turned away, focusing on the marching rows of vines, vibrant green with fresh growth.

A new start, that's what she needed. She'd cure herself, somehow, of her feelings for Aurelio and—

'I'm sorry, Amber.' His voice, deep and rough, smashed through her thoughts.

'Sorry?' She swung round, frowning.

'For what I said, how I behaved when you arrived.'

Amber stared up at him, but all she read in his troubled features was regret.

'I was harsh.'

'You were insulting and unreasonable.' She squared her shoulders, watching his eyes widen. But instead of anger at her plain speaking, she saw acceptance.

'I apologise. I behaved badly. I was wrong.' His body language, including his rigid stance, told her he wasn't used to apologising. Once she'd have said that was because he'd have little to apologise for. Now she wondered which was the real Aurelio – the witty, decent, charming man she'd fallen for, or the scowling, selfish ogre.

'Can we call a truce?'

Despite the instantaneous spring of hope, Amber didn't trust his motives. 'Why?

He smiled and to her horror Amber registered that all too familiar melting sensation deep down inside.

One smile. Is that all it takes?

Instantly she stiffened, and the smile bled from his face. He shook his head. 'I hurt you, I'm sorry, Amber. There's no excuse, I know. I saw you and thought you'd come here deliberately to…'

'Chase after you?' The words squeezed from her tight throat. So much for her fantasy that he'd welcome her with a passionate embrace and the news he'd missed her.

'Something like that.' He frowned. 'It was stupid and selfish of me. I have no…inclination for a long-term relationship and I reacted badly.'

'That's putting it mildly.' Vaguely Amber was surprised at her ability to converse when inside it felt like she'd broken into tiny pieces. Just as well he didn't know yet about the long-term relationship he'd embark on in seven or eight months' time when their baby arrived. She didn't have the stamina to tell him about that yet.

'So.' He paused, tilting his head as if to survey her better. 'Can we work together?'

He held out his hand. It was large, callused and tanned. But Amber remembered how gently it had moved across her flesh, how tenderly it had traced her body, how easily it had brought her pleasure.

A shiver ran up her spine and she locked her knees.

'We can work together.' Breathing deep, she put out her hand and let his engulf hers. Tingles rippled through her, echoes of old delight, tinged with the sadness of loss.

Stoically Amber told herself it was a first step towards friendship. For her baby's sake she'd just have to learn to accept that and not yearn for more.

Chapter Five

HE SHOULD NEVER HAVE TOUCHED her. Aurelio knew it was a mistake, even as he reached for her hand.

Why had he done it? There was no need to seal their understanding with a handshake. Especially when he'd read Amber's reluctance, swiftly hidden by that characteristically bold stare. Clearly she defied him to find any weakness in her beautiful, determined face.

He'd reached for her for the same reason she'd haunted him since her arrival at the vineyard. Or, if he was truthful, every night for the past six weeks.

Because he wanted to touch her.

He'd missed her.

The need to connect with her was a craving in the blood that even reason couldn't vanquish.

Her handshake was firm and short. Businesslike. Yet the touch of her soft skin on his evoked memories that blasted his composure to smithereens.

Yes.

This.

The hungry beast within him woke in an instant, demanding more.

Usually he kept his libido under tight control, burying himself in work and the ridiculously long hours it took to turn a neglected old vineyard into a lauded state-of-the-art winery. When the need for release grew too much, he allowed himself a short liaison. A night or two with a woman who, like him, didn't want more.

His mistake had been bedding Amber. For there'd been nothing simple about what they'd shared. No matter how often he told himself it was simple sex, part of him knew it wasn't true.

This woman had the power to undo him if he let her.

Abruptly he released her hand and stepped back, fixing what he hoped was a smile on his face. It was probably a grimace, but it was the best he could manage, torn by competing impulses to retreat as fast as he could, or haul her close and kiss her till she melted against him.

It was as he pulled away that he saw something new in her expression. Something other than pride, challenge or impatience. In that moment as her hand dropped back to her side he read...hurt.

It was a flare, a widening of the pupils, a tightening of that lush, gorgeous mouth. It lasted only a second before she looked away, lifting her hand to shade her eyes and turning towards the sunlight spilling over the ridge to the east.

But Aurelio had seen it and he couldn't unsee it.

He'd hurt her with his sudden withdrawal.

How much more had he hurt her earlier, when he'd ordered her away from the vineyard, demanding she leave the job she'd won on her merits?

Or when he'd turned his back on her in Rome? He'd left so abruptly, in the middle of a torrid affair that showed no signs of ending. There'd been passion and physical gratification but there'd also been laughter, tenderness and companionship, and it had been that which had sent him, literally, running for the hills.

How much had she hurt then?

He'd told himself Amber knew the score. He'd made it clear he only wanted a short fling.

But then he'd broken his own rules, hadn't he? He'd stayed. He'd talked and shared himself in ways he hadn't shared himself in a decade.

'Just tell me one thing, Aurelio, then I'll never probe again.' She didn't turn to look at him. Her gaze was still fixed on the rows of vines, vibrant in the early morning glow.

He squared his shoulders. 'Yes?'

'Why do you think you don't want a long-term relationship?'

So he'd been right. She *had* wanted more. Or if not wanted, at least wondered.

Guilt was a bitter stew in his belly. He should never have seduced her. Even if the seduction had been mutual and all the more thrilling for that. And he should never have allowed it to last more than a single night.

'I don't think it.' He paused, forcing his gaze from her profile, so pure and proud it made him ache inside. Instead he too surveyed the orderly rows of grapes that he'd made his work, his dream, his whole life. 'I *know* it.'

'I see.' Just two syllables but they held a sombre gravity that told him she really did understand now, at least enough to back off for good. Her next words confirmed it. 'You've already tried it.'

'And it didn't work out.' How bland the words sounded, like he'd tried a new grape variety and hadn't liked the taste. No words could describe the gut-cleaving pain of loving and losing. Of having a soul-mate and then, in one tragic moment, having the person who mattered most in your life torn away.

Aurelio had been lost, grieving and rudderless, for a long time. He hadn't cared about anything, until his old friend Paolo had bullied him into work again. The unrelenting rhythm of hard labour had forced him to begin sleeping. Eventually the work of growing and making had driven him into a routine and from routine, into awareness and appreciation. Into life.

His family worried that he buried himself in his work. Just recently his brother Matteo, inviting him to one of his parties, had accused him of turning into a hermit. Aurelio hadn't bothered to explain that the winery was his life now, for they all knew it. Even so, he'd found himself hinting to his little sister, Lia, that he might bring a friend to their brother Gennaro's engagement party. He'd said it to get her off his back, since she'd been concerned about his withdrawal from the world. But her disappointment when he'd arrived alone had made him more determined to stand his ground.

'Well, now we've sorted that out.' Amber's voice was brisk as she swung round. Instead of avoiding his gaze, she looked straight into his eyes, her own an unreadable grey that made him think of misty mornings in the mountains.

Whatever she'd once hoped, she was ready to bury the past and move on.

In that instant, a surge of admiration swamped Aurelio. He'd never met a woman like Amber, so strong and feisty, despite the warm, caring nature he'd been drawn to from the first. Even Valentina, who'd been his other half, hadn't had Amber's courage. But then she'd had him to protect her. Until that last day.

Pain scoured Aurelio's gut, fast and savage as a mountain torrent.

'I'd better move on.' Amber's words came to him through the rush of his blood. 'I've got a lot to do and so have you, I'm sure.' Her smile was perfunctory, almost scornful, and Aurelio knew he should be glad she'd accepted the way things were.

She turned, pulling her jacket closer, and began walking away.

There was something stoic about her, so determined and controlled. Yet lonely too. Aurelio had seen it in that earlier flash of hurt, and though he tried to tell himself he imagined it, it was there in the too-upright way she held herself now.

The sight tugged at something inside him. The need to lessen the bitter pill of his rejection. Guilt at his brutal treatment of her.

He settled for telling himself she was here to work and that work would go better if he followed through with his earlier decision.

'Wait.' She paused on his word but didn't look back. 'If you've got time I'd like to show you the vineyard.'

Amber was still so long he wondered if she'd heard. When she turned, lithe in slim fitting jeans and boots, her expression was guarded. 'Paolo has already taken me on a tour.'

'I know.' He walked towards her, ignoring the delicate beauty of her features and instead focusing on those wary eyes. 'But I'd like to show you what

I see here. *My* vision for the place.'

It was true. He wanted to share that with Amber. Aurelio told himself it was so she could understand his utter devotion to the place, to the exclusion of personal relationships.

'It might help with the PR campaign.'

That persuaded her. Whatever she'd once hoped for, business took precedence for her now. Aurelio could relate to that.

The tightness around the back of his neck and shoulders eased as he turned up into the grapevines. Amber tramped beside him as slowly he began to talk about what he loved, the vines and the challenge of nurturing them and turning them into premium wines.

The sun rose higher and the aroma of honeysuckle and woman blended with the scents of earth and green, growing things. He found himself relaxing as they talked, not about personal matters, or even the new PR campaign, but the soil, the new growth, the potential for the future.

Amber was a good listener. Her questions revealed not only a quick mind but an appreciation for this world of his. It was one of the reasons he'd initially wanted her for the job. Now, her responses to him and her understanding of the challenges and opportunities here confirmed he'd been right to want her.

For the job.

As she surveyed the vineyard now spread below them, Aurelio looked down at her exquisite features.

His heart thundered against his ribs. The want hadn't gone away.

If anything, it grew as his admiration grew.

All he could do was hope that familiarity really would breed contempt. Otherwise he was in big trouble.

Chapter Six

'WHEN WERE YOU GOING TO tell me about the gala premiere?'

Amber had tracked him down in the oldest part of the winery. Here, instead of new stainless steel vats, he was surrounded by old barrels. The dark, echoing chamber was rich with the scent of wine and oak. And now sweet honeysuckle and warm sunshine.

He couldn't explain the sunshine scent. As far as he knew mankind hadn't found a way to bottle such a fragrance, but he inhaled it every time Amber came close.

Aurelio drew in a furtive breath, telling himself he was impatient at the interruption. Not pleased at the sight of Amber in her skinny jeans and white shirt. With her hair up and her hips swaying, she strode the length of the barrel hall like a catwalk model with more than the usual share of attitude.

His gaze dropped to the curve of those lithe hips, till he caught himself and dragged it back up, past a waist so narrow he could span it in his hands. Over firm, plump breasts that made him—

'Aurelio? Did you hear me?' Impatience sharpened her voice. But not nearly as much as it would if she realised he'd been ogling her. Just as well he stood in the shadows.

She shook her head. 'You really are in another world when you get involved in work.' This time when she spoke, something like affection softened her words and Aurelio felt a throb of inexplicable emotion rise.

No, not affection. Understanding. This week they'd achieved the truce he'd offered. More than a truce, really, for they'd worked well together, fine tuning the comprehensive strategy she'd developed. They'd also achieved again a level of easy companionship. That surprised him since awareness bubbled beneath every interaction he had with Amber.

'Were you even going to *tell* me about the premiere?' She jammed her hands on her hips in an attitude he found ridiculously attractive. So much for familiarity breeding contempt! He must have been out of his mind.

'Sorry? What premiere?'

She drew a deep breath as if fighting for patience. This time Aurelio kept his gaze on her face, but that didn't stop him being aware of the rise of those luscious breasts. Heat eddied down in his groin, a reminder that with Amber on the premises, he'd been battling arousal for days.

'The first showing of your brother Matteo's new film. His directorial debut. The one all of Italy and half the world is talking about, especially with that story about him being reunited on set with his wife after a long separation. It's tipped to be the biggest box office success in a decade.'

'Oh, that premiere.'

Amber tilted her head, trying to read him better. 'You don't care about your brother's film?'

'Of course I care.' Aurelio folded his arms over his chest. 'It was a massive gamble for him. We all hope it will be the beginning of a successful career in directing as well as acting.' And there'd been jubilation in the family that Matteo, who'd spent twelve months scowling, was now reunited with Angela. The pair were so patently in love it was painful to watch.

Aurelio felt a stab of shame. He didn't begrudge Matteo and Angela their love. He just wished the sight of them so wrapped up in each other didn't remind him of something precious he could never have again.

The past was the past. He'd fought hard and long to free himself from it and make a fist of living day to day.

'So you're going to the premiere?'

A frown settled on his features. The last thing he wanted was to spend more time in Rome. He had so much to keep him busy here. But his was a close family, even if they didn't live in each other's pockets, and he was proud of all his siblings. He'd just have to find time to spare a night in the city.

'I'll be there.'

'Good. Let me work on the publicity angle and you can focus on networking.'

'Publicity?' Aurelio scraped a hand over his unshaven jaw, dragging himself back from memories of last time he stayed in Rome, sharing Amber's bed.

'Of course.' She moved closer, all vibrant energy. 'Paolo tells me the after party will be in a stunning hotel owned by your brother, Luca, and that your wine will be featured.' She paused, apparently waiting for him to say something. 'So it's a golden opportunity to stir a little publicity for the winery.'

'This will be Matteo's night.'

'Absolutely. And what could be better than having your wines showcased at such a glamorous event to celebrate the work of one of Italy's sexiest men?'

Aurelio stared at her eager face. Did Amber have a soft spot for his movie-star brother? The thought shouldn't bother him. He was used to women swooning over Matteo. He used to rib his brother about it mercilessly till Matteo separated from Angela and jokes about being a sex magnet didn't seem appropriate.

Yet Aurelio felt a tightening within, as if his tendons shrank back against hard bone. He felt something might just snap at the excitement in her bright eyes.

'You're interested in Matteo?' The words ground from between clenched teeth.

Amber's stare grew fixed. 'As a means to give your business a higher profile, definitely.' Her jaw lifted. 'You have a problem with that?'

'No.' So long as that's all it was.

He'd denied himself any right to an interest in Amber's love life. Yet that didn't stop the swirl of unease in his belly as he imagined Amber with someone else. Not Matteo, obviously, but some nameless, faceless guy who'd revel in her beauty and passion. Who'd enjoy that stunning body and…

Aurelio yanked his thoughts back to the conversation before his imagination had him beating that unknown man to a pulp. This simple sexual frustration, he told himself. Sex with Amber had been phenomenal and here, alone with her, it was natural his body responded to the allure of hers. This was merely a matter of testosterone, nothing more.

'What was that about networking?' Anything to keep his mind off the twin ideas of Amber and sex.

'Obviously you'll be networking at the party to promote the business, right?'

Aurelio said nothing. He was attending as Matteo's brother, that's all. He knew the value of networking of course. He'd developed excellent links in the wine industry as well as in distribution and the restaurant trade. But working the room at some glittering social event was his idea of hell.

Attending the recent industry awards night had been his limit, but since the winery had won a slew of awards he hadn't been able to avoid it.

Inevitably his mind zoomed straight back to sex because that was the night he and Amber had finally hooked up. Before that, when he'd seen her in the crowd at a wine expo, his need to go to her had been so strong he'd actually left the event rather than succumb to what felt more like compulsion than desire.

Amber sighed, her shoulders and breasts rising. 'I see. Even that's too much to expect.' Her gaze shifted from his as she apparently took an interest in their surroundings for the first time. 'At least tell me you've got some beautiful date to take with you.' Her husky voice quickened. 'Someone who'll look good on the red carpet for the photos.'

'No.'

Abruptly her silvery eyes meshed with his and he felt a sting of heat right through his body.

'I don't do dates.' When she just stared he added. 'It's not necessary that I take someone.'

He had no interest in a date with another woman. Look at the trouble this one still caused him.

Never before had it been difficult to sever ties with a temporary lover. Yet even before Amber had turned up at his vineyard she'd caused havoc, distracting him from work and undermining his concentration, not to mention destroying his sleep. She'd even made him wonder what might have happened if he'd been a different man, a man able to invest in a relationship.

Hell!

His backbone froze, vertebra by crackling vertebra, at the direction of his thoughts.

Dismay raced through him and he drew himself up straight, scowling at Amber's ability to mess with his head.

He'd learned to his cost that permanent relationships could be anything but permanent. He couldn't again go through pain like he'd suffered ten years ago.

Silently Amber studied him, her expression impenetrable. Then she lifted a hand to her hair in its usual immaculate style, and grabbed at it like she wanted to yank it out.

'You don't think it's necessary!' She shut her eyes and Aurelio saw the pulse pound at the base of her neck. 'And you can't be bothered promoting your own business.'

'I didn't say that. I spend a lot of time promoting it. Just not schmoozing people in dinner suits. Anyway, isn't that what we're paying you for – to promote us?'

Amber spun on her heel and paced away, then spun round and stalked straight back. The impatient energy radiating from her zapped at his blood, making his pulse quicken. It was a wonder he didn't see sparks as she moved.

'Aurelio.' She paused as if searching for words then slicked her lower lip with her tongue. Instantly Aurelio's attention was fixed on her mouth and the memory of her sweet taste. 'This is the sort of opportunity businesses *dream* of. A high class hotel, one of Rome's most exclusive. A film by Italy's hottest leading man.' Sternly Aurelio ignored the sudden blaze of jealousy at her words. 'An A-list party that everyone will be talking about. The press will be out in force. You *need* to make a splash.'

'I'll be wearing a dinner jacket,' he offered, watching Amber roll her eyes. That was a major concession. He hated formal clothes and bowties were the work of the devil in his opinion.

She opened her mouth then snapped it shut, clearly speechless.

Perhaps he was being unreasonable. His siblings all accused him of burying himself here and ignoring the outside world unless it suited him.

The vineyard had become not just his home but his sanctuary, the thing that had kept him going in the empty days after his world shattered. But he *was* going to the premiere and he did want to do what was best for the business. He didn't want to scupper their PR campaign before it got off the ground. He just didn't want to do the marketing himself. Give him his vines and his vats any day. Amber could handle the rest.

'How about this?' He paused, reassuring himself

it was a sensible solution. 'You're the expert on all this so you take my spare ticket. You come to the premiere and the after party with me. Plus you can organise whatever publicity or photos you want. But you can do all the schmoozing. Agreed?'

One evening in Rome with Amber at his side. Surely he could manage that. Besides, she'd be too busy flitting here and there chasing down VIPs and spreading word about the marvellous wines to tempt him with that delectable body.

It wasn't like he invited her on a date.

Yet Aurelio felt nervous about her response.

For long moments those stormy eyes stared up at him, as if trying to fathom his motives. Then, abruptly she nodded. 'Agreed.'

Chapter Seven

IT HAD BEEN A MAD decision. Amber should have known better than to accept Aurelio's suggestion she accompany him to the premiere.

But what choice did he give her? If she hadn't stepped in he'd waste this perfect opportunity to promote his wines. To promote *himself*. For Aurelio De Laurentis *was* the brand. Young and sexy with those stunning dark looks and brooding air, he looked like any woman's dream in a tuxedo.

His wines were all about quality, refinement and the allure of knowing you were drinking the very best.

To Amber's mind, nothing spelled out the best quite the way Aurelio did with his broad shoulders and tall frame filling out those formal clothes to perfection.

Unlike most handsome men, he didn't even seem to realise the effect he had on a woman, just by looking at her. He certainly didn't deliberately tease or tempt, at least not outside the bedroom.

Amber sucked in a tremulous breath and surreptitiously checked the bodice of her strapless gown. The young designer who'd eagerly lent it to her for the red carpet event publicity had assured her it wouldn't slide down. Yet Amber was acutely aware of how the fitted bodice revealed more of her décolletage than usual. And the way her breasts, more sensitive with pregnancy, felt the scrape of stiffened fabric with every breath.

It had to be that, *not* a reaction to Aurelio standing so close beside her.

She was aware of lingering stares even in the crowded, exclusive party. Women loved the elegance of the gown and her charismatic escort. But the men obviously appreciated how the figure-hugging dress clung to her curves, only flaring out from her thighs.

She'd chosen the ultra-sexy dress in shimmering silver because she wanted to look glamorous for the cameras. And because she was accompanying Aurelio, who, in a tuxedo, was breathtakingly mesmerising. She might be just his PR advisor, but Amber was determined to hold her own amongst the swarm of sophisticated women at tonight's party. The ones watching Aurelio so avidly. Amber had jaw ache from biting back warnings that they keep away from him.

Not the way to make friends and influence people! She was supposed to encourage them, not scare them away. Yet tonight she found it almost impossible to focus on work.

Part of the trouble was the dress. It didn't just make others look, including women wanting the designer's name. It clung in a way that made Amber more than usually aware of her body and its reaction to Aurelio. The close clasp of stiffened fabric in the bodice recalled the possessive way Aurelio used to fondle her breasts. The nipped in waist, his avid delight at discovering he could span her waist with his large hands. The whisper of the long skirt as she walked, the rustle of bed sheets and the soft scratching sound of his early morning whiskers against her fingertips.

Amber shuddered as erotic memories awoke. Of sharing Aurelio's bed. Of him using his tongue to tease her in the most wicked ways.

She couldn't afford to think of that.

Or of Aurelio's appeal as anything other than a marketing tool to exploit. She hadn't spelled that out to him because if he suspected *he* was the secret weapon in tonight's marketing plan, he'd hightail it back to his precious grape vines and bury himself in one of the wine cellars. It had been like prising a bear out of its cave to get him to the city.

Besides, dwelling on his attractiveness was destructive. He wasn't for her, could never be for her again. The best she could do was continue to work at establishing trust and respect between them so that when she told him about the pregnancy they had something to build on.

And it *had* been working. Since his apology they'd been together every day. Amber sensed he even enjoyed her company, as she did his. Though of course he had the advantage of not being distracted by a yearning for more.

'Are you okay?' Aurelio's deep voice was a buzz of warmth through her veins, making her snap her head round towards him.

How did he know she was unsettled when they weren't touching? He couldn't feel her tremble. He wasn't even looking at her.

All evening he'd barely glanced her way, except for that single, scorching survey when they'd met. He'd scrutinised her from head to toe then back up again in a deliberate stare that made heat lick at her belly, her breasts and in all the secret places he'd once caressed.

'I'm great. It's such a fabulous party.' She lifted a crystal glass of sparkling water to her lips and swallowed deeply.

'But you're not enjoying yourself.' He turned, his ebony gaze capturing hers with an intensity that made everything in her still. 'You're not even drinking wine. *Not* a good advertisement for the brand.'

Amber pinned on a smile. 'That's because I'm here to work. Remember? I need to keep my wits about me. You're the one here solely to enjoy your brother's triumph.' She nodded to the mob of people on the far side of the opulent room, clamouring for the attention of Matteo De Laurentis and his talented screenwriter wife, Angela.

'You can go and chat with your family and leave me to my own devices.'

Maybe if he did that for a while she'd regain her equilibrium enough to focus on pursuing valuable contacts.

Besides, much as she'd liked the family members she'd met, she'd been conscious of their speculation about her. She'd expected Aurelio to explain they were just work colleagues, a point she was at pains to tell herself, when he stood at her side looking, in her opinion, far more attractive than his celebrated movie-icon brother.

But Aurelio had ignored his siblings' curious glances and subtle questions as if impervious to them. Even when Lia, his gorgeous sister, had kissed Amber on both cheeks and said fervently how happy she was that Aurelio had finally shown up with a special *friend* in tow.

Amber turned away, knowing she really should concentrate on the job she was here to do. But before she could move Aurelio's fingers closed around her wrist, a warm, unbreakable manacle, tethering her to him.

Her eyes snapped up and there it was again, that dark velvet gaze that felt like a caress. A tremor ran the length of her body and she bit her bottom lip. She shouldn't be feeling this. She had to get past this desire.

Nothing good could come of it. He wasn't in the market for anything more than physical pleasure. And though that pleasure was starkly, stunningly addictive, further intimacy would only make it harder to accept he didn't want her the way she wanted him.

'I need to work, Aurelio.' Her voice was husky, not like her own at all.

'I'll help you.'

Amber felt her forehead pucker in astonishment. 'What's caused the sudden change of heart? You made it clear you were leaving that to me.'

Something she couldn't interpret flickered in his eyes, then he shrugged, making her even more aware of those wide shoulders. Had those sexy grooves in his cheeks deepened too? Usually they were only evident if he smiled or, she recalled, during moments of intense passion.

'It's my wine. I need to do my bit to promote it.'

'Even though you hate bowties and socialites?' she whispered.

Those creases deepened in his lean cheeks as he

gave her a smile that did something terrible to her pulse. 'Even then.'

Aurelio was as good as his word, never leaving her side despite the numerous invitations from women who wanted a private chat with him.

Together they spent the next hour circulating and, in the process, subtly getting word out about the latest, magnificent vintage. To Amber's delight Aurelio was charming, witty and engaging, putting himself out, not just to join in the conversation, but draw others out too.

She shouldn't be surprised. She'd thought him all those things and more the night they'd shared a table at the wine awards dinner. It's just that the last ten days, since she'd turned up at the winery, he'd given a good impression of a recluse who only grudgingly gave time to the outside world.

Had Aurelio always been like that? Having met his siblings Amber thought it unlikely. Members of the De Laurentis family were clever and driven but they were all sociable.

Yet if this was an intrinsic part of Aurelio, why did it surface so rarely? What had happened to make him shun the world and people as much as he did?

'Ah, little brother, how are you?'

Luca De Laurentis, host of tonight's party in his flagship luxury hotel, approached them. It was the first time Amber had met the eldest of the De Laurentis siblings and she was struck by the family resemblance. Seriously, they all had the tall, dark and handsome thing down pat. Except to her mind Aurelio outshone them all.

She had to stop that line of thinking.

She had to separate herself mentally and emotionally from him.

Which was hard to do when he was glued to her side.

'...introduce Amber Moncrieff.' Amber blinked as Aurelio mentioned her name, realising to her horror, she'd zoned out for precious seconds. Truly, the sooner she made a clean break from Aurelio the better. He was messing with her head as well as her heart now.

Luca smiled and shook her hand. 'I'm very pleased to meet you. I've heard a lot about you.'

Before Amber could question that, he turned to the woman just crossing the room to join them. Voluptuously beautiful with raven hair and blue eyes, she wore a dress of blue-grey that might have been demure but for the thigh high slit up one side and the way it scintillated under the lights, showing off her figure. Amber sucked in a furtive breath, so pleased she'd pulled out all the stops with her outfit tonight. It would be easy to feel dowdy in such company.

The woman stopped and grinned directly at her. 'You must be Amber. I'm so pleased to meet you at last.' She reached out and shook Amber's hand.

'Allegra?' Amber recognised that voice from several phone calls prior to the party, organising the wine and checking details to do with the press. Allegra Davis was Luca's super-organised and incredibly helpful personal assistant. It had been a real pleasure working with her.

Allegra nodded. 'That's right, I've been looking forward to meeting you in person but we haven't had two minutes to ourselves this evening, have we, Luca?'

To Amber's silent astonishment Luca lifted his hand to Allegra's face, drawing his knuckle down her cheek in a gesture of infinite tenderness. 'Something we need to remedy soon,' he purred and Amber watched in amazement as the ultra-efficient Allegra swayed towards him, a slightly dazed look in her eyes.

Obviously this pair were far more than boss and PA.

Aurelio cleared his throat. When he spoke his tone was pointed. 'Don't let us interrupt you two. The hotel rooms upstairs are the last word in luxury. Perhaps you should get one.'

Luca took his time turning around to his brother. When he did there was a devilish glint in those dark eyes so like Aurelio's. 'You don't fob me off so easily, brother. We have some catching up to do.'

Did she imagine that Aurelio stiffened beside her?

'Excellent,' said Allegra. 'That will give us a chance to get to know each other better. If that's okay with you, Amber?'

'Of course.' Then, before she knew it, the two men had stepped away, already in conversation.

Clearly the closeness she'd felt with Aurelio tonight had been illusory. He left her without a backward glance.

Which is a timely reminder that tonight is all about business. Remember? No matter how tempting it was to believe he'd stayed at her side because he enjoyed being with her. Or that the rapport she'd built with him, where they seemed so often on exactly the same wavelength, meant anything other than that they were committed to working together.

'Don't worry,' Allegra said, reading the hurt Amber tried to hide. 'I don't think Luca will keep him too long. We're all so glad to see him here with you! The family's abuzz with excitement.' Her meaningful look made Amber's heart shrink.

'I'm afraid you've misinterpreted...' She gestured inarticulately, then gathered herself. 'Aurelio and I aren't an item.' Amber stood straighter as she said it, coiling her hands together before her. 'We're just business associates. I'm not here as a real date.'

Allegra considered her for a long moment. 'Funny. That's not the way it looked. And the back-off vibe Aurelio gave when that slimy media mogul tried to chat you up seemed pretty personal.'

Amber's mouth twisted in a parody of a smile and her hand rose to her hair, nervously checking it was still in its elegant updo. Her stupid heart had somersaulted with pleasure at that apparently possessive gesture by Aurelio. Until he'd whispered in her ear that the guy had harassed Aurelio's sister Lia and he wouldn't trust him close to any woman, not even his *nonna*. Protective he might be but it wasn't anything personal.

'Despite appearances, our...relationship is strictly *im*personal.'

Those blue eyes surveyed her so long Amber wondered what they saw. 'And that's why you're upset?'

'I'm not—' Abruptly Amber's throat closed and she swallowed hard. It had been simultaneously wonderful and terrible, standing beside the man she loved tonight, acting the part of his date, knowing that he was only with her under sufferance. For the sake of his business.

But the tiniest hint of a sympathetic look was all it took for her façade to crack.

'Oh, Amber, I'm so sorry.' The other woman stepped close, putting her hand on Amber's elbow and turning them both away from the crowded room so no-one could see their faces. 'It was rude and thoughtless of me to ask. It's just that Aurelio is special and his family has been concerned for him for so long. Ever since—' She broke off, clamping her lip with her teeth.

'Ever since…?' Did Allegra know the reason Aurelio brooded alone in his vineyard, turning his back on any chance of a relationship? Amber's pulse quickened.

'I'm sorry. I shouldn't have spoken. If Aurelio hasn't told you about his past I don't feel it right to share something so personal.' Allegra grimaced. 'Me and my big mouth. I keep putting my foot in it, don't I? I'm not usually so gauche, but you looked miserable and I know how awful it is working with the man you love when you think he doesn't care for you.'

Amber gasped, quivers of shock running through her. She opened her mouth to deny it but her companion looked so earnest and so sympathetic, somehow she found herself saying, 'Am I really so transparent?' Pain jabbed straight to her heart. 'Do you think Aurelio realised…?'

'No, no!' Allegra shook her head. 'He's been too busy tonight trying *not* to look at you.' At Amber's hiss of disbelief she nodded. 'Truly, he worked so hard, but whenever you turned to someone else he stared at you like he wanted to eat you all up.'

Heat crept up Amber's body, from her womb to her ears. She felt her face flame and her belly tighten.

As if reading the longing she refused to give voice to, Allegra went on. 'I'm not mistaken. Believe me, I'm not the only one to notice.'

For a second jubilation fizzed in Amber's veins. Maybe, despite his determination to fight it, he *did* feel something for her after all.

Then reality, like a wave of icy water, sluiced over her.

There was, of course, a rational explanation. And it had nothing to do with love or affection.

'That doesn't mean anything,' she said, miserably. For now her mask of insouciance had been breached, Amber found it impossible to dissemble. Or maybe she just longed for a sympathetic ear. Even from a stranger.

She sucked in a breath and forced a smile that felt as brittle as her emotions. 'Aurelio does lust very, very well. What he won't do... *can't* do is relationships. He might *want* me.' Despite the pain engulfing her Amber shivered with arousal at the idea. 'But he'll never... care for me.'

'Ah, you poor love.' Allegra put her arm around her, her body warmth in contrast to the chill eating Amber from the inside. 'Let's get you away from here. You've had enough for one night.'

She urged Amber towards a door and Amber was only too happy to leave. She'd put in hours tonight at Aurelio's side, on the red carpet then at the premiere film screening and now at the party. But she couldn't do it any longer.

As the two women stepped from the crowded

reception room into the blessed quiet of a wide corridor, Allegra murmured, 'Things always seem darkest before the dawn. Just you mark my words.'

But Amber said nothing. Finally she confronted the truth. It was time to walk away from Aurelio. It was too self-destructive to torture herself, working closely with him when they had no future together.

Chapter Eight

'WHERE'S AMBER?' AURELIO LOOKED FOR that sleek figure in silver as Allegra Davis walked back to join him and Luca.

The crowd was as thick as ever, but amongst the black suits and vibrantly coloured dresses he could see no silver. Aurelio turned, scanning the far side of the room with increasing impatience, ignoring his brother's curious stare.

Aurelio didn't care. He should never have let Luca pry him from Amber's side. She might be clever and sassy but he didn't like to think of her as prey to some of the wolves here tonight. He hadn't missed the lascivious looks she'd received, which partly explained his decision to stay with her, rather than leave the networking to her as he'd intended.

Somehow, when he'd read the carnal interest focused on her, his aversion to socialising didn't seem to matter anymore. He wouldn't trust some of those men within five metres of her. If one of them had—

'She left.' The word cleaved through his composure, making him swing back to his companions.

'Left?' He scowled. Bad enough to have to suffer his eldest brother's oh-so-subtle questions about Amber, thinly disguised as a business discussion about his PR campaign and how it might integrate with Luca's expanding hotel interests. But now, to discover Amber had left, without even telling him?

'Alone?' The single word sliced from his tongue and he saw Allegra's eyebrows lift as if he'd revealed something surprising, instead of asking a perfectly simple, reasonable question.

'Alone.'

Without saying anything? That wasn't like Amber.

Aurelio's gut churned. Something bad had happened. He *knew* it.

'What happened? Is she okay?' He tried without success to read Allegra's expression.

The woman was a miracle of organisation, according to Luca and knew how to play her cards close to her chest during business negotiations. But why the poker face now in answer to a straightforward question?

'Nothing happened,' she said coolly. 'Amber has been working hard and it's almost the end of a very long night. She was tired. I gather it's been a busy couple of weeks for her.'

Yet there was something disturbing in that unreadable slate blue gaze. Beside him Luca stirred, picking up the jarring vibe too.

It was true there'd been a lot of work to do organising the new campaign and getting ready for tonight, but Amber had been more than up to it. He hadn't been driving her into the ground. Far from it, they'd worked together with an ease and a common purpose that had initially surprised him.

Aurelio stared at the bland, beautiful face of the woman before him, reading the tightness at the corners of her mouth that hadn't been there before. The high angle of her chin reminded him of Amber in confrontational mood.

Was Luca's partner angry with him? Momentarily curiosity stirred. But that didn't matter. All he cared about was Amber.

'Did she say anything before she left?' He stepped closer and saw Allegra's expression alter. Was that... sympathy in her eyes?

Damn it, now he really was worried. Something must have happened. Amber was a professional to the core. She'd never just walk out of an event like this. Unless some guy had persuaded her to go with him...

Nausea swirled in Aurelio's belly at the idea.

'Just that she was very tired. She was going to her room.'

Aurelio stared. That didn't sound like Amber. The woman could face anything for the sake of her work. Look at how she'd bearded him at the winery, even threatening him with legal action if he reneged on the contract offered to her.

He was torn between worry and relief that at least she hadn't gone far.

Luca had provided rooms for them both upstairs. At first Amber had demurred, saying it would be better to return to her own apartment, pretending it wasn't convenient to stay in one of Rome's most luxurious hotels. She'd only changed her mind when Aurelio reminded her they had an early meeting scheduled in the hotel tomorrow with an advertising executive who'd flown in to attend tonight's function.

'Right, in that case I'll go and check on her.'

A speculative look passed between Luca and

Allegra but Aurelio didn't give a damn. His family, and their lovers for that matter, could speculate about him all they wanted. They'd been doing it for years after all.

He wouldn't feel happy till he'd seen Amber for himself and checked she was okay.

'She's ordered room service,' Allegra said, stopping Aurelio in the act of turning away.

Room service? After an evening of waiters offering wine and delicacies every time they turned around? Unlikely that she was hungry.

Aurelio stilled, his heart ramming up against his ribs as an explanation surfaced. Even as he told himself it wasn't Amber's style, he couldn't stop his brain racing ahead, torturing him with possibilities. Perhaps the room service order wasn't about hunger but setting a mood. Champagne perhaps, to share with some man. Or maybe Aurelio's own premium prosecco. Bile burned the back of his tongue at the idea of her entertaining a lover in her room.

Ridiculous, he knew. After their flaming hot affair he'd spurned her. He had no claim now on her affections or her body. Besides, despite the way they'd come together so quickly, their need so explosive, Aurelio sensed she wasn't the sort of woman who made a habit of picking up strangers. Their torrid affair had surprised Amber, he knew, even as she'd revelled in it.

Yet he couldn't banish the thought of her with another man. It drew a veil of hot mist across Aurelio's eyes. His hands clenched at his sides, his jaw grinding tight.

'A pot of herbal tea, I believe.'

Gradually Allegra's words penetrated. Tea. Not a sensual midnight celebration but the restorative Amber favoured when she worked long hours.

So it was tiredness after all, not some midnight tryst. Logic had told him Amber wouldn't turn her back on him for an assignation. He'd just been… worried. He needed to check on her. Amber's actions didn't sit right with what he knew of her.

Murmuring goodnight to Luca and Allegra, he crossed the still-packed room, avoiding the people eager to catch his attention. He wouldn't be able to settle till he knew Amber was okay.

Amber heard the knock on the door and wrapped the voluminous bathrobe more tightly around her. She'd already undressed, ready for the bath she'd run, only to remember belatedly her room service order.

Actually, Allegra's order, not hers. The other woman had steered her back to her room, given her a sympathetic hug and decided she needed something soothing. She'd been the one to order room service with a no-nonsense solicitude Amber found surprisingly reassuring. It made a nice change from being independent, from hiding her hurt beneath a can-do outlook and a façade of imperviousness.

It had been nice, just this once, to let someone else take charge.

Life recently had been full of shocks and upheavals. Her affair with Aurelio, so out of character yet seemingly so *right* at the time. Discovering herself in love and then, hard on the heels of that recognition, learning how heartbreak felt. Finding herself pregnant and prey to so many fears for the future. Being brutally rejected by the one man in the world who had the power to hurt her. Then trying to find a way to establish some middle ground on which to base a friendship with him.

She didn't want friendship. She wanted Aurelio!

Amber pursed her lips against a wail of hurt, regret and longing. Anger too, that he'd cut off any chance of a future for them.

She told herself not to be a fool. He might accept her now as a work colleague, but that was all. There could be no going back.

The knock sounded again and Amber crossed the suite, feeling the soft antique carpet beneath her bare feet, then the coolness of marble in the small foyer.

She unlocked the door, opened it, then froze.

'Aurelio!' Her heart jammed high in her throat. She felt her breath escape then heard a wheeze as her cramped lungs tried frantically to drag in air.

Despite his debonair tuxedo and the tea tray he carried, he looked hard-edged and determined, not at all like the suave, mainly superficial set who'd attended tonight's party. His square jaw, already darkening with the shadow of a beard, was set and those jet black eyebrows were lowered in a brooding frown. Long grooves carved his cheeks, but not from smiling this time. He looked…

Dangerous was the word her tired brain conjured.

But that was crazy. Aurelio wasn't dangerous to her. He'd already wreaked too much damage on her foolish, poorly guarded heart. He couldn't hurt her any more than he already had.

If she kept telling herself that she might even come to believe it!

His eyes met hers and that frantic sizzle started in her blood. Instantly Amber clasped the bathrobe tight at her collarbone, standing as tall as she could in bare feet.

His attention fixed on the tell-tale movement.

'Aren't you going to invite me in?'

'I'm tired, Aurelio.' Was that her voice — that high, breathy thing?

'I won't stay long. And,' he lifted the tray in his hands, 'I've brought room service.'

Frowning, Amber reluctantly stepped back, allowing him into the room. 'How come you're delivering it?'

He shrugged and her gaze slid inevitably to that vast expanse of powerful muscle and bone beneath his jacket. Amber gnawed her lip and looked away as he crossed the room to put his burden down on a table. 'I met the waiter and suggested I bring it to you.'

'I'm pretty sure hotels frown on guests doing that.' What about her privacy?

Aurelio turned, his gaze catching hers and holding it, making her rapid pulse grow haphazard. 'One of the perks of being the owner's brother.'

She opened her mouth to argue, then snapped it shut. She was tired, more weary than she'd let herself admit. Once she'd stopped playing the part of perfect professional with Allegra, she hadn't been able to pretend anymore. She needed time to erect that façade again before tomorrow's meeting with the ad guru.

Forget tomorrow's meeting. She needed to pull

herself together again before facing Aurelio. Yet here he was.

She felt rubbed too thin, as if the time pretending to feel nothing for him had scraped layer after layer away, leaving her raw and bleeding. Her emotions were too close to the surface. Too…volatile.

Amber folded her arms across her chest. 'Thank you for the tea.' She took a step towards the door. 'I'll see you in the morning.'

Aurelio didn't budge. Instead he crossed his own arms, parodying her gesture. But on him it didn't look like a defensive movement. It looked aggressive.

'You didn't say you were leaving the party.' His jaw jutted, accentuating that frown.

Amber returned his stare, refusing to feel guilty. 'Allegra said she'd pass on the message.'

Slowly he shook his head. 'Not good enough, Amber.'

'Sorry?' Anger stirred. 'I've worked myself to the bone making sure tonight was a success for your business and fine tuning the details of a complete new strategy for the winery.' Her hands found her hips in a rush of indignation. What did he want? *Blood*? 'I've been working since the early hours this morning and it's after midnight now. I decided to clock off.'

'You think I'm accusing you of clock watching?' He unfolded his arms and paced towards her, anger simmering in his stare. She felt his restless energy like a force field. Like a brewing thunderstorm on a summer evening.

'Aren't you?' Now she had to tilt her head to meet his eyes. He was far taller than her and in her shoeless state he towered over her. But she was in no mood to be bossed about. Once she'd revelled in his masculinity and the physical differences between them. Now they annoyed her.

'No.' His frown became a scowl. 'I was worried about you.'

And just like that, as if he'd pierced a balloon with a pin, Amber's storm of indignation deflated in on itself. Leaving her with that scoured-too-close-to-the-bone feeling, knowing her defences had fractured and fallen.

His concern, like Allegra's sympathy earlier, undid her.

To Amber's horror, as anger fled, other feelings rushed in to fill the void. She stood, transfixed by his hot gaze, and all the emotions she'd worked so hard to suppress, or at least hide from him, welled up.

Aurelio peered down into stormy silver eyes and was stunned to see them suddenly awash with unshed tears.

Because he said he'd been worried about her? No, it must be something else. Something *had* happened tonight. He'd been right to worry.

'Amber? What is it?' Urgency roughened his voice, made it harsh and demanding when he wanted to be supportive.

But he'd never seen this woman close to tears before. Ever. Not when he'd walked out on her in Rome. Nor during their confrontation when she arrived at the vineyard. Or more recently when she'd put in ridiculously long hours, trying to finish everything before leaving the vineyard. Through it all Amber had been astonishingly resilient. He didn't know another woman who'd have stood up to him as she did.

He'd become a reclusive grouch lately and it took a strong personality to put up with him, much less inveigle him into letting down his guard.

Amber had done it.

Yet here she was, bright eyes glazed and mouth trembling.

An unseen fist punched him in the chest. He felt winded, like something vital was unravelling inside him.

'Amber? Talk to me. Did someone hurt you?' He closed his hands around her upper arms. If some guy had—

'No! I'm fine, I told you.' Her voice wasn't her own either. It was a meagre shadow of her usual firm tones.

Aurelio stared down into her taut face, watched her blink to clear her eyes and felt…useless. How could he help if she refused to say what was wrong?

But one thing he knew for certain. Something *was* wrong. Badly wrong.

If she didn't explain he couldn't fix it for her and Aurelio knew without doubt that he wanted to fix things for her. He hated seeing her silent suffering. Enough to cross boundaries he usually avoided at all costs.

'Tell me, Amber. I care about you.' The words spilled out, uncensored and unplanned. But they were true. Hearing them, Aurelio realised how true they were. Amber was special. Her distress tore at him. 'I want to help.'

Yet instead of easing her hurt, his words seemed to have the opposite effect. He watched her mouth drag down in a grimace and felt a rough shudder pass through her as if she fought a mighty internal struggle.

Stymied, Aurelio considered his options. If he couldn't fix the problem, for now all he could do was look after her. There was no way he could simply turn around and leave Amber like this. Remarkably for a man who shunned complications, the thought of her crying alone in her room was even worse than the possibility of her crying on him.

He knew the sort of comfort women liked. Hadn't he been a rock for Valentina, for his little sister, Lia, and even for his widowed mother through the years?

Silently, Aurelio released his hold on her and instead wrapped his arms around her, drawing her close.

Amber stiffened in his embrace, jerking her head back to stare up at him. Her mouth worked, ready to protest but then she apparently changed her mind. Another shudder ripped through her, her shoulders sagged and the fight left her.

Strange, the feeling of peace he felt as she finally gave up fighting him and let her head sink against his chest. He gathered her even nearer, tucking her right against him, stroking her hair in a slow, soothing rhythm.

He wished he could be a bastion between Amber and whatever had sent her into an uncharacteristic meltdown. Aurelio's heart hammered at the idea of her so distressed. When he found out who'd hurt her he'd make them pay. In the meantime, he'd cuddle her till she quietened.

They stood so long he lost track of time. But he was in no hurry. He could stand here all night if it meant holding Amber in his arms.

He'd missed her. Keeping to his hands-off policy had driven him crazy.

Was it selfish to enjoy the feel of her in his embrace when she was still obviously hurting?

Probably. But Aurelio refused to follow that train of thought. Instead he concentrated on moulding her to him, hoping she'd find comfort in his warmth and strength, palming her slippery silk hair in long strokes and fighting to ignore the trickles of heat radiating through him at that sensual caress.

This is about Amber, not you.

He planted his legs wider, suddenly restless. Not with holding her, but as his body responded to the proximity of Amber's sweet body against him. To those breasts pushing against his ribs with every shuddering breath she took. To the sunny, floral perfume filling his nostrils. To the feel of her hands tucked up flat against his chest.

He tried but couldn't stop thoughts of how those delicate hands had moulded his bare body, exploring, awakening, teasing and ultimately pleasuring.

His groin tightened and once more he shifted his weight. But instead of helping, Amber moved closer, as if wanting to burrow into him.

Aurelio gritted his teeth, dragging in a sustaining breath. If he wasn't careful it wouldn't be simply comfort he offered her. Already he felt heat drive down into his loins. That all too familiar strain in his lower body. It might have been two months since they'd had sex but he reacted to Amber's proximity like they were still lovers.

He had to end this now, to draw back and give her space.

Exhaling, he let his hand drop from her hair. But instead of falling to his side somehow it anchored in the thick toweling robe covering the swell of her hip. His hand moved, splaying possessively, holding her to him.

A judder of heat passed through him.

On the next breath he'd make himself step back.

Except on the next breath Amber lifted her head.

Her pink lips were parted, as if she too had trouble drawing in enough oxygen. The tears were gone but her eyelashes were spiked with wetness. Her eyes were clouded with turbulent emotion.

Aurelio looked into them and felt himself falling, drawn closer and closer.

There was a gasp, a flare of brilliance in her gaze, then his mouth closed on hers and for the first time in two months, the world felt right.

Chapter Nine

AURELIO'S MOUTH COVERED HERS AND Amber's eyes drifted shut as she gave herself up to his kiss.

This shouldn't be happening. He didn't want to renew the relationship they'd had. He'd made that abundantly clear.

And she…well, she had more sense than to crave kisses from the man who'd rejected her.

Yet instead of stepping back or jerking her head aside, Amber leaned closer, rising on tiptoe, trying to scale his tall frame.

From the moment his lips touched hers, gently, tenderly shaping themselves to her mouth, she was lost. All the reasons why this was a bad idea were banished by the triumphant, silent shout of joy reverberating through her.

Higher she moved and the powerful arm lashing her waist slid lower so his palm covered her buttock, drawing her up against the hard column of his erection. Instantly heat spilled and spread, pooling and circling through her womb, leaving her damp and aching between the legs.

It was bliss being so close to him, tasting him on her tongue, breathing in the salt, male scent of him.

Bliss, but surely a betrayal of herself?

Bravely her beleaguered brain fought to make

her pull back. To regret this intimacy and her weakness in opening for him. Yet she sucked his tongue hard into her mouth and caressed him greedily. As if she'd never taste him again.

Perhaps she wouldn't.

He hadn't planned this, she was sure. In another moment Aurelio would come to his senses, drawing back to reject her again.

At the thought pain seared, making her tremble.

Yet even that didn't stop her. If Amber had a shred of pride left she'd pull away and end this now. Pride was about all that had got her through the last weeks. She couldn't yield to him just because for a moment he'd forgotten that he didn't want a relationship.

But it wasn't so simple.

Her heart was engaged. And where the heart ruled, it was hard to put pride first, now her defences were breached and she felt so…raw.

She'd pretended not to be hurt, pretended it didn't matter that the man she loved didn't want her. But it did. She craved him with a desperation that had grown rather than diminished during the time they'd spent working together.

That desperation made her lean in to soak up the very essence of him into her bones, imprint him on her body as he'd imprinted himself on her heart. Amber was determined to absorb every sense memory she could against the time when Aurelio was gone from her life.

But the kiss didn't end. He didn't pull back or push her away. Instead, with a low sound of need that rumbled from the back of his throat, he tugged her higher, closer, and she grew dizzy on him. All her senses were on overload after being starved of him so long.

She shifted her hand, moulding his powerful chest, and discovered his heart sprinted as fast as her own. Shock smote her. She could, eventually, have resisted, but for the discovery he needed this as much as she did.

With a sigh of surrender Amber slid her hands up to channel through the thick hair at the back of Aurelio's skull. She'd give herself to the decadent pleasure of his kiss, now hungry rather than gentle. She'd enjoy the moment, knowing it would be brief. After this she must walk away for the sake of her sanity.

Finally, when the blood roared in her ears from lack of oxygen and sheer sensual overload, he shifted, put his hands on her arms and lifted his head.

For a second longer Amber clutched at him then, recognising it was over, let her arms slide down over his heaving chest, to her sides. Her legs were wobbly but Aurelio held her steady, clearly realising she'd have trouble standing alone.

She waited for regret to engulf her, or embarrassment, or even shame. But they didn't come.

Finally she opened her eyes to meet his hot, dark gaze. Fire spread through her at that kindling look but Amber didn't turn away. She refused to hide now, no matter what he might read in her expression.

Aurelio's breath was warm on her face, his body hot and hard beneath the fine weave of his tuxedo. Pain squeezed her chest as she looked up into his taut features. Even after all that had happened she wanted this man as she'd never wanted before.

The pads of his fingertips grazed her cheekbone in a trailing caress that made her eyelids flicker. Gossamer threads of delight spun through her from that touch, winding like silk round her heart.

'Amber.' His voice was hoarse and urgent and something within leapt at his loss of composure.

His caress moved to her mouth, his thumb planting itself on her slick bottom lip and tugging it down till she opened for him. Instantly darts of flame shot through her body. He rubbed his thumb across her mouth and she licked it, eager for the taste of him again.

So much for pride. Or control. Or even self-respect.

But the tiny voice of protest inside couldn't conquer what she felt.

Aurelio's breath was an audible hiss and he shuddered as he withdrew his hand to her shoulder.

'I want you, Amber.' The words seemed dragged from him. 'I have no right to, after how I treated you, but I do, more than ever.' His voice hit a low note like mountain thunder, its vibration tracking right through her belly.

She told herself she'd misheard. That she'd projected the words she wanted to hear, but the way his eyes ate her up told their own story.

A pulse flickered hard and fast at the base of his throat. 'Tell me to go, Amber, and I will.'

There it was, the moment she could exact revenge for the distress he'd caused, turn the tables and make Aurelio feel just a tiny bit of the aching loss she'd endured.

The thought only lasted an instant. For Amber

didn't care about vengeance. Just that Aurelio wanted her. It wasn't love. For him it could never be love. A pang of loss filled her at what might have been, if only Aurelio could—

No! There was nothing to be gained dreaming of what was clearly impossible. But this was a chance to experience one last time the bliss of being with him, before she turned her back on him once and for all and moved on. As she had to do. She couldn't keep working with him, she'd decided tonight. Even if they shared the parenting of their child in years to come, they could do that at a distance. Being so close to Aurelio, loving him as she did and not being able to have him was too much.

She captured his hand in both of hers, tracing the calluses and scars of more than a decade of wine-making. He had strong, capable hands that could nevertheless be incredibly gentle.

'I don't want you to go,' she whispered. The admission was a release. The weight of tension pressing down on her eased and relief welled.

Amber pushed his hand under the lapel of her bathrobe till it reached her breast. Instantly his hand moulded to her. There was no need for her to press her fingers against his, anchoring them there, except that she liked it.

Amber watched the burst of shock in his face, the wide flare of his nostrils and the way his veins stood proud in his neck.

'I want you to stay and make love to me, Aurelio.'

Her lips were still shaping his name when his mouth slammed onto hers.

This kiss wasn't gentle or tentative. It was urgent and needy. His grip on her breast tightened to that point of shocking pleasure just this side of pain. His other arm wrapped her close and his mouth pressed against hers, ravaging and demanding.

A shiver of carnal excitement sped down her spine as she arched against him. Their loving had always been passionate but never before had she felt this frantic urgency.

He powered her backwards, half carrying her across the carpet till she felt the mattress at the back of her legs and then they were falling together in a tumble of bodies. It wasn't graceful or coordinated. But it was magic.

Hands plucked at his shirt buttons, ripped off his bowtie and pushed her robe aside.

For what seemed a full minute Aurelio was still but for the heave of his chest as he sucked in more air, his gaze transfixed by her bared body. When he touched her again his hand was unsteady as it skimmed from her collarbone to her breast, across to her other nipple then down to her waist and hip.

'You're beautiful,' he breathed. 'Even lovelier than I remembered.'

Amber *felt* beautiful in a way no makeup or jewels or designer gowns could achieve. The fierce adoration in his dark eyes made her feel like a queen.

'Take me, Aurelio. Now.'

His urgency as he tore his clothes off fed Amber's arousal. Before, even in the throes of passion, Aurelio never totally lost control. Now he looked like a man functioning at a purely primal level. She adored it. The sound of cloth tearing. The sudden fumble as, in his eagerness, he realised he'd forgotten to take his shoes off before trying to strip away his trousers.

She reached out to help but he shook his head. 'No. Don't touch me. I don't trust myself.' His voice was strained and unrecognisable.

For once Aurelio wasn't in command of himself and the thrill of that was headier than any draught of fine wine, more exquisite than any gift she'd ever received.

But before she had time to revel in the knowledge, Aurelio was prowling back up the bed towards her, caging her with his naked body. Instantly her satisfaction died as urgency climbed. What was he doing? He was so close yet held himself above her, not touching.

Amber tilted her hips, slid her thighs wide and felt the solid muscle of his legs against hers. A quiver ran through him. She saw his shoulders shake and his lips thin. Then, as if she'd given a signal he'd been waiting for, Aurelio lowered himself onto her.

Fire scorched from the contact. He was burning up and so was she. But it was a delicious fire, the friction of his chest with its smattering of hair against her nipples detonating tiny explosions of pleasure. The weight of him pressing her into the bed, the urgent way he invaded the space between her legs with those powerful thighs — all ramped up her desire from need to desperation.

Amber curled her arms around his ribs, feeling the rise of each laboured breath, drawing him hard against her.

When their mouths meshed it was unlike any kiss she'd ever had. There was no finesse, no teasing, just a dive straight into bliss.

As their tongues tangled and she swallowed the rich taste of him, Aurelio settled his erection against her. Then, without pause, there came the sure, steady thrust of his body entering hers.

There was no need for foreplay. Amber was primed for him, only him.

To be together again was so perfect it took just one thrust, one growl of approval from Aurelio, for sensation to bombard her. Like fire in her blood, heat roared through her. There were no tiny ripples to signal an impending climax. There was simply a blast of rapture, so strong, so all-encompassing that Amber could do nothing but give into it and hang on.

It was the same for Aurelio. His hips bucked against her, hard and needy as he spilled himself deep within, his whole body taut and shivering with the force of his orgasm.

Amber's hands clawed his back as the world dropped away and there was only the pair of them left in a swirling, dizzying, stunningly beautiful galaxy of shooting stars.

Chapter Ten

SLUMPED ON TOP OF AMBER, Aurelio felt his body judder and jerk in the aftershocks of the most explosive climax he'd ever experienced.

He resisted the temptation to analyse why it had been so perfect. Instead, with the ability to compartmentalise his thoughts that had kept him sane, just, through the dark years, he blanked his mind to everything but Amber and the lush welcome of her sweet body.

He groaned against the fine skin at the base of her neck and was rewarded with a little, voluptuous shiver that jiggled her breasts against his chest and moved all that cushiony softness beneath and around him.

It was a reminder that he was crushing her. Yet it was beyond him to leave her. Instead, gathering the last of his strength, he rolled onto his back, taking her with him, keeping them joined.

She sprawled, boneless, over him like a sensual blanket. Her inner thighs were silk against his hips and her mouth, pressed now against his collarbone, moved in a phantom caress that evoked a buzz of reaction.

His penis stirred and Aurelio's laboured breathing faltered as a ripple of pleasure coursed through him.

Again?

Even for a man with such a healthy sexual appetite, that was unusual. It had to be some aberration,
a lingering sensation from that white hot orgasm
and not—

Amber wriggled a little getting comfortable and
his penis stirred again, swelling towards arousal.

Stunned, Aurelio swept his hands over the curve
of her back, past the softness of her unbound hair,
down to her buttocks. She shivered as he pulled
her closer, harder onto him. There it was again. The
unmistakable tightening in his groin. Slowly he
tilted his pelvis, prodding deeper into those slick
depths and a sigh broke from his lips.

Amber lifted her head.

Eyes bright as gems surveyed him. Her lips were
the colour of crushed raspberries, her skin flushed,
her hair wild and tumbled. She was the most gorgeous thing he'd ever seen.

Aurelio opened his mouth to tell her but the
words disintegrated when she moved, levering
herself up off his chest, and sitting back, knees at
his side.

They were still joined, locked together so that the
movement was exquisitely arousing. She knew it.
He saw it in the tiny smile flickering at the corners
of her mouth, and the way her pulse thrummed.
Slowly she licked her lips and he couldn't prevent
his body's jerk of appreciation.

Amber smiled then, like a cat surveying a bowl of
cream. She planted her hands on his ribs to steady
herself and then she was moving, slowly drawing
herself up high until at the last moment dropping
down in a sensual slide that made him see stars all

over again.

Aurelio grabbed her hips, clutching her tight. He knew she wouldn't leave him, not when she was clearly enjoying this as much as he, yet he couldn't fight the need to hold her tight. Possessiveness as well as pleasure surged. With every slow, sensual slide of her body against his, with every shattered breath and gasp of delight, it intensified.

He didn't just want Amber. He *needed* her. She was vital to him, she was—

Amber circled her hips, driving down hard against him and Aurelio's thoughts fractured. Unable to stop himself, he thrust high and hard, clamping her to him, driving himself and her towards a peak of acute pleasure that was unattainable, exquisitely unreachable, until suddenly it was there.

Fire stormed his body as he lost his rhythm and shuddered his way into an explosive completion just as Amber's eyes shut and she screamed his name.

Sensation flared across every pleasure point in his body, branding him with a bliss unlike anything he'd known. It seared his very soul. And at the centre, inseparable from the storm of rapture, was Amber, head flung back, breasts thrust towards him as she rode him.

Beautiful, delectable Amber.

The woman who'd made him feel again.

Aurelio didn't leave that night. He could no more have dragged himself back to his own room than he could have moved the Colosseum single-handed.

Through the night that followed, as they sheltered in each other's arms and even, occasionally slept, and when they made love again, slowly but with the same profound sense of the world shifting around him, Aurelio felt...

At peace?

That was passive, too ephemeral to describe his bone-deep satisfaction.

At home?

A shiver scudded down his backbone at the idea. It wasn't—

'Aurelio?' Amber's hand slid down his arm and the word was a breath of warm air across his chest since she was snuggled up against him, her head on his collarbone. 'Are you okay?'

Aurelio dragged in a deep breath and opened his eyes, taking in the sunlight around the edges of the curtained windows. He didn't need to look at his watch to know it was late. So late they'd probably missed this morning's meeting. For the moment that paled into insignificance.

'I'm...okay.'

His voice didn't sound right even to his own ears. So it didn't surprise him when Amber wriggled against him, turning so she could prop herself up above him. Prop her smooth, naked, soft body against him.

Inevitably, as if they hadn't spent the night having sex, arousal stirred. She did that to him every time. Made him eager and ready. Made him even think about wanting more than sex, though he knew more was impossible. He couldn't, wouldn't go through that again.

'You're a bad liar, Aurelio.' Her lips curved into a

smile but her eyes were wary.

Who could blame her? He was wary too. He didn't understand these emotions Amber stirred up. They stole his peace and confounded all his certainties.

She moved and a swathe of dark hair spilled across him, an abandoned caress. Aurelio planted his palms on her hips, as much to stop his hands roving her body as to stop her moving again.

Yet her soft skin distracted him. With difficulty he yanked his mind from her body. He couldn't give voice to his disquiet, but there was one difficulty he had to raise.

'There is one thing.'

Amber nodded, her gaze steady, waiting. Guilt shafted through him. This was his fault. Utterly, completely his. He'd never been in this situation before.

'I forgot to use a condom last night. Twice.' Because the second time had come so hard upon the first. He hadn't even pulled free of Amber's body before he was powering into her again, filled with a desperation to claim her that went beyond any bounds he'd previously known.

After that he'd used protection but there was a chance it was already too late.

That realisation stirred a jumble of feelings. There was disbelief at his uncharacteristic behaviour and fear that one lapse was enough for consequences that would last a lifetime.

But there was more. Thinking through what happened stirred even more disturbing revelations. Including a deep-rooted emotion he couldn't name at the idea of impregnating Amber with his seed. It couldn't be satisfaction, could it? That didn't make sense to a man whose path in life was as a loner.

Aurelio became aware, finally, that Amber hadn't reacted, except for a slight widening of those bright eyes and a quickening of her breath.

'Amber, did you hear me? I'm clean. You wouldn't catch anything from me, but it's just possible I've made you pregnant.'

The words sounded unreal.

Unreal but strangely...

No! He was imagining things.

Finally he got a reaction. She blinked, her eyes clouding as the news sank in.

'Don't worry.' The words spilled out. 'If anything happens I'd look after you.'

Even saying it made his chest tighten as if caught in a huge vice. But he meant it. Even if the very idea was almost too catastrophic to contemplate.

'You mean that?' Amber's voice wobbled, her mouth turning down at the corners as if tugged by strong emotion.

Aurelio swallowed, trying to moisten his suddenly parched mouth. The idea of a baby, of commitment and permanency was the stuff of nightmare. But at the same time it was obvious she needed reassurance.

'You'd stick by me?' She looked so intense, her gaze needle sharp.

'Of...course.' He smiled, but suspected it didn't reach his eyes. For he sensed her idea of him sticking by her and his were different. Aurelio knew he could never commit to a permanent relationship. The thought of it iced his bones. But he could provide money to support her. To provide for a baby.

Bright eyes scrutinised him so intently he was sure his face must be burned on Amber's retinas.

'Say something,' he said finally, discomfited by that stare.

'What do you want me to say? Tell you it's okay because I'm on the pill and there's no chance of pregnancy?' Her words were tight, almost confrontational.

Amber slid away, breaking his hold and sitting up on the side of the wide bed, turning her shoulder to him. Aurelio couldn't read her expression from this angle but his body protested the loss of her closeness.

He sat up too, drawn by something in her tone, in the sudden stiffness in her luscious body that now seemed all angles instead of curves. Her legs were crossed he realised, and her arms too, her shoulders hunched forward.

'Amber?' Concern rose as he leaned close and saw the colour bleed from her face. Surely her breathing was too rapid. 'What's wrong?'

Desolate eyes turned to meet his. 'I can't reassure you, Aurelio.' Her tongue swiped her bottom lip and as he watched, dampness beaded her forehead. Her pale skin turned the colour of curdled milk.

Instinctively he reached for her but he was too late. One hand to her mouth, the other to her stomach, she stumbled to the bathroom.

Stunned, Aurelio got to his feet and strode across the room. She'd looked distraught, almost sick and—

The sound of retching reached him.

'Amber?' His stride lengthened but he pulled up short as the bathroom door slammed in his face.

What was going on? She'd been fine earlier. Was this nerves, some extreme anxiety reaction to the idea of a chance pregnancy?

Aurelio frowned, propping himself up on the wall beside the door. That wasn't like Amber. She was a fighter, not the sort of woman to be laid low by the mere possibility of bad news. She had more gumption that any woman he knew.

Again the sound of retching, this time partly masked by running water. Nevertheless, it made the hairs at his nape stand on end.

Gut instinct said this wasn't some simple nervous reaction. Or food poisoning.

Aurelio stared blankly across the room at the bright morning sunlight filtering around the side of the curtains. She'd been fine last night. More than fine — energetic and enthusiastic. It was only this morning…

Aurelio's breath caught in his chest and his heart stuttered as his brain catalogued things he'd noticed but not attended to.

Since the day Amber arrived at the vineyard he hadn't once seen her drink the strong coffee they both enjoyed.

Nor had she tasted any wine. First she'd claimed it was too early in the day. Then that she'd already tried the wines he wanted her to savour. Then last night at the gala she'd drunk nothing but sparkling water.

She hadn't reassured him about being on the pill, even though she'd been using a contraceptive that week they spent in Rome.

She was sick in the morning.

Aurelio sagged against the wall as intuition filled

in the blanks.

She was pregnant.

It should be a slim possibility only, yet it felt like certainty.

Bile rose in his throat.

He couldn't do this. Fate wouldn't be that cruel.

He remembered Valentina sweet-talking, trying to convince him to have a child, to bring forward the date of their wedding and start a family. Her disappointment when he'd stuck to his guns about finishing one last vintage away, building up the experience he'd need for his career. The career he'd need to support a family.

They'd been sweethearts forever and the one thing she wanted as much as their wedding was a big brood of kids. Kids he'd delayed giving her till it was too late.

The sounds stopped in the bathroom but Aurelio didn't make a move to enter. He stood rooted to the spot, staring at the luxurious room but not seeing it.

Guilt and anguish enveloped him, pressing down from all sides, driving away the last vestiges of the well-being he'd known was too good to be true.

He'd refused to give the woman he loved a child when she wanted one. And now, when he'd turned into a man unable to love, he was going to be a father.

Chapter Eleven

AMBER DRAGGED AN UNSTEADY HAND
through her tumbled hair and wished she had
something to tie it back from her face.

Her eyes caught her wan reflection in the huge
mirror and she grimaced. A hair tie was the least of
her problems.

She'd spent the night doing what she'd vowed
she'd never again do — making love to Aurelio.
Now her emotions were in complete disarray.

Time and again lately she'd told herself that she'd
be okay once she could get away from seeing him
every day. That she'd start afresh and one day learn
to be heart whole again.

Last night had changed that. She felt...connected
to him in ways she couldn't explain. Ways that were
stronger than the sex they shared. She watched her
reflection as her hand covered her belly. Logic told
her she and Aurelio were linked by the fact they'd
soon share a child. Yet her stubborn heart hummed
that there was more even than that.

Spinning away, she reached for a fluffy robe and
slipped it on, tying it tight around her middle.
There was no time for daydreaming. She had to go
back in there and face Aurelio. Explain...

Talk about timing! Her first ever bout of morning sickness would hit when she was in bed with

him.

Had it been morning sickness? Or was it nerves, facing the man she loved, seeing his utter dismay at the idea they might have made a child?

Again her hand crept protectively to her abdomen. Whatever the future held, she was sure of one thing. She'd do whatever it took to give her baby a wonderful future.

She needed all her determination as she opened the door and saw Aurelio propped on the wall nearby, his expression bleak.

There was nothing soft in his face at all. His dark brows sat low, scrunched over his eyes. His jaw was set and deep grooves bracketed a mouth that was a thin twist. Even those wide shoulders seemed rucked up high.

'When were you going to tell me?' His voice was low and soft but with a rough edge that scored her conscience.

'Tell you?' Amber clutched the neck of her robe close around her throat. He was utterly, gloriously nude and she was almost fully covered by the concealing robe, yet under that brooding glare she was the one who felt naked.

'That you're pregnant. You *are* pregnant, aren't you?'

Amber's hand clawed at the door frame as her already weak knees buckled.

'How did you know?' She'd only been nauseous once. She was nowhere near showing. The only other symptom she'd had was sensitive breasts, which far from being a problem had made Aurelio's lovemaking last night utter bliss.

She shivered as a trail of erotic heat coiled languidly through her middle. Just as if the man scowling down at her was about to ravish her instead of grill her for information.

'It's mine, isn't it?'

No mistaking that hollow tone. Aurelio wasn't anything like thrilled at the news. He sounded utterly grim. Even worse than the day she'd turned up at the vineyard and he'd ordered her away. Then he'd been cold and angry. Now he sounded...desolate.

A shiver ran through her, icing her skin under the thick robe. Anger she could deal with, and obstinacy, but the blankness in those dark eyes, and the starkness she read in his expression, those filled her with fear.

Again she paused to wonder at his acceptance of the situation. They'd barely known each other when they'd had their affair yet he hadn't bothered to ask if there'd been anyone else.

'If you want a DNA check—'

He cut her off. 'If you tell me it's my child that's enough. I know you, Amber. You're not the sort of woman to foist another man's child on me.'

It didn't sound like a compliment though she supposed it was proof that he believed in her honesty. That should comfort her. Instead she felt on the edge of a precipice, leaning out, awaiting the final push that would send her plummeting into nothingness.

'It's our baby, Aurelio.' She stood straighter, releasing her hold on the door frame. 'I haven't been with another man in—'

His slashing gesture cut off her words. 'I don't need to hear about your lovers.'

Was that anger she heard in his voice? If so it was gone again in an instant. He looked stern, but not furious.

'I know it seems unlikely.' Even though he hadn't questioned, Amber felt the need to explain. 'I was on the pill and you used condoms but—'

'But these things can still happen.' He sighed and she watched as he drew in a breath so huge it made his chest and shoulders rise.

Amber stared at this big, beautiful, powerful man, so superior in physical strength, yet looking so utterly lost, and was overcome by the need to protect. Was this some latent nurturing instinct awakening with pregnancy? Or was it because Aurelio, who could infuriate her as easily as he made her sigh with pleasure or laugh over some light-hearted remark, had become precious to her?

The time they'd spent working together, each bringing their own expertise and enthusiasm to the project, had been as exciting and satisfying as their original affair. More so possibly, for there'd been something wonderful about sharing more than sex with him. About learning more of the man who made her heart race whenever he smiled at her.

She reached out and took him by the elbow, his flesh hot against her chilled fingers.

'Come and sit.'

Amber ignored the designer chairs grouped by the window and led the way to the bed, sitting on the end of the mattress and pulling him down beside her. He sank without a word and Amber had the impression he didn't really take in their surroundings.

But then she remembered her own shock at discovering she was pregnant. It had taken ages even to process the fact, much less start thinking about the future.

'Are you okay?'

That dragged him from his reverie. His laugh was a short husk of sound, devoid of humour. 'I should be asking you that.' He sat straighter, turning to view her, his knee pressing into her thigh. 'Are you well? Are you sick often?'

Amber shook her head. 'This morning was the first time. I've been fine.'

'You've been to a doctor? Everything's normal?'

'So far so good. And yes, I've seen a doctor.' With such momentous news, she hadn't trusted in a store bought pregnancy kit.

Warmth filled Amber at Aurelio's concern for her. See? It was just the initial shock of the news. Things weren't so bad after all. In fact, his response to her news was, she suspected, far better than most men's. No demands for a paternity test, no grilling about her non-existent affairs. Aurelio De Laurentis had swept her off her feet and into an unplanned liaison, making her forget her usual caution. Right from the first there'd been something about him that *got* to her. A fizz of attraction, a crackle of energy, a sense that this man, amongst all the ones who'd made a play for her over the years, was different.

Hers.

That's how it felt. As if Aurelio was hers and she was his.

'That's why you were so determined to work at the vineyard.'

Amber shrugged. 'I'd won the contract so of

course I wanted the work. But yes, the pregnancy was a factor.'

After he'd spurned her, part of her had wanted never to see him again. It had taken every ounce of courage and determination to front up that day and pretend to be strong.

Dark eyes held hers. 'When were you going to tell me?'

There it was again, that hollow sound in his deep voice, like he was lost in a vast, empty space. It was…unsettling.

Amber rubbed her hands up and down her arms, cool despite the warm gown. In her peripheral vision was a broad, delicious expanse of bare skin and solid muscle that was Aurelio. Physical work in the winery had honed his body into impressive lines. All that taut muscle must explain why he didn't feel the chill that enveloped her.

Or perhaps she had a premonition of impending disaster.

'I don't know. Soon. My only plan was not to dump the news on you as soon as I arrived. I was waiting for a suitable time.'

There could never be a suitable time to break such news. After all, they weren't committed to each other, long-term lovers with a future.

Yet, after last night, after the glory of being in Aurelio's arms again, tucked close against him even as they slept, Amber couldn't help but hope there was a chance—

'And you're keeping the child.'

Aurelio's words cut across her dreamy thoughts like a razor through soft flesh. She jerked upright, her heart racing. 'I am.'

He nodded. 'I couldn't imagine you getting a termination.'

Heart still sprinting, Amber sank back a little, one hand propped on the bed for support. She waited to feel pleasure, something, at his understanding of her, and his acceptance that there *would* be a child, but it didn't come. His stony face, the sense she had that he was...disengaged, was too disquieting.

'You're shocked by the news.' Stating the obvious, of course, but Amber felt the need for words. Preferably words from Aurelio. So far he hadn't expressed any feelings whatsoever about the fact he was going to be a father.

She told herself it was far too early for that. He was still grappling with the news. Yet his unnatural stillness, his lack of strong reaction was almost more disturbing than if he'd protested and stormed about asking for proof the baby was his.

Amber reached out and covered his fisted hand with hers. His skin was hot, the flesh hard and the fine sprinkle of hairs on the back of his hand tickled her palm. But he didn't seem to register her touch. He was lost in his own world.

A sombre world if his expression was any mirror. He wasn't scowling but he didn't look happy.

Amber stroked her fingers along his taut flesh and abruptly he moved, jerking his hand away. For a long moment that ebony stare held hers, then in a surge of movement he was gone, rising from the bed and striding away.

Despite the wrenching pain in her chest, Amber found herself mesmerised by the sight of Aurelio, so strong and athletic, as he marched across the room and then back. He was completely uncaring about his nudity as he grappled with the implications of her pregnancy.

Finally he turned towards her. But instead of coming over to sit beside her, or even drawing up a chair to face her, Aurelio propped himself against the wall, feet wide and arms crossed, as if needing to brace himself.

'There's something you should know.' His voice wasn't harsh, but there was something about it that made Amber hug the robe tighter round herself.

Silently she nodded.

'I can't be a father.'

'But it's your baby! You already accepted that.' Was he now going to demand a paternity test after all?

'I don't mean that. I'm not talking about getting you pregnant.' He paused and hefted in a deep breath. Amber watched as the throbbing pulse at his temple quickened. 'I'm talking about the ability to act as a father. To be there, all the time, for a child.' His eyes narrowed on her and she felt his regard like a physical weight. 'Or for a wife, for that matter.'

Confused, Amber latched onto the one statement she did understand. 'I wasn't asking you to marry me!'

Yet, try as she might, she couldn't stir indignation at his implication. She was too caught up in the distress she read on his face. It was like a mask had been peeled back off his features, revealing something that looked horribly like pain.

'Aurelio? What's wrong?' She was on her feet before she'd even thought about it but in that same moment he stretched out his arm, palm out towards her, warning her off. She halted, mid stride, the hand she'd half raised towards him falling at her side.

She'd never expected him to leap with instant joy and embrace her when he heard about the baby. But his reaction, not anger or suspicion, but something far more visceral, worried her. 'What are you talking about?'

His mouth jerked up to one side in what might have passed for a smile, except it looked like it hurt him.

Amber felt the echo of that hurt in her own chest where her ribs seemed to tighten, making it difficult to draw breath.

'I can provide financial support.' He nodded, confirming his determination to do just that. 'You and the baby can count on me for that.' He paused and Amber felt her pulse pound as she waited for him to continue. Finally he did, his eyes meeting hers. 'But that's all I can do. I can't...' He waved his hand in negation. Finally he went on. 'I can't do any more than that. Don't expect me to be there, sharing custody, or at your side.' Something glittered in his eyes then disappeared. 'I'll have no role in the child's life.'

The child.

Not 'our baby'. Even his choice of words distanced him. As if their baby didn't matter.

Anger brewed, stirred by his dismissal.

'I never expected to have you at my side, Aurelio.' Even if she'd dreamed that perhaps, after all, it might be a possibility one day. 'But that doesn't stop you being a father to our baby.' She paused, dragging in a shuddery breath. 'Our baby,' she emphasised the word, 'deserves a mother and a father. It will be better—'

'No!' Aurelio's hand cut the air between them. 'It will do better without me in its life.'

Stunned, Amber stared, taking in the quick rise and fall of his chest, the rapid pulse, the beading of sweat across his upper lip. If she didn't know better she'd almost think him sick.

'How can I believe you if you don't tell me what's going on? I know you're shocked but—'

'It's not shock, Amber.'

He lifted a hand and raked it back through his thick hair. Even from here she saw his fingers were unsteady. Despite herself, she wanted to reach out to him, hold him close.

'It's the simple truth.' Finally, as if his strength failed, he turned and subsided into one of the lounge chairs beside him. Amber hesitated a moment then took one opposite him, her gaze locked on his taut features.

'I can't do…love.' His eyes met hers and she saw without doubt that he wasn't making excuses. This was no stunt to try avoiding parental responsibility, even if she'd believed Aurelio the sort to try that.

The man looking back at her was haggard, flesh pared back against bone and eyes haunted. He looked like a man in anguish. 'Not again.'

'Again?' Shock jolted her. Then she remembered — he'd tried love and it hadn't worked.

An aching emptiness opened up inside, hollowing her belly, carving chasms through those optimistic hopes she'd clung to, even when they seemed impossible.

They *were* impossible! Amber wrapped her arms

around her torso, holding in the hurt as her silly, stubborn heart finally cleaved in two. For the implacable light in his eyes told her, even more than words could, that he couldn't give his love to her.

'I was in love once, long ago. But I let her down and she died.' Aurelio's tone held a finality that spelled the end of any hope of happiness. 'I haven't been whole since. I can't go through that again.'

He paused and when he spoke again his voice was cold as hardened steel. 'I *can't* love.'

Chapter Twelve

AURELIO SAW AMBER FLINCH THEN draw in on herself, shoulders hunching forward, arms wrapping tight around her waist.

But it was her eyes, dazed and clouded, that undid him, made him want to gather her close as the little colour she'd acquired drained, leaching her skin.

He hated seeing her like this. Hated knowing he'd shattered any hopes she might have harboured.

But, with a mighty effort of control, he held himself in check. Going to her, comforting her, would only prolong what should be cut short now. A shudder ran through him as he fought the impulse that tightened his muscles, to leap up and gather her to him.

He ploughed his fingers back through his hair, cursing his inability to keep his hands off her, the weakness that made him keep turning to her, not just for sex, but because he wanted to be with her. Despite knowing his own limitations he'd craved her warmth and smiles, he'd revelled in working with her, enjoying the shared understanding and common purpose. There was so much—

No! There he went again, losing himself in feelings for Amber that could go nowhere.

He didn't deserve Amber.

He'd only let her down. And their child. Just as

he'd let down Valentina.

He didn't deserve happiness.

With Amber he'd forgotten that. He'd almost let himself believe…

'I'm sorry, Amber.' Sorry wasn't enough, but he had no words to express his regret, or the ache of loss ripping through him. 'You deserve better than me.'

It was true yet he had to force the words out. Even though he'd spent a decade cutting himself off from relationships, trying to erase the word love from his personal dictionary. In that time he'd shunned the world as best he could by burying himself in work.

'Tell me.' Her eyes had lost that foggy look and instead skewered him like silver needles. 'I want to understand.'

Silently Aurelio nodded, swiping a palm over his unshaven jaw. Amber deserved to know. He cleared his throat.

'I knew Valentina all my life. We grew up together, went to school together. Her family and mine were neighbours.' He paused, remembering that hazy golden past. 'We'd always been friends but by the time school finished we were in love, inseparable. Except Valentina was happy to stay in our little town and work in her parents' restaurant and I had other plans.

'For years I'd been working during harvest at a winery not too far away. I knew it was what I wanted to do, but I wanted more than just to work as a cellar hand all my life.' His aim was to make more of himself, partly because of his fascination with winemaking and partly to support Valentina and the family they'd have together.

'So I went away, working harvests in other vineyards in Italy and overseas, getting experience. I studied winemaking, building up my theoretical knowledge as well as my practical skills. But that meant being away from Valentina most of the time.'

He stopped to drag air into tight lungs. Amber had moved back in her seat, her gaze still fixed on him.

'Valentina was patient through all those years. She put up with me being away, pursuing my dream. She put up with short visits home because in the long run we'd be together for the rest of our lives. We were planning to get married and start a family when I finally came home.'

Aurelio hadn't been fussed about having kids early, though he knew he'd love them when they arrived. But Valentina was positively clucky for a child and counting the days till he was home for good so they could make a baby. Persuading her to accept that final year of separation had been difficult. They'd debated it so long but eventually Aurelio had got his way.

'I was working in California. There'd been a delay with the grape harvest and I worked right up till a couple of days before the wedding, weeks later than originally planned.'

He'd missed all the wedding preparations that he'd assured Valentina he'd be around to help with. But his professional reputation had been on the line. He'd assured his employers he'd see the harvest through.

So instead he'd let down his fiancée.

He'd never forgive himself for that.

Valentina had tried to involve him in the minutiae of the wedding plans though he was on another continent but he'd been so exhausted from long days of hard labour getting the grapes processed, he hadn't been able to focus. He'd resented her insistence on asking about feminine stuff he didn't understand and she'd snapped that he cared more about his grapes than their wedding.

In the end she'd stopped asking for input. He'd heard the hurt in her voice and vowed to make it up to her when he got back. His aim was to have enough saved to put a deposit on a place of their own.

But he'd never got the chance.

Recently, watching his brother Gennaro and his soon-to-be-sister-in-law Chiara plan their wedding, it hit home how much he'd disappointed Valentina. Gennaro hadn't a clue about colour schemes or wedding flowers but Chiara positively glowed as she shared every tiny detail with him.

Another thing Aurelio had denied his fiancée.

'Aurelio?'

He blinked and saw Amber frowning, waiting for him to continue.

'I flew in late in the evening.' Aurelio drew a sharp breath, the metallic taste of despair filling his mouth.

'I was going to arrange transport home but Valentina wanted to collect me herself.' He looked down at his hands, clasped before him, feeling that familiar weight of guilt pressing down on his shoulders and crushing his lungs.

That last phone call had been…stiff. He'd apologised and she'd accepted, both stilted and wary.

He'd heard how tired she was and said he'd make his own way from the airport. Valentina had been hurt, actually thinking he wasn't eager to see her after their long distance quarrel. So he'd capitulated, even though he knew she didn't like night driving.

'What happened?' Amber's voice was soft, breaking through the memories.

He jerked his head up. 'I waited and waited. I rang her phone. Nothing. Then, hours later, I got a call. There'd been an accident on the autostrada, a three car pile-up. Valentina in her little car had been in the middle. She hadn't a chance of surviving.'

Even now he could recall every word of that phone call. He remembered the sour scent of airport coffee left to go cold. His complete disbelief as he grappled to take in the news the woman he loved was gone forever.

'I'm so sorry, Aurelio.'

He nodded, losing himself in the sympathy he read in Amber's silvery eyes.

His throat was tight, his heart pounding. But for once it wasn't just from the memories. Even worse than that old loss was the here and now, reading the defeat in Amber's face and the slump of her shoulders. Bright, beautiful Amber, who usually glowed with life and deserved only good things, looked ashen.

His fault. It was all his fault. Because he'd dared to break his rule and get involved, choosing to ignore his own limitations. Now Amber paid the price for his selfishness.

'I'm sorry too, Amber.' He took a slow breath,

making himself stop rather than blurt out how much he cared for her. That didn't, couldn't matter in the long run. Pain radiated from his jaw as he ground his molars.

'I lost a part of myself when Valentina died. I didn't think I'd survive.'

'So you devoted yourself to work.' Amber leaned towards him, obviously trying to understand. 'That's why you've got a reputation as a recluse, only coming out of the winery when you have to.' She tilted her head in that endearing way and Aurelio clenched his hands into fists to stop himself reaching for her. Even now she made him wish…

'But you did survive, Aurelio.'

He blinked, watching as Amber sat back in her seat, her expression unreadable.

'Grief is a terrible thing, but you survived it.'

Aurelio frowned. 'But Valentina didn't. I let her down, delaying and delaying and…' He shook his head.

Amber stared at those bold features, etched now with suffering.

'Do you mean you blame yourself for her death?' When he said nothing she plunged on, the idea of Aurelio blaming himself when he clearly wasn't at fault was too appalling. She hated seeing his obvious grief.

'You weren't driving, Aurelio. It was an accident. You weren't at fault.'

He shrugged and spread his hands. 'I let her down. I should have agreed to marry and start a family earlier. She never lived her dream. Don't you see? Because of me she never had that chance.'

What Amber saw was a man whose guilt was skewed out of proportion. She bit her lip. Saying that wouldn't help.

'I knew then I'd never love again. There'd never be anyone like Valentina for me. Besides,' his gaze seemed to sharpen on her, 'I wouldn't trust myself not to let them down. I just can't do love again.'

A great wave of emotion smashed into Amber, submerging her in a jumble of feelings, pummelling her and leaving her breathless. It reminded her of her first visit to the beach when she was six. She'd been caught by a rogue wave, a dumper that jerked her feet out beneath her then rolled and rolled her right into the shallows till her lungs almost burst and her skin stung from sand abrasion.

Amber blinked and shook her head, trying to clear her thoughts.

It was tough hearing Aurelio say he'd never love again because there'd never be anyone as special for him. She wanted to cry out that *she* was special. But what good would it do? You can't force someone to care.

But just as dreadful was his declaration that he didn't trust himself to love again in case he let his loved one down. Her heart ached for him, the man she'd tried to reach yet couldn't. And for their unborn child, doomed to miss out on a father's love.

'Aurelio.' She halted and licked her lips, searching for words. 'My dad died when I was thirteen and it messed with my head for ages. For a while there I wondered if it was my fault. If I'd been better in some way maybe he'd have survived.'

Horror rounded Aurelio's eyes. 'No! You shouldn't—'

'I don't, not anymore. But for a while I did.' She leaned closer. 'But there's not a day goes by that I don't give thanks that I had him for thirteen years. He was a terrific father, a special man. I loved him with all my heart. I'm so lucky I had him while I did. There are a lot of people who don't get even that much time.'

'He sounds like a good man.'

'He was. A wonderful man, and my life would have been poorer if I hadn't known him.'

She waited for Aurelio to say more, but he remained silent. Gradually, as the silence lengthened, annoyance tempered her sympathy. The man was so stubborn. She understood grief, she'd been through it herself. Watching the man she loved choose to cut himself off, not just from her but from their child, tore her apart. Dully she wondered if anything could put this right.

Her blood hammered in her arteries, adrenaline pumping at the sheer waste of it all. Aurelio had cared so much he didn't dare admit love into his life again. Yet in the time she'd known him he'd proven himself not only passionate but considerate, gentle, encouraging and just plain fun.

When he wasn't being blinkered and obstinate.

No wonder his siblings had been beside themselves with excitement last night, seeing him apparently with a partner in tow. They must have given up on him ever finding love again.

Or more precisely, ever risking his heart.

'So that's it?' Amber curled her fingers around the arms of her chair. 'You blame yourself for your fiancée's death and you're determined not to risk your heart again?'

'Isn't that enough?' For a second, fire glimmered in his dark gaze, making Amber catch her breath.

Seconds spun out to a minute, to more, as she grappled with mixed emotions. She understood how he felt. Right now the thought of ever caring for someone else was enough to scrape her skin raw. She *never* wanted to feel this way again.

But she still cared for Aurelio, damn it. Even if he didn't care for her. She hated to see him like this, giving up on life.

And then there was the baby. Her hand slid to her belly to comfort that tiny life in the face of its father's rejection.

That, finally, broke the dam of words in her throat.

'I feel sorry for you, Aurelio. You must have loved your fiancée so much.' She paused, swallowing. 'But I can't agree with you. You say you can't do love again because you might get hurt or might let someone down.' She shook her head so vehemently her hair swung like a dark curtain around her face.

'We all just do the best we can. Of course we make mistakes. Of course there'll be hurts along the way. But it's better to care for people, to be part of love than to cut yourself off from everyone.'

He opened his mouth to speak then closed it again, his expression impenetrable but for the frown furrowing his brow.

Amber's impatience rose. He was so determined to go it alone!

She surged to her feet. 'So our child, *your* flesh

and blood, is supposed to be thankful never to know its father! You expect it to be grateful you send money for expenses. That could never make up for a parent's love.'

Her breath came in pants as she struggled to hold herself together. Even the sight of Aurelio's tall frame jerking in response to her words as if he'd been slapped couldn't stop her.

'It's all very well to hide away in your winery and tell yourself the world doesn't exist. That emotions don't exist. They *do*. Love isn't a *choice*, Aurelio. You don't make a decision to love. It's what happens when you connect with someone. When you care.'

She hefted a shaky breath but ploughed on. 'It doesn't matter if you spent years getting to know them or whether you looked, just once, across a room and met a soul mate.'

She caught his eye and stopped, seeing the shock in his eyes. But she refused to back down or hide. *She* wasn't a coward. Nor was she ashamed.

'I…cared for you, Aurelio. Very much.' Her voice wobbled betrayingly and she had to swallow past a knot of emotion before she could go on. 'I thought you were at least the sort of man who'd care for his own child instead of rejecting it.'

Her lip trembled and she bit it hard, the salt tang of blood sharp on her tongue.

'I thought better of you. But it seems I was wrong. If you're the sort of man who's too scared to even *try* loving his own child, it's far better if you don't have anything to do with our baby.'

With one last searing glare she turned around, ignoring the aches that plagued her body. She'd aged a lifetime in just fifteen minutes.

'I'm going to have a bath. Don't be here when I come out.' She walked towards the bathroom, then paused in the doorway. It took everything she had not to turn back as she spoke again. 'I never want to see you again.'

Chapter Thirteen

AURELIO DIDN'T MAKE IT AS far as the winery. He'd planned to check out of the hotel and hit the autostrada north as soon as possible, telling himself once he was back at the vineyard he'd get his perspective back again.

It had worked before, when Valentina died and his world collapsed.

But this was different. This wasn't about trying to deal with grief. He found himself at the window of his suite, watching the light play across the old buildings surrounding the piazza, unable to summon the energy to move.

He was in stasis, Amber's words ringing in his ears. The accusation. The distaste. She hadn't said the word aloud but it had been there in her eyes.

She thought him a coward.

Was she right?

The idea was so foreign his mind reeled.

Scared, she'd said. Scared to love.

All this time he'd thought himself sensible and prudent, and in his own way, caring, by not initiating a long-term relationship because deep inside he feared he'd let another woman down as he had Valentina.

Yet Amber implied he hadn't let his fiancée down.

Of course she didn't know all the facts. Valentina had longed for babies from the time she was in her late teens. She'd sacrificed what she wanted so he could achieve *his* dream.

She'd lost her life because he'd felt so guilty after their unaccustomed row he'd let her drive in conditions she hated rather than insisting on taking care of the transport himself.

He braced one hand beside the window, staring at the swirl and ebb of pedestrians and traffic below.

Suddenly something Lia had said popped into his head. While his brothers had been silently supportive all these years, Lia was more outspoken. She'd known Valentina well and guessed at the guilt he usually refused to speak of. She'd chivvied him about burying himself in his winery and said Valentina would have hated to see him cutting himself off. For Valentina had loved him and loved life, always revelling in the chance to be with people. According to Lia, Valentina had been proud of her fiancé and the way he was following his dream, working so hard to build a future for them. She'd never been happier.

Aurelio thought of Amber's words. About being grateful for the time she'd had with her father, rather than dwelling on his loss.

Lia in her forthright way had told him no-one could have made Valentina happier than he had. And now thinking back he remembered her laughter, her animated chatter, and her comment that it was worth the wait to have him return, qualified and ready to build his career.

In the intervening years he'd cast her as a suffering victim, denied the one thing she'd wanted.

Yet they'd discussed the future over a long time and made their decisions jointly. Now he thought about it, despite her eagerness for a child, Valentina had been glad to get more experience in hospitality, ready for the day they'd have their own vineyard and winery restaurant.

Somehow over the years he'd forgotten that.

When had he let grief become a habit? An excuse to cut himself off?

When had he become so selfish?

A shudder racked him as he recalled Amber's eyes, overbright with emotion. Yet she'd been so valiant with her chin hiked high, accentuating the slender fragility of her neck.

She was stronger than he'd ever been. No hiding for her. She confronted life with the same determination she used to tackle her work and her recalcitrant employer.

All through the discussion in Amber's room, even while reliving the pain of losing Valentina, it wasn't past pain that gutted. It was the torture of being eaten alive by guilt as he watched Amber shut down before him.

Amber who said she'd cared for him.

The ever-selfish, unregenerate part of him wondered what that meant, hoped it meant far more than he deserved. Even now when he'd lost her.

He scoured his palm across the back of his neck, where the muscles were hard as concrete. But nothing eased the ravages of guilt.

She was right.

What sort of man rejected his unborn child?

Rejected the woman who'd dragged him, kicking and screaming out of his cave of self-pity and back into the light?

He'd so disgusted her she never wanted to see him again.

The pain ripping at his insides made him stagger.

The question was, what, if anything, was he going to do about it?

Amber leaned on the balustrade of the viewing platform on top of the Palatine Hill. The sun warmed her as she stared across the ancient forum of Rome towards the Capitoline Hill and *Il Vittoriano*, the Victor Emmanuel Monument. This was her favourite spot in the whole city. From here she was high above the bustle of the capital yet able to drink in the spectacular views.

Now they barely registered. Her mind was back at this morning's confrontation with Aurelio. She'd come here seeking peace and a clearer head but it hadn't worked. Instead she felt muddled, wondering if she should have tried harder to change his mind.

But Aurelio hadn't been interested in her or what she had to say. That had hurt even more than she'd thought possible. Because she'd naïvely believed last night proved there was something strong and unbreakable between them.

She'd done the right thing, the only possible thing, severing all ties with him. It could only be self-destructive to try maintaining a relationship with a man who just didn't care about her or their child.

Yet the anguish of doing right almost undid her.

Coming here hadn't helped. She'd be better off

going to the office and seeing what had to be done before she could hand over the contract to someone else.

She spun around and walked back the way she'd come. Gravel crunched underfoot as she passed through the bright roses of the Farnese Gardens. Their perfume mingled with the scent of pines that she'd always associate with Rome, even if she moved back to Australia.

She'd have to consider that option carefully if she was going to raise a child alone—

'Amber.'

Her heart leapt then plummeted.

The voice, low and distinctive, stopped her in her tracks, making her notice for the first time the man blocking her path. The sun was behind him, casting his face in shade, but she knew him. Not just because of the wide, straight shoulders or the voice that caressed like suede across her skin. She'd know Aurelio anywhere, without sight, smell or sound. Her body was totally attuned to him.

'What are you doing here?' Surely they'd said everything that needed saying. Aurelio had been gone when she finished her bath. Obviously he'd been only too glad to get away. Part of her had died when she walked into that empty room and realised he'd taken her at her word.

'I'm here for you. I've spent hours tracking you down.'

Mute with shock, Amber stared up at him, trying to read his expression and failing.

'I tried your office and your apartment. Even your favourite café. Then I remembered you saying you liked to come here.'

Amber's mind reeled. He remembered that? A chance comment made months ago?

She wanted to be firm and simply walk away, not torture herself by listening to him, knowing whatever apology he made there'd be no happy ending. Yet she wasn't that strong. So she stood her ground and waited. A few metres away a young woman pushed a stroller. This time next year that could be her, though not, she decided in that moment, in Italy. There'd be too many memories of Aurelio here. She'd return to Australia, even though it meant giving up the business she'd worked so hard to establish.

'I'm sorry, Amber.' Before she realised what he was about, Aurelio reached out and took her hand, his much larger one engulfing it in heat. A tremor shot through her at the contact and she shuddered.

'Don't!' She made to step back but found he held her tight. 'We've said everything that needs to be said. I don't want to rehash it all over again.'

When he still didn't move she bit out, 'I'm rather busy. I've got a business to close up and a move to Australia to plan.'

She yanked her hand and this time it slid free of his grasp.

'You're migrating?' His voice was sharp, his mouth thinning.

'Returning home. I've decided there's nothing worth staying for in Italy. I'd rather bring up my child where I'll have support.'

Setting her chin high she stepped past him.

'I'll look for winery work there too.'

'Sorry?' She swung round. This time the sun shone full on his face and Amber saw determination in the angle of his jaw and the lines that ploughed down beside his mouth. He stared straight back at her, those dark velvet eyes so serious her breath hitched.

'I'll get work in Australia. I've had offers before but I wasn't interested.'

Amber shook her head. 'And you're not interested now. Your business is here, remember?' What game was Aurelio playing at?

'My business is wherever you are, Amber.' His gaze softened and his nostrils flared as he breathed deep. 'You and our baby.'

Amber backed a step on wobbly legs. Her bruised heart gave a mighty lurch as if trying to leap out into his open hands. She pressed the heel of her hand to her sternum, trying to ease the pounding beat.

This was too much, too unbelievable. 'Don't be ridiculous. You can't give up your winery. It's your life.'

Even before he revealed how he'd clung to his dream like a lifeline after his fiancée's death, Amber had seen how much the place meant to him. If ever there was a man living in harmony with his environment it was Aurelio.

He shook his head. 'You think a winery, or any business, is a fit substitute for love?'

Amber frowned. He was talking in riddles. The sooner she left the better, because he was tying her in knots. Just standing close to him made her weak with all the longings she fought so hard to repress.

'You obviously think so. It's what kept you going all this time.'

'Maybe that's the problem.' He speared a hand

through his hair in a jerky gesture that spoke of impatience. 'If what you said is right, I've been hiding there too long. It's time I concentrated on what really matters. Time I stopped running and faced my feelings.'

Amber swallowed hard at the fierce light in his eyes. She'd seen Aurelio vibrant with passion and laughter, racked by pain and determined in his rejection. But she'd never seen him look like this.

Look at *her* like this.

She faltered back another step at what she saw in his face. Her foolish heart swelled.

'You're absolutely right, Amber. I've been hiding, not just from the world, but from you, and from emotion. I've been fighting not to feel but it didn't work. Ever since we met I've felt…different. Connected. Engaged. You turned my world upside down and I didn't know what to do about it so I did what I'd done for years and buried myself in the winery. But it didn't work.'

'It didn't?' Amber crossed her arms over her waist, hugging in the burgeoning hope that sprang out of nowhere at his words. Surely he couldn't be saying what she thought he was?

'If you hadn't turned up that day at the winery I'm not sure how much longer I'd have withstood the temptation to return to Rome and see you.'

'But you didn't want me there.'

His mouth crooked up at one corner in a half-smile that weakened her jelly knees even further. Did he know? Is that why he reached out to cup her elbow, holding her steady? The warmth of his hand on her bare arm sent delicious heat coursing through her. This time she didn't pull away. Just stood, staring up at him, needing to hear more.

'Of course I didn't. Because you threatened my cosy world. You made me feel things, want things I'd convinced myself I didn't deserve.'

'Oh, Aurelio…'

'Don't you dare feel sorry for me!' His scowl was brutally hard. 'I've been a totally selfish bastard. I hurt you.' His other hand lifted to her face, then paused a moment. Did he expect her to push him away? When she didn't, his knuckles slid in a tender caress down her cheek.

'I'm so sorry, Amber. For all the hurt I've caused. It's going to take a lot to make it up to you, I know.'

It was heaven standing here, listening to his soothing words, feeling his touch. But it wasn't enough.

'Why are you here, Aurelio? Is it guilt over what I said about not being a fit father?'

She wouldn't really deny him a part in their child's life if he wanted it.

'Why am I here?' He paused and this time when his mouth curved up it was in a full, wide smile, transforming his features from brooding to stunningly charismatic.

His grasp slid from her elbow to her hand just as he dropped to his knees before her. Amber's eyes widened.

'I'm here because I love you. I love you and I want to persuade you to forgive me, or at least persuade you to give me a chance to prove myself.' His smile faded, replaced by a solemn expression that made her heart roll over.

'Please, Amber, give me a chance to prove myself to you. I love you and I want to be in your life.'

'Aurelio?' She couldn't believe she was hearing this. Or seeing him on his knees before her. But he was so intent, so engrossed, she had to believe he was serious.

Out of the corner of her eye she saw a couple of tourists on the far perimeter of the garden watching, enthralled. One even held up a phone to get a shot of them. But Aurelio didn't notice. His attention was all on her.

She swiped her tongue over her lip. 'I wouldn't really stop you from seeing our baby.'

'I'm glad. I want to be part of its life. But that's not enough.' He raised her hand and pressed it to his mouth. 'I love you, Amber. It sideswiped me because I didn't believe it could happen to me again. And because it was so different from what I felt before. Valentina and I knew each other all our lives. We just grew into affection gradually. But when I met you it was like mountain lightning, striking in an instant, hard and inescapable. A force of nature.'

Stunned, Amber nodded. It had been like that for her too.

'That day you gave your presentation in Rome I couldn't believe what I felt. It was all too much, too soon. Then when we spent that week together I felt myself falling further and further under your spell. I kept telling myself I could break away. That it was just sex, not emotion, but I lied to myself.' He shook his head, his expression stern. 'I've discovered I've done a lot of lying to myself, and to you. I'm sorry for that, Amber. If I'd been more honest I could have avoided hurting you.'

Amber stared down at the gorgeous man before

her wearing such a regretful expression. Desperately she tried to still her rioting senses. She wanted so much to believe him but some instinct for self-preservation made her hold back.

'I don't know what to say.'

For a second something flared in his eyes. It looked like desolation, and she felt the sudden judder through him as if rocked by an unseen blow. Then he nodded. 'I understand. It will take far more than a simple apology to put right all the wrongs I've done you. But give me hope that you'll let me stay in your life and try to win you.'

'Win me?'

He nodded. 'Of course. I love you, Amber. I want to spend my life with you. I'll come to Australia to support you and our baby. But have no doubt my main aim is to convince you to love me too.' He paused, his grip on her hand tightening. 'One day I hope you'll marry me, not for the sake of the baby,' he said quickly, 'but because you love me too.'

That did it. Amber had been strong and sensible so long but how could she withstand that?

'Ah, *tesoro*, don't cry!' Aurelio surged to his feet and wrapped her close against him. Beneath her cheek she felt the quick sprint of his heart. 'Please, don't. It breaks my heart to see you unhappy.'

Amber snuffled into his shirt, inhaling the scent of warm male flesh and spice that was uniquely Aurelio's. Her skittering pulse eased as she sank into him. Finally, when she found her voice she tilted her head back to meet his worried eyes.

'I'm crying because I'm happy.'

'Happy?' His frown cleared. 'My sister Lia does that too. It's supposed to be a good thing.' He said it carefully as if waiting to be corrected and Amber's heart squeezed at the sight of him so unsure. She wasn't used to Aurelio being hesitant.

'I'm happy because you love me.' She drew a deep breath. 'I've been in love with you so long, Aurelio. I never thought—'

Her words died when his mouth covered hers, at first lightly, reverently, as if, like her, he'd feared they'd never kiss again. Then, as their bodies clung closer, his hand lifted to her hair, his spread fingers holding her so he could feast on her.

Joy and love and something like triumph, or maybe relief, filled Amber as she kissed him back. Her arms crept to his shoulders, her own hands welding to the back of his head, tugging him down to her level as she strained up towards him on tiptoe.

When, finally, they drew apart enough to breathe, Amber became aware of an unfamiliar noise. Not the birds in the pine trees or the distant hum of traffic, but applause from the large tourist group watching from the other side of the garden.

Amber caught smiles and the glint of cameras.

'Do you mind?' Aurelio's voice rumbled up to wrap around her like an embrace.

'I don't care one bit.' She tilted her head back to see him smiling down at her. He looked so different from the brooding man she'd first met.

'You really love me?' Was that anxiety she heard still in his deep voice?

'I really do.' Her mouth curved up as the darkness that had clung so long faded away, banished by happiness.

'I'll devote my life to making sure that never

changes.' This time his kiss was a gentle salute that stole her breath with its tenderness.

When he finally lifted his head Amber was dizzy with happiness. She wasn't even surprised when Aurelio scooped her up against his solid chest.

'I could get used to this.' She curled her hands around his neck.

'That suits me down to the ground. Now,' he turned towards the path, 'let's go somewhere private and book our flights to Australia.'

Amber didn't bother to protest that he couldn't carry her all the way down off the Palatine Hill. She'd stay in his arms forever if she could. 'I've changed my mind. I want to stay in Italy.'

The look he gave her told her just how much that meant to him. Now he didn't bother to guard his emotions, the love she read in his expression was so strong, so open, Amber felt it surround her, warmer than sunshine. Happiness bubbled inside, even her bloodstream felt effervescent.

'And risk wondering, even for a second, whether the vineyard business means more to me than you do?' Aurelio shook his head. 'I think not.'

Amber's eyebrows rose. 'I'm serious, Aurelio. We can make a wonderful life here with our child.' When he didn't nod his agreement she persisted. 'I put a lot of work into that marketing plan. I don't want it to go to waste.'

'What's a marketing plan compared with our whole future?' His words were serious but Amber caught the twinkle in his midnight eyes. Suspicion dawned.

'Aurelio, are you deliberately provoking an argument? You are! But why?'

His smile turned smug as they passed a couple of people who watched them bemused as Aurelio hugged her even closer.

'Because I love your passion when you're aroused, *anima mio.* I intend to reap the rewards.'

'Aurelio De Laurentis, you're impossible!' But she was grinning, already looking forward to sharing that passion with him. Besides, how could she resist him when he called her *his soul*? 'It's a good thing I love you so much.'

He stopped in the middle of the path. 'It is. Believe me, I know just how lucky I am.'

Then that devilish gleam reappeared in his eyes. 'And I know just how to celebrate my good fortune.'

Epilogue

De Laurentis Vineyard, almost a year later

AURELIO SHOULDERED THE DOOR OPEN, his hands full with chilled bottles of premium prosecco.

A burst of laughter reached him and a wave of voices. Happy voices talking across each other and mingling in several simultaneous conversations.

He smiled. Across the courtyard a long table was set up under the shade of a leafy pergola. Family members, vineyard workers and old friends were gathered there, helping themselves from the vast platters of food that Amber, with her sisters and mother, plus all the women in his own family, had spent the morning preparing.

The scent of charcoal-grilled meat made Aurelio's nostrils twitch. He glanced to the shady spot where Matteo and his best friend Niccolo were paying more attention to their argument about rival football teams than to their barbecuing. Fortunately Gennaro, his arm wrapped around his wife Chiara's waist, looked up from nuzzling her hair just in time to save the meat.

Aurelio shook his head. It would be a miracle if the grilled meats weren't overcooked. He'd have to go and save them. He didn't want to let Amber down. She'd been so delighted at the thought of their two families coming together to celebrate.

He was detouring across the courtyard to the grill when Chiara poked her brother-in-law and his friend in the ribs and took control of the situation, ordering them about with an assurance that made him smile. Matteo and Niccolo were both heartthrobs to millions of women, but since settling down with Angela and Lia they'd become almost domesticated. As for Chiara, she might have been born with a silver spoon in her mouth but she'd become one of the De Laurentis family in no time.

Knowing all was under control, he strode across to the table, passing over the chilled bottles.

Instantly his eyes went to the middle of the table, to Amber, stunning in a simple white dress that accentuated her slender figure and pure features.

His heart thumped against his ribs, taking up a fast, familiar rhythm.

Happiness washed through him. Gratitude. Love.

He'd never thought to be so lucky. How many ever got such a second chance?

And there was nothing second-hand about what he felt for his beloved wife. With Amber everything was fresh and new, gilded with the magic only true love could create. Every day he woke with her in his arms, wondering what he'd done to deserve such happiness. Every night, as he gathered her to him, he knew himself the luckiest man in the world.

Last night, counting his blessings, he'd been so filled with emotion he'd struggled to find the words to tell her how much she meant. For Aurelio was learning that sharing with Amber, even speaking about his feelings, was far better than hoarding them to himself.

Amber had surveyed him with understanding in her eyes and told him he brooded too much. She'd slid her palm down his naked body and demanded he make love to her. And their loving had been as rapturous as ever.

As if sensing his gaze, Amber looked up. Bright silvery eyes snagged on his and a bolt of energy arced between them. Her pupils dilated and she smiled, that private, loving smile, just for him, and desire coiled tight in his belly.

But it wasn't just desire. It was love.

'Aurelio.' The way she said his voice, low and husky, had him wishing they were alone.

Why had he agreed to such a big party? Then Amber's smile widened and he had his answer. Because she'd wanted, no, *they'd* wanted to share their joy.

He circled the table, responding automatically to the comments directed his way, smiling and nodding and agreeing it was the perfect day for a celebration.

Yet all the time he was aware of his wife, waiting for him.

She rose as he approached, leaning up on her toes to kiss him. Her lips were soft and delicious, her warm, honeysuckle scent tickling his senses.

Desire rose, but more too, far more. He lifted his head, looking down into crystal-bright eyes. 'Everything okay?'

'More than okay.' Amber shone with an inner glow and he followed her gaze down to the precious bundle cradled in her arms.

Silky black hair covered their daughter's head, her tiny rosebud mouth and pink cheeks so perfect the sight of her made Aurelio simultaneously awed and protective.

Their child.

His family.

Their daughter shifted in Amber's arms and Aurelio grinned. Their little girl had already managed to kick off one of her satin christening booties. Perfect, tiny toes wriggled in her sleep and it struck him suddenly that here, in this sunny vineyard, was everything he cared about in the whole world.

'*Tesoro.*' He lifted his hand to his wife's soft cheek. 'Have I told you lately how much I love you?'

Before Amber could answer, his brother Luca's voice drawled from nearby, 'Yes, you have. Constantly.'

'Sh, Luca. Let them be.' Aurelio turned to see his new sister-in-law Allegra nudging her husband.

Luca just grinned and hauled her close. 'Isn't it time for a toast, little brother?'

'You're right.' Aurelio reached for a bottle of prosecco, pouring the pale wine into a couple of glasses while others around the table followed suit then rose to their feet. The group at the barbeque came over bearing platters of food and each collected a glass.

When everyone was ready Aurelio surveyed them all, the friends and family who'd stood by him through the difficult years, and who'd welcomed his wife and child into their midst with laughter and warmth.

Finally he turned to the woman beside him, her

radiant happiness so bright it made him blink.

'To Laura Maddalena De Laurentis. May she be blessed with love all her days.'

Around them dozens of voices echoed 'To Laura Maddalena De Laurentis.'

'And to my precious wife, Amber. Thank you for dragging me out of my cave and into the light.' His smile was for her alone, though he didn't care in the least who saw the emotion in his eyes. '*Ti amo.*'

'And I love you too, Aurelio. With all my heart.'

He knew he was the luckiest man alive and he felt no guilt at all about that.

IF YOU ENJOYED THIS STORY please tell your friends or consider writing a review.

YOU MIGHT ALSO LIKE OTHERS IN THIS SERIES:

HOT ITALIAN NIGHTS ANTHOLOGY,
BOOKS 1-3
Back in the Italian's Bed
Bought by the Italian
Bound to the Italian Boss

BOOK SEVEN –
The Italian's Marriage Bargain
BOOK EIGHT –
Burning for the Italian

For other Annie West titles visit
www.annie-west.com

About Annie

A NNIE WEST LOVES WRITING SEXY, emotional stories about charismatic heroes and strong heroines, and not just because it gives her a chance to ignore housework! She is a USA Today Bestselling author, published in 25 languages, and has won the Romantic Times Reviewers' Choice Award and the Romance Writers of Australia Romantic Book of the Year.

She lives on the east coast of Australia between wonderful beaches and glorious wine country. When not writing and avoiding housework she can be found walking, enjoying good food and good company, travelling or reading. Annie loves chatting with readers as far apart as Brisbane, Bremen and Bermuda.

Visit Annie at *www.annie-west.com*

Sign up for her reader newsletter for advance notice of new releases, giveaways and behind the scenes info via her website.

Or follow her on Facebook at
www.facebook.com/anniewest.author